My Forever Christmas

Marion Rhines

Copyright © 2021 Marion Rhines

All rights reserved.

ISBN 9798507567829

DEDICATION

To every foster child who dreams of finding their Forever Home…

CONTENTS

Acknowledgments	i
Chapter One	1
Chapter Two	10
Chapter Three	17
Chapter Four	25
Chapter Five	38
Chapter Six	49
Chapter Seven	63
Chapter Eight	80
Chapter Nine	91
Chapter Ten	104
Chapter Eleven	118
Chapter Twelve	132
Chapter Thirteen	149
Chapter Fourteen	158
Chapter Fifteen	166
Chapter Sixteen	180

ACKNOWLEDGMENTS

I want to thank my wonderful husband, Darrin Rhines, for his encouragement and inspiration as this was the first novel I wrote. Thank you for letting me live my dream of writing stories to inspire others. Thank you to my dear friends Irene Clements, Vanessa Addington, Susan Spalding, Nancy Mitchell, Sandra Fields, Beth Nelson, and Jerelene Perryman for reading my work and providing insight. I want to say a special thank you to J.P. Peach for being the real-life Julie Patterson for me…the friend who pushes me to be better. She also served as my content editor, of sorts, for this story. As always, thank you Rebekah Wood for the awesome cover art.

CHAPTER 1

Monday mornings at Juvenile Court always meant the docket of cases was completely full. It was November and there were always children coming into foster care. There were new cases to be heard and permanency plans revisited, so the social workers presented the progress of the cases to the judges. Charity Walters passed through security with all her stuffed animals and placed them in the box. Juvenile court had a custom of giving stuffed animals to children who were working through not being home with their families.

"Hello, Daniel," Charity greeted the clerk. Daniel checked in all participants and directed them to the rooms where they would sit in on the cases.

"Hey, Charity," Daniel replied. "You start out in Room Four for the Ferguson case. Then you'll need to check back for the other one. I don't know where it will be yet."

"Thanks! And, oh, I brought in the stuffed animals I promised last time. Sorry it took so long to get them here," Charity explained, a little embarrassed.

"You always think of the kindest things to do for these children, Charity.

Thank you very much," Daniel declared, shaking his head, and smiling. "Take care and see you next time."

"See ya," Charity waved as she turned to find a seat.

Charity weaved through the lobby and sat in a chair by the vending machines. Though she knew the date was Monday, November 2nd, she didn't realize today was the anniversary of one of her most important court dates- the day she aged-out of foster care. Although youth typically age-out after their eighteenth birthday or when they graduate from high school, Charity had a special situation that allowed her to wait a few months longer. The clanking sound of the drinks coming out of the machine transported her back to the day she waited with Jennifer Ryan, her own family service worker, to have her last appearance in juvenile court. She had asked to do this on her own and not have her foster parents, William and Monica Avery, come with her to see the judge. The Averys had taken good care of Charity and set her on the path to journalism, but she had to do this on her own.

"Charity, you realize this is your last time in court?" Jennifer queried as she sat beside Charity, eyes fixed on chairs in the next row.

"I understand," Charity replied. "How much longer before we go in to see the judge?"

"Well, we just have to wait for them to call our case," Jennifer replied.

Twenty minutes later, the clerk announced on the intercom, "All participants in the Charity Walters case please make your way to Room Four."

Charity and Jennifer walked to into Room Four. Jennifer sat at the seat with the microphone and Charity sat in the seat to her left.

The clerk said, "All rise for the judge," as Judge Amy Winters quickly took her seat.

Judge Winters looked at Jennifer and began, "Ms. Ryan, we are here today to close out the final chapter in the case of Charity Walters. After this meeting, she will be considered an adult and out on her own in the world. Is she prepared for these new challenges?"

Jennifer sat upright, "Judge Winters, Charity understands that after today she will no longer be a ward of the state. Since she made the decision four years ago to not seek adoption, she has prepared herself for a career in journalism. She is currently enrolled in the January semester of journalism school and has secured lodging and a lead on a job. Transportation is still a barrier she hopes to have handled by the time she begins school. She is ready to move forward with her future."

"Wow," Judge Winters considered, "Charity, this is one of the most prepared aging out situations I have ever presided over. I understand you chose this path instead of trying to be adopted and have your forever family. Do you have anything you want to say at this time?"

Charity stood up and confidently spoke, "Judge, I did decide to forgo adoption as I could not deal with further disappointments as the chances of a forever home fell through. Though Mr. and Mrs. Avery have loved me and taken good care of me, I want to make my own way, choose my own path. I feel I have been made a stronger person because of the things the Averys have taught me, as well as my own experiences. I don't expect to be free of problems, but I will strive to be self-sufficient."

The judge considered her words and asked Jennifer, "Do you have any other comments before we end this meeting?"

"No, judge, I have presented all the information relevant at this time," Jennifer stated.

After a few moments of silence, Judge Winters announced, "Charity Walters, at the conclusion of this meeting, you will be on your own. You will no longer be required to check in with the Department of Children's Services or attend any further court meetings. I must say I am incredibly pleased with the situation you are in as you are leave state's custody. I feel good about your chances of making it out there in the real world. If there is nothing else, case dismissed," the judge banged her gavel. "Congratulations, Charity."

"Charity…Charity!" Barbara Fredrickson called as she shook Charity's shoulder bringing her back to the present. "It's time to head into Room Four."

Charity stood up and followed behind Barbara. As the participants of the previous case exited that room, Henry Thompson, a Family Service Worker for the Department of Children's Services (DCS), almost knocked her down.

"I am *so* sorry," Henry exclaimed, extremely embarrassed he didn't see her. "Glad you weren't holding any hot coffee." He held out his hand to help steady her.

"I don't drink coffee," countered Charity meeting his gaze as she accepted his hand. "I prefer a nice, cold Diet Mountain Dew." Charity righted herself and smoothed her clothes, picked up her sunglasses and placed them back on her head, using them as a headband.

"Well, the least I can do is treat you to one," Henry offered as he handed her her briefcase.

"Next time, maybe. I must go in now. Judge Grimsby doesn't like to wait," Charity lamented. "Are you even going to tell me your name?" Extending her hand to shake his, "Charity Walters, nice to meet you."

Taking her hand for a second time, Henry responded, "I'm Henry Thompson, Family Service Worker. I was here to give an update on a case. Good news. The kids get to return home. I guess I was a little too happy with how things had gone that I wasn't paying attention to where I was going," Henry explained as he looked at her for a moment. He tilted his head, realizing that something about her had piqued his curiosity.

"That's wonderful," Charity celebrated with him a moment. "I wish all cases ended up so well. I really have to go. And truth be told, it wasn't completely your fault. I was coming out of a daze from a triggered memory and not paying attention to where I was going either. Well, I'm glad you are okay, but I *really* need to be going. The judge will certainly be grim if he has to wait much longer."

"Take care, then," Henry waved as he watched her disappear into Room Four.

Charity walked into the room and spied the Hendersons with Amanda and Peter. She walked over and hugged the children. "It's nice to see you today. How are you?"

"Great," chimed Amanda. "We got loads of candy Trick or Treating." Peter just flashed a big smile.

"Let's take our seats. The judge is ready to begin," announced the clerk.

Everyone stood up as Judge Grimsby walked slowly to his seat and sat down. "Ms. Frederickson, go ahead with your update, please."

Barbara Frederickson occupied the chair with the microphone. "Good morning, Judge Grimsby. The court terminated the Ferguson's parental rights, and we're almost to the end of the thirty-day appeal period. We're approaching fifteen months since Amanda and Peter came into custody and need to get them to permanency. The Army has also given Mr. Henderson transfer orders to Hawaii effective the first of the year. We're not sure what to expect next, your honor. You know the extenuating circumstances that prevent the children from staying with their foster parents."

Judge Grimsby crinkled his brows and inquired, "Mr. Henderson, how do you feel the children have been doing since the last review?"

"Well, your honor, Amanda is doing well in school. As always, she's very loving and respectful. Peter, on the other hand, still isn't talking. We've tried everything. He just won't say a word," reported Mr. Henderson.

"Does anyone have anything else to add to this case before we set a date for the next progress review," the judge paused, looking at his calendar, "for December 21st?"

Observing the silence, the judge took his gavel and said, "Case continued until December 21st. Have a Happy Thanksgiving."

Everyone gathered their belongings. Peter ran up to Charity, hugging her one more time. "Oh, thanks, Pete. I'll be in touch with you soon, okay? Maybe we can do a fun day some Saturday, just you, Amanda, and me." Peter nodded vigorously giving Charity another hug as the Hendersons left the room. Charity left the room without a word and headed off to work.

****

It was eleven-thirty when Charity arrived at her desk at *The Standard Banner*. She sat down, ready to work when Rachel Peterson approached.

"How was court today, kid?" Rachel was forty-eight years old and worked as the paper's sports expert. She had taken Charity under her wing when Charity was first hired. Rachel and her husband, Adam, had two children. They had a biological son named Joey and an adopted daughter named Ophelia. Experiences with foster care were what drew Rachel and Charity together in the first place.

"It was a tough day. I didn't connect the date today and the only seat available in the lobby was next to the vending machines…Let's just say that I relived the last time I had a court appearance," Charity revealed.

"I'm so sorry, kid," Rachel consoled. "How was the rest of it?"

"Well, the case I'm most concerned about isn't turning out well at all. You know I can't give specifics, but I really hoped something would change for these kids. And on top of that, I almost got knocked down by a DCS worker on his way out of Room Four. Luckily, we didn't hurt each other," Charity expressed matter-of-factly, noticing an official envelope on her desk. "I wonder what this is. I'm caught up on all my bills and my stories for the paper." She opened the envelope and pulled out an official document that looked like something from an estate attorney. The letter read:

Dear Miss Walters:

The law firm of Lovejoy, Wilkins, and Thomas, hereby inform you that you have been named the sole beneficiary of your great uncle and aunt, Francis and Marion Ledford, and hereby inherit the Silver Horseshoe Ranch, located in Jefferson County, Tennessee. Please contact me at our office as soon as possible to sign the papers. Mr. Charles Hobby, the ranch foreman, awaits your arrival to give further instructions.

Sincerely,
Arthur Lovejoy

    Charity was stunned, "This can't be right. Maybe they have the wrong person." She never knew she had a great uncle and aunt, let alone ones that lived so close by. Why had they never reached out to her? Her eyes were still glazed over when Rachel finally spoke.

    "Whoa! You have inherited a horse ranch. Aren't you allergic to horses? Need someone to go with you when you see Mr. Lovejoy?" Rachel offered thoughtfully.

    Rachel's voice jarred Charity back to the moment, "Yes, I *am* allergic to horses. After this morning, I think that may be a good idea as I haven't seen a lawyer since I aged-out of foster care," she remembered. "I'll let you know when I go see him. I need some time to think this over." Rachel hugged Charity then went back to her desk.

    Not able to concentrate, Charity flipped half-heartedly through her notes, trying to decide what public interest story to pen next. There were a few things to choose from and she still had a little bit of time.

    Five o'clock signaled the end of the workday. She gathered her stuff then headed home. Charity pulled into her apartment complex and parked in the space in front of her building. She saw Max, her black cat, fixed between the curtains, looking for her.

    "Hello, Max. I missed you," Charity said stroking Max on the head. "Today was very strange. I forgot what day it was, I almost get knocked over by a stranger, then I found out I had relatives who couldn't take me. I don't understand what happened. Want to order pizza and put on a good movie?"

    Charity ordered her favorite specialty pizza, a cheeseburger pizza. She added on the double chocolate brownies. She selected her go-to, pick me up movie, *The Polar Express*. She needed a night of emotional comfort. Though she knew you should never use food for emotional issues, this made her feel much better.

Charity and Max fell asleep on the couch. The television was still on, as *The Polar Express* was one of those movies that played over and over continuously. Charity dreamt of horses, prancing around an arena. Suddenly she woke up, then remembered she was in her apartment…alone. Her mind worked to unravel the aunt and uncle mystery.

****

On Tuesday, Charity called in to work so she could do some thinking. When she couldn't stand it any longer, she looked up the address for the Silver Horseshoe Ranch and planned an incognito drive by. She put her hair up in a ponytail and put on a ball cap and her sunglasses. That always works…

It wasn't a long drive from her apartment to the turn off for the Silver Horseshoe Ranch. She had driven past this road so many times, never thinking it would one day change her life.

As she turned down the road that led to the house, Charles "Chuck" Hobby, was riding a horse in the front part of the property. She had been driving very slowly, looking hard at the property when he flagged her down. Chuck was a slender older man of about fifty-five, with salt and pepper black hair and a cowboy hat. He was clean-shaven and had piercing, blue eyes. He was muscular from all the hard work with the horses and equipment. She rolled down the window.

"You must be Charity. I had a feeling curiosity would get you before the papers were officially signed," Chuck smiled. "Come on in here and let me show you around." He rode off ahead of her, opening the gate as she followed him through to the house.

She parked in the driveway. The house sat in the middle of the property with the horses, barn, and arena all in the back. It was a gorgeous two-story farmhouse that had an old-fashioned hitching post out front. On the right side of the porch was a swing large enough for two people. The tall, second story seemed to reach up forever. There was a lovely weeping willow tree off to the side. There was an enormous garage to the left of the house. She realized she was staring like a codfish with her mouth open, so she closed it quickly.

"Come on inside and let me show you around," Chuck invited. "We'll start out back near the barn."

Charity followed Chuck through the house, just briefly seeing the living room, hallway, and kitchen before going out the back door. It was the most peaceful place Charity had ever seen. Horses grazed on the oats that had just been put out. Birds were flying south as they migrated for the season. A few horses nickered as Chuck walked past, obviously wanting his attention.

"I bet you are wondering why your great uncle and aunt never tried to take you in," Chuck began. "It wasn't because they didn't want to. They couldn't because of their age. They both were over fifty years old when you went into care. At that time, it wasn't a common thing for older folks to take in smaller children. Your uncle was still well enough, but your aunt was a little more fragile. They kept an eye on you, you know, from a distance. They were extremely proud of how hard you worked at that newspaper of yours."

Charity remained silent for a moment then found the words to say, "I just wish I had known I had family. Especially living this close to me. You have no idea what it feels like to think you don't matter to anyone. Why did they want me to have the Silver Horseshoe Ranch? Didn't they have children of their own?"

Pushing his hat back on his head, Chuck answered, "They had a son, Jeremy, but he died in a car accident fifteen years ago. He never married, and there was no other heir. There were no other extended family members to pass the ranch on to. After that, they decided to save the ranch for you, to take over after they both were gone."

Charity quietly asked, "What happened to them?"

"Your Aunt Marion died from pneumonia six years ago. Then about a year ago, your Uncle Francis, Frank, was diagnosed with a brain tumor. We were devastated to see him struggle like he did. He missed your Aunt Marion terribly. He remained sharp as a tack until the end, even amidst getting the papers prepared for your inheritance. He just didn't want to go on any longer the way he was. Then, two weeks ago he died during the night. We carried out his arrangements, just as he specified. Then, we had Arthur Lovejoy send you the letter."

Suddenly, Charity heard a high-pitched sound in her ears. Her face flashed a bit of heat. It must have been noticeable because Chuck put his hand on her shoulder and asked, "Are you okay? Here, let's move to the kitchen."

Charity felt a little faint from the overload of emotion. Why did she always feel so weird when she got overwhelmed? Luckily, Chuck held on to her as he offered her a seat on a stool at the bar. "I think I need to head back home. This is all too fantastic to believe. I never thought they would have wanted to make a future for me. I don't know what to say. All this time, I believed I was alone."

"I can't rightly say I know how you are feeling, but I do know about needing time to ponder what you learned." Chuck reassured Charity as he walked her back to her car, "Just be sure to call that Mr. Lovejoy and get those papers signed. We have some work to get done around here."

Charity nodded as she climbed back into her car. Her head ached a little from the surge of unexpected emotions. A ranch, full of horses. What would she do about her allergies? She was lucky she hadn't sneezed while there. But she may not be so lucky next time. She queued up her Christmas music playlist and drove home.

CHAPTER 2

By the time Charity got to her desk on Wednesday, the news spread to the others on her team. Marcus, a strikingly handsome, Black man about thirty-eight, leaned on her desk. He worked as the paper's financial expert. "Good morning, Charity," he grinned. "How in the world did you inherit a horse ranch? I thought you were an orphan or something."

"Your guess is as good as mine. Apparently, I had a great uncle and aunt out there who couldn't take me, but made provision for me when they died," expounded Charity.

"Hold up, now, don't say anything else until we can hear it, too," boomed Mr. Cooper, with Rachel on his heels. Mr. Cooper, "Buzz" as he was known by the people at *The Standard Banner*, was very loud, extremely fair, and always sharpening pencils in his office. Though he was well-versed in technology, he preferred to write down all his stories and ideas on paper. He kept a pencil behind his ear and a notepad with him all the time. "Give us all the juicy details," he pressed.

"Well, I haven't learned everything yet. I still need to meet Mr. Lovejoy and sign the official papers," Charity commenced slowly. "I had a fight with curiosity and lost. Yesterday afternoon I drove out to the Silver Horseshoe Ranch. I was in disguise, or so I thought, but the foreman saw me from a mile away. I never saw anything so peaceful in my entire life."

"Don't you have this love-hate thing with nature? You know, you love it, but it hates you. Aren't you allergic to just about everything? I hope this works out for you," Marcus uttered with a concerned look on his face.

"Fortune was on my side yesterday as I didn't sneeze once. But I left before I spent too much time near the horses. The foreman, Chuck, seemed nice enough. He advised me to get the papers signed as soon as possible. There was work to get done and I needed to help," Charity mused as she wondered how she could give sound advice about a horse ranch.

"Let me know when you've made the appointment with Mr. Lovejoy, and we'll go together," Rachel nudged.

"All right, everyone, get back to work. The paper doesn't run itself you know. You all have deadlines to meet," Buzz ordered as he winked at Charity, putting his hand on her shoulder for support. Everyone scattered to their desks and returned to work.

Charity eyed the letter from Mr. Lovejoy and decided to bite the bullet and call him.

"Mr. Lovejoy? This is Charity Walters. When can I come by and sign the papers for my inheritance?" she paused. "This afternoon? Oh, that is soon. What time? Four o'clock it is. Thank you. I know the address," Charity declared as she scribbled the information down on her notepad. She hung up the phone, pricked with fear.

Charity strolled over to Rachel's desk. Rachel was listening to a replay of a high school football game and pulled out the earbuds when she saw Charity approach.

"Hey, kid, what's up? Rachel inquired.

"Mr. Lovejoy set the time for this afternoon at four o'clock to sign the papers. Can you still come with me? I didn't think it would be so soon," Charity voiced shakily.

"Sure, I'm almost finished with the replay of this past week's high school game then I'll be ready to go," Rachel assured her.

Charity believed herself to be a strong person. She had endured so much while in foster care. She couldn't recollect anything before she was four years old. She was told trauma sometimes did that…blocked out things.

Usually thought to be things too painful to remember. When she was fourteen, she decided to not seek adoption. Though the Averys took good care of her, she worked through the next four years then got out on her own. She had a dream of becoming a children's book author. That dream was what led her to the newspaper.

Rachel drove Charity to the lawyer's office. Though she wouldn't admit it, Charity was shaking like a leaf deep down inside. Rachel pulled up to the office and put the car in park.

"You ready, kid?" Rachel probed.

"It's now or never, huh? Let's go see what Mr. Lovejoy has to say," Charity verbalized with all the courage she could muster.

They walked into the lobby of Lovejoy, Wilkins, and Thomas. Addressing the receptionist, Charity inquired, "Can you please tell us where to find Mr. Lovejoy?"

"Down the hall, third door on the left," the receptionist countered with a smile.

The door was open, but Charity knocked anyway. Mr. Lovejoy looked up and beckoned them inside. Still on the phone, he motioned for them to take a seat at the table. He was finishing up a conversation when she saw the papers with her name on them.

"Okay, thank you for doing business with Lovejoy, Wilkins and Thomas. Good-bye," Mr. Lovejoy said hanging up the phone. "Ah, ladies, thank you for coming here today. I presume you are Charity Walters?" Arthur queried looking at Charity.

"Yes, that's me," gulped Charity. "Thank you for seeing me, well, us this afternoon."

"Here are the papers. I expect you want to examine them before you sign. They are straight-forward. In addition to the Silver Horseshoe Ranch, you also inherit the sum of thirty-five million dollars," announced Arthur matter-of-factly.

Charity almost fell out of her chair. "I'm sorry," she said in total shock, "did you say thirty-five million dollars?"

Rachel gasped as she heard the amount of Charity's inheritance.

"Yes," Arthur commenced, "your uncle dealt in real estate. He owned rental properties all over Jefferson, Blount, and Sevier Counties. It's a funny thing, he was showing the Silver Horseshoe to another family when he decided to keep it for himself. He had a friend who owned horses and offered to let him board them at the Silver Horseshoe. The man did so until about five years ago. When Francis was diagnosed with the brain tumor, he sold off all the properties and collected the revenue for your inheritance."

Charity read through to the last page when she noticed money set aside to cover the ranch hands that worked on the ranch as well as a house caretaker. "What does this mean about the house caretaker and the ranch workers?"

"Francis knew it would take some time for you to learn the routine, working the ranch and all. He set aside an additional fifteen million for the purposes of salaries and other expenses. It should last you a good long time. At least long enough to decide what you want to do with the ranch," concluded Arthur as he gave Charity a pen. "Ready to do this?"

Charity looked at Rachel. Rachel gave her a wide-eyed look and said, "Kid, this is the most incredible thing I've ever witnessed. Do you think you can handle this?"

"I don't know," she whimpered. "I have never had more than one paycheck's worth of savings to my name. Now, I will never want for anything as long as I live." Resolve restored, she signed her name at the bottom of the paper. "There, I did it."

Arthur took the papers from her and made a copy on the printer. He placed several other papers together in a big envelope. "Here you are, Charity. You are now the sole owner of the Silver Horseshoe Ranch." He gave her a set of keys and the alarm codes to the front gate and rest of the house.

"Thank you very much, Mr. Lovejoy," Charity sincerely expressed as she and Rachel stood to leave. Arthur escorted them from the room and down the hall back to the door.

"It's been my pleasure, Charity. I know your Uncle Frank would be happy to know you are making your own way but also taking care of what he loved for so long." Arthur extended his hand and shook Charity's hand first, then Rachel's. Arthur bid them good-bye, and they left the building.

"Whew, what are you going to do first?" Rachel solicited.

"Well, we're going to stop at a gas station. I need a stiff drink. I'm getting the coldest Diet Mountain Dew I can find," Charity explained.

Rachel stopped at the nearest gas station. They went in and got their drinks. "Oh, I need to get you back to your car. It's still at work."

"Oh, yeah. Hey, I don't want to be alone tonight. Can I take you and Adam out to dinner somewhere? I need to ask him a few questions." Adam was a banker and could advise Charity about inheritance rules.

"You don't have to do that," Rachel scolded. "Just come over and we can order take out. We'll send Adam to get it."

They made it back to *The Standard Banner*. Charity got her car and followed Rachel to her house. They enjoyed Chinese food and conversed about inheritance rules.

****

Thursday found Charity a little anxious to pick the public interest story for the week. She decided to pursue the story of two children who were reunited with their parents after being in foster care. The relatives of the family were holding a celebration event at the local bowling alley. Friends and extended family were welcomed. Reunification with family deserves the biggest salute possible. The event was to commence Friday night and she needed to be in attendance.

Across town at the DCS office, Henry Thompson was in a meeting with his team. Another team member was Randi Young. She was fresh out of college and had only been on the team for two months. Alex George was present, as well as their boss, Erica Longmire. Erica had been a Family Service Worker for a long time, and really wanted to retire. Now just was not the best time. They were already short staffed. If she left, she didn't know who would be able to step into her role as team leader.

"Okay, folks, let's get this meeting started," Erica initiated. "We have two new cases and need to get a jump on them as quickly as we can."

It was a fact that during the fall, especially before and after holidays, the number of child referrals went way up. Some of the referrals got screened out, meaning there wasn't enough substance to them to investigate. Some referrals were situations where the parents needed educational services to improve family safety or supplement their lack of knowledge. They didn't realize that their children were at risk. The last kind of referrals were the ones that showed a clear and present danger to the children. They must be removed from the home until the situation could be rectified. Once removed from the home, the children were assigned a Family Service Worker. That's where Henry's team entered the picture.

"Alex, take Randi with you and go out on the first case. Henry, you take the other one. It may be a bit tense and you're the toughest guy we've got," Erica pronounced as she gave them the folders with the referral notes.

"This can't be right," Henry said as he read the case notes. "Wasn't this the case we put wrap around services in six months ago? Wasn't that situation doing much better?"

"Apparently, Mrs. Barlow decided that she didn't want to take the parenting classes. In fact, she said she really didn't want to deal with her children anymore. Ever since Mr. Barlow walked out on the family, Mrs. Barlow struggled with keeping the family going. She hasn't been taking them to school. It was the school who contacted me directly when Robert and Cynthia missed almost two straight weeks," Erica explained with frustration. "You're right, Henry, it was going well. Something must have triggered defeat. The next-door neighbor said the children came over while Mrs. Barlow was at work and said they didn't have any food in the house."

Henry pounded his fist on the table, "I hate it when people refuse to take a little help. Couldn't she understand we were just trying to help them succeed? Is Mrs. Barlow home now, or do we need to wait until this evening to get the children?" Henry questioned.

"She is home now. We sent for the court order yesterday and Judge Grimsby gave us the approval to act. We just need to locate a foster home that has an opening. The children need to be kept together, if possible," concluded Erica.

"Randi, our case looks like only services are needed for additional support. They are young, first-time parents and have no idea how to take care of a baby," Alex said as he looked over the notes.

"Henry, don't you have a celebration to attend tomorrow night? The Anderson children were reunified with their family for the trial home placement thanks to your report at the review board last week," Erica declared patting Henry on the back.

Henry knew from an early age he wanted to become a social worker. He was twenty-eight and worked the last six years with DCS there in Jefferson County. His mom and dad had adopted his brother as a small child. His brother came from a horrible place and found his forever home with the Thompsons. Henry and his biological siblings never viewed their adopted brother as anything but their brother. Henry had delusions of grandeur that he could save all the children and make their stories turn out right.

"I completely forgot about that," Henry smacked his forehead with his palm. "The Anderson family is having a thing at the Last Pin Standing Bowling Alley. I think *The Standard Banner* is covering the event for the paper this week. I'll be sure and give a good interview," joked Henry as he winked at Erica.

"Just don't be too cheeky. They may not realize you're just kidding," Alex rebutted as he threw a side-armed punch at Henry's shoulder.

"Hahaha, I promise to be on my best behavior," smirked Henry sarcastically.

"Okay, then, let's get out of here," Erica uttered as she shot up from her chair. "Have a good afternoon and send me updates as you take care of these cases." They waved as they headed out the door.

CHAPTER 3

On Friday afternoon, Charity prepared for the event at the Last Pin Standing Bowling Alley. It was almost five o'clock and she was looking through her bag. She had her camera for taking pictures, the voice recorder for recording interviews, and the gift card to give the Anderson family. Charity knew first-hand the challenges this family had overcome and how hard they had worked. It was great the community gathered around them to show support. She packed up all her things and straightened up her desk. She wanted to arrive at the bowling alley a little early and talk with the Andersons before they were bombarded with friends. She slid into her car and headed out.

Charity made a mental list of the questions she wanted to ask…First, what was the hardest thing you had to overcome? Second, do you think the foster family took good care of your children? And finally, do you feel you received the services you needed to ensure success? She always tried to keep the questions short because she wanted to celebrate the victories with the people she interviewed, not grill them about their apparent mistakes.

Charity also had a mental list of who else she wanted to talk with at the event. Of course, her list could change depending on who showed up. She usually talked with either the Family Service Worker, a CPS person, or the foster parents. She didn't know who she would be interviewing beyond the Andersons.

It was already dark, so the bright lights of the bowling alley made the place look like a happening hang-out. Since it was past Halloween, but not yet Thanksgiving, the bowling alley had white lights hung up on the outside of the building. They generally changed to colored Christmas lights on the day before Thanksgiving, putting people in the holiday spirit. She snatched her bag out of the car and walked inside. She made sure her name tag for *The Standard Banner* was visible.

As she walked in, she was bombarded by a wave of different aromas. She smelled pizza, the leftover hint of the aerosol the bowling alley attendants used to disinfect the shoes, French fries, coffee, and popcorn. Charity had always been fascinated by the smell of a bowling alley.

She ventured past the counter and was greeted by Charles Anderson, the father of Heather and Catherine Anderson. Yvette, his wife, also walked up to greet her. She could hear children's laughter in the background.

"We are so humbled that *The Standard Banner* wanted to do a story on our family. We are so grateful we got the children back home," said Yvette, as tears started to line her eyes.

"We never thought people cared so much about us until this all happened. We're incredibly lucky," Charles added.

Charity pulled out her voice recorder and hit the record button. "Right," she started. "I have a couple of questions for you then I will let you get to celebrating. First, what was the hardest thing you had to overcome?"

Trying to hold back tears, Charles finally confessed, "It was realizing that I had a depression issue that caused me to neglect my wife and children. I quit trying to work at all, and left Yvette to take care of everything on her own. That caused her to start taking pills to try and keep up with everything. It was only when Heather accidentally swallowed the pills that we knew we needed help. We are so grateful for the rehab treatment program that Yvette went through, as well as the counseling for me. I don't need medicine for the depression. I use supplements to help with my mood. I was able to get my job back at the same rate of pay. We are truly blessed."

"Do you think the foster parents took good care of Heather and Catherine while they were not at home," Charity pressed further.

"We couldn't have asked for better foster parents for the girls. They made it clear that they were only loving on them until they could get back home to us. We never felt threatened by them or that they were trying to take our kids from us," Yvette said proudly.

"Okay, final question. Do you feel like you received the services you needed to ensure success?" Charity inquired.

Before she could even think, both Charles and Yvette said in unison, "Yes." Then Charles took over, "I never thought of myself as someone people would go out of their way to help. The doctors and the counselor, and even my boss, have all been so encouraging. I just didn't know how to ask for help."

"I learned that I could feel better naturally, not depending on drugs to be able to handle daily life. I walk every day and take vitamins. I cut out the caffeine from my beverages and it has really made me feel better," Yvette offered happily.

Charity turned off the voice recorder and pulled out the gift card from her bag. "Here," she said, extending her hand, "I wanted to make sure you had a little something extra. I know how hard you both have worked to get your children back. Heather and Catherine are lucky."

Tears welled up again in both of their eyes as Charles took the gift card from Charity. All they could do was give Charity a group hug. Charity smiled and left them to go find the next person she needed to talk to for the story.

Charity knew someone from DCS was supposed to be there. She was on her way to get a bottle of water when someone called her name. When she turned around, Henry Thompson was standing there.

"What are you doing here?" Charity asked, recognizing him from court.

Henry grinned, "Well, I was the Anderson's Family Service Worker. I told you that, but I guess you didn't remember."

"Well, duh," she said slightly embarrassed. "Then I need to ask you a few questions. *The Standard Banner* is covering this story for the paper. Let me get the voice recorder, hang on."

As Charity fumbled through her bag to get the recorder, Henry had forgotten how cute she was. She had long, brown hair. Big, brown eyes. A few well-placed freckles dotted her nose. And she smelled of…Christmas.

As Charity turned back around to face him, Henry quickly shook the thoughts from his head. She turned on the recorder and asked, "What is your major focus when you have to take children to a new foster home?"

Henry thought for a moment then answered, "My major focus is to make sure the foster home meets the required standards of the children having the space for their belongings and a bed of their own."

Charity moved on to the next question," What do you feel is your most important contribution in the child and family team meeting and the foster care review board?"

"I feel that my most important contribution to both the CFTM and FCRB is that I stay as neutral as possible, but testify to the facts, good or bad. When the permanency plan is being worked hard by the biological parents, I make sure to shout their praise and tell of their hard work. And on the flip side of that, when they are not working the plan, I make sure the judge knows that as well. I must make sure those children are safe," Henry finished.

Charity looked melancholy for a minute. She could tell Henry really took his job seriously and wanted to do what was best, for both the children and the parents.

"Okay, final question. What would make you decide tomorrow that you would leave your job and not continue in this line of work? I can tell from your responses that you are the job, that you take this very seriously," Charity said admiringly.

"Whoa," Henry scratched his head. "I can't say I know the answer to that question. The right situation hasn't presented itself. I currently plan to 'Save the World' forever. I love what I do, and I'm good at it."

"Thank you, Henry, that was very informative." Charity put the voice recorder back in her bag as she queried, "I wonder if the family service worker who handled my case had as much conviction and compassion as you do."

That comment caught Henry off guard. No wonder she was at the court hearings, he thought. She must have been in the system. Not knowing what to say, he just grinned awkwardly and shrugged his shoulders.

"Sorry," Charity pouted, realizing he was looking at her with a strange expression on his face. "You have been helpful. I have one last person to talk to then I have to head home."

"Will I see you around?" Henry asked earnestly. "Maybe at the foster care review board?"

Channeling her absolute best Jack Burton impression, Charity backed up as she replied, "You never can tell." She turned and left to find the last person she needed to speak with.

****

Buzz Cooper arrived early Monday morning to find Charity working furiously on her computer. She was putting the finishing touches on her public interest story about the Anderson family. "Charity? Why are you here so early?"

Charity didn't look up from her keyboard when she responded, "I need to get this done and send it to you. I need to be at the Silver Horseshoe Ranch around one o'clock. I wanted to make sure my assignment was completed. I should have finished this over the weekend, but I have had a lot of things on my mind. Shoot," she pounded her fist on the desk angrily, "I just realized I didn't take any pictures. Will that be a problem?"

"No, it will be fine," replied Buzz. "Your story is the last one I need to get the paper out by this afternoon. Marcus and Rachel gave me their assignments yesterday."

"Thank you, I appreciate that," Charity replied, embarrassed she forgot. Buzz waved to her as he headed into his office and closed the door. He must have been working on something big because he immediately began sharpening his pencils. Charity clicked her story back up to the beginning and read it out loud. She read the article again and was happy with the result. She saved it as a PDF then sent it to Buzz. She didn't feel like working, as she couldn't concentrate. She texted Buzz asking if she could head on out. He gave her a "thumbs up" emoji on her phone. She replied, "TY," and left the office.

Later that day in the Jefferson County DCS office, Erica was reading the afternoon edition of *The Standard Banner*. She was looking for the public interest story, finding it on the second page. She almost finished it when Henry, Randi, and Alex walked in the room. "Henry Thompson is a conscientious worker for child welfare and makes absolutely sure the situation is safe for children to return home," Erica read out loud as she glanced at Henry, whose face flashed red at that last line. "I didn't know you were so conscientious, Henry," she joked.

"Yeah," Alex chimed in, "how much did you pay the girl to say that about you?"

"Come on, guys, you know I have no influence with the paper, and besides, I don't even know this girl. Well, unless you count almost knocking her down in the lobby of juvenile court last week," Henry said defensively.

"Well, she obviously seems impressed with how you handled the Anderson case. We may have to make you our PR person when dealing with *The Standard Banner*," Erica said approvingly.

Henry sat down at the table and pulled the paper toward him so he could read the entire story himself. As he read it, he could almost sense the sadness in her writing. It was a happy story, to be sure, but her words expressed something different. He remembered how she looked that night. Her cute, freckled nose. Her big, brown eyes, and the fact that she must have spent time in the system. She was a puzzle, and he found himself thinking about how to help her. Charity Walters…had she had that same name this entire time? He snapped back to reality and realized he had some papers to process before leaving for the day.

****

As Charity pulled up at the house of the Silver Horseshoe Ranch, a woman she had never seen before met her at the front door. "Hello, Charity, my name is Theresa Wilson. I worked for your uncle and aunt. I didn't get to meet you last week. Please come inside." Theresa was a lovely woman around fifty years old with brown eyes and slightly graying brown hair. She was a little taller than Charity and had a medium build. She was impeccably dressed, wearing a red apron.

"Thank you, I still can't believe I had family, and this is, uh, was their place," Charity said incredulously.

"Well, you mean it's your place," corrected Theresa

"Yeah, that will take some getting used to," confessed Charity.

"Let me show you around the house," Theresa said as she led Charity further into the living room. "We will start here."

Charity saw a big living room filled with normal sized furniture. The floors were hardwood, but a large rug covered the center of the room. Pictures of green, rolling pastures with trees in their autumn colors of orange, yellow, and red hung on the walls. It was obvious Fall had been their favorite season. Uncle Frank and Aunt Marion also apparently loved books. There were two bookcases, that went from the floor to the ceiling, with books of all kinds, poetry, classic stories like *Frankenstein*, and so many others. There was no television in this room, so it must have been a sitting room to converse with visitors.

"Wow, this is a great room," Charity stated in awe.

"They would sit in here for hours talking to each other and reading a few pages in between," teased Theresa. "They loved each other very much."

Next, they walked down the hall where pictures of beautiful flower arrangements hung on both sides. From there, they toured the huge kitchen. It had a breakfast bar and an eat-in kitchen table that sat eight people. The appliances were state of the art and the fridge blended in with the cabinets. Off to one side was the formal dining room with a china cabinet filled with beautiful dishes. The table sat ten people. The walls were decorated with scripture verses. There was also a bonus room, a full bathroom downstairs, and an office. Theresa opened the French doors to the office and Charity saw a huge, solid wood brown desk. The walls in the office were decorated with maps. There was a large tapestry map of the United States, taking up almost one entire wall. On another wall was a map of Tennessee enclosed in a brown wooden frame. And finally, there were pictures of what must have been the places Uncle Frank owned before he died. Sevier, Jefferson, and Blount counties were written on the bottom of the maps. A giant globe was in the corner next to a set of fancy, green leather armchairs. It looked so formal. She wondered what kind of business deals were made in this room. The master bedroom was also on the main floor. Theresa opened the door and they walked in. The bed was the biggest bed she had ever seen. Pictures of both her uncle and aunt were still on the bedside tables. The rest of the room was decorated with beautiful Italian villa scenes, the waterways of Venice, opulent grape vineyards, and touristy port cities. The bathroom was equally impressive with both a shower and a deep, garden-style bathtub. She could see herself soaking in the tub after a long day with Max watching over her.

Exiting the bedroom, Charity bravely asked, "Theresa, if it was only just the two of them, why are the tables in both the kitchen and dining room so large and this house so big?"

"Your folks always had the men who worked the ranch for them eat with them at the table. They wanted to make sure all the men knew they were greatly appreciated for who they were, not just that they tended to the horses and the grounds," Theresa explained. "As far as the house size and that story, Chuck can explain more about that when you talk with him."

Theresa walked Charity upstairs where there were five bedrooms-yes, five. There were also two full bathrooms, one on each side of the hall. They were all meticulously kept and had beautiful décor. Theresa could see Charity was getting overwhelmed, so she suggested she go check in with Chuck.

Chuck was outside when Theresa walked Charity out to meet him. He was grooming a horse named Maverick. Maverick was a chestnut-brown color. Chuck rode Maverick most of the time. Charity always wanted horses, that is until she found out she was allergic to them. How was she going to make this ranch thing work?

"Chuck," Theresa began, "I think Charity has absorbed all the information she can right now. I just showed her the house. Why don't we have her spend the night and you can talk things over tomorrow?"

"What, are you sure you want me here overnight?" Charity said in disbelief.

"Well why in heaven's, not? You are the owner now. You may as well get acclimated some time," Chuck said authoritatively.

"Good thing I have a cat, and not some other animal at my apartment. Cats are used to fending for themselves. Max will just make me work a little harder for attention when I get home. Sure, I would love to stay," Charity reasoned. "I just need to let my boss know I will be a little late tomorrow."

CHAPTER 4

Charity was amazed at how well she slept in an unfamiliar house. Since she was the owner, Theresa and Chuck insisted she sleep in the master bedroom, though she would have been happy sleeping on the couch. She and Max did that on a regular basis. While she didn't drink coffee, the smell of it in the morning always gave her a warm feeling inside. She put her hair in a messy bun and brushed her teeth with the toothbrush she kept in her purse, then wandered into the kitchen.

Theresa was rattling pans, about to start breakfast. "Good morning, Charity," Theresa smiled. "I didn't think to ask, do you prefer bacon or sausage? And how do you like your eggs?"

"Bacon, always, over sausage. When I do eat eggs, I like them scrambled with cheese. And I will never turn down waffles or pancakes," Charity replied rubbing her hands together, thinking about waffles.

"Got it, you are so unfussy," Theresa laughed. "You would be surprised at what some of these guys eat."

As if on cue, Chuck walked into the kitchen, "Are you going on about that again, Theresa? You know us, we need a big, hearty breakfast, and not those muffins and bagels? We get hungry again before we even get two horse stalls mucked out. And no one wants to think about food after standing in horse manure," Chuck reasoned with a bit of sarcasm.

"Well, I guess that makes sense," Theresa relented as she declared herself the loser of that battle. "No more sugar breakfasts, that is unless Charity eats them."

"No, don't look at me," Charity remarked holding her hands up defensively. "I skip breakfast most of the time. There are cases to be involved with and stories to write for the paper. I eat when I get hungry."

"Theresa will be a few minutes. Let's finish looking around outside on the grounds," Chuck said as he motioned her outside. He had a cup of coffee in his hand but held the door open for Charity as she walked through behind him.

Charity hadn't noticed yesterday, but there was a small, cottage-size house attached to the back of the main floor of the house. There were also two vehicles parked off to the side, a green El Camino, and a black Cadillac Escalade "What is that for?" Charity asked.

"That is the staff living quarters. In the past, Theresa and I spent almost all our time here on the property. Neither of us have close family, so we decided to stay here on sight permanently and work with your Uncle Frank and Aunt Marion. It is bigger than it looks. Theresa and I have our own separate rooms, each with a huge bathroom. Since we were always here, Frank just built an addition to the house. There is a secret door between the formal dining room and the kitchen. We were all a great team. We were equals in their eyes, not just hired help," Chuck said with a slight catch in his throat. "There is one other fella who works here during the day and go home. All the other fellas have fallen away over the last while to work somewhere else."

"I saw Maverick. How many horses are on the ranch, and who do they all belong to?" Charity asked with curiosity.

"Well, the barn is large enough to hold ten horses. There are only five that belong to the Silver Horseshoe. Your Uncle Frank had a soft spot for underdogs, horses most people would give up on. There is Ginger, which is a big, rusty-brown mare. Lightning, a sleek, black gelding, who is terrified of everything. Mr. Whiskers is a miniature pony with a bunch of unruly hairs around his mouth. He is a good-natured fella. And last, we have Sinbad, a white stallion that was delivered to Frank just about three weeks before he died. Sinbad is still having a little trouble adjusting here. He seemed to have formed a quick bond with Frank. And with him gone, he isn't interested in many people," Chuck finished with a sad air in his words.

"I don't know why, but can you show me Sinbad? I can't promise I won't sneeze on you, but I want to see him," Charity said, shocked the words came out of her mouth.

They walked over to the fence that lined the pasture. Chuck whistled. Nothing happened. He whistled again. Finally, a white horse came trotting timidly over to the fence. "Whoa, boy," Chuck soothed, extending his hand to let Sinbad sniff him. "That's a good boy."

Charity slowly reached out her hand. First, Sinbad pulled his head away from her. She tried again and he sniffed her palm. She heard you should always extend an open palm to a horse. "Wow, he's letting me touch him. That's a good boy," she whispered as she stroked the side of his face. She had been around horses before, so she knew a little, but when her allergies got so bad, she had to give them up. She was even allergic to Max, but decided she wasn't going to abandon him. They needed each other...but Max didn't make her sneeze as much. She was touching the felty part of Sinbad's muzzle when, suddenly, "Achoo." Then she sneezed again. And again.

"Okay! Enough horse petting for one day," Chuck intervened. "You really do have it bad, don't you?"

Charity felt terrible. She sneezed six more times before she got back to the kitchen. Since she hadn't gone back to her apartment last night, she didn't have any allergy medicine. She had used up the stash she kept in her car.

"Here, take a spoonful of honey," Theresa exclaimed as she brought over a heaping spoonful with her hand underneath to catch any spillage. "Honey is nature's remedy for allergies. It is locally grown, so it should work faster than any pill."

Charity grabbed the spoon and swallowed it down, "Ugh, this tastes terrible." Though she didn't like the taste of it, she could feel an almost immediate sense of relief. She drank a little water to help get the taste out of her mouth.

Theresa had breakfast ready and motioned Charity to the breakfast bar where she had a plate of pancakes and bacon waiting for her. "Here, go ahead and eat your breakfast. It will help to get food in your stomach along with that honey."

Charity realized she had not washed her hands after petting Sinbad and went to the sink and washed. She sat back down and before she knew it, she had eaten her food very quickly. Theresa had just gotten Chuck's breakfast on the bar as Charity put her plate in the sink.

Charity sat quietly as Chuck ate his eggs and bacon. She knew it was hard to answer questions and eat at the same time. When he finished his last bite, she asked, "When we met the first time, you mentioned we had business to take care of and you needed my input. What kind of business?"

Chuck wiped his mouth with his napkin and said, "Every year, the Silver Horseshoe hosts a Christmas event for hardship families. Families where both parents work but have a hard time making ends meet. They have jobs, but you know around here, people must drive a ways to have the good paying jobs. We need get the preparations going for the party. It happens on Christmas Eve."

"But that's a little over a month away. What could possibly take so long to need to start this soon?" Charity inquired.

"You'll be surprised. We don't start until the Monday after Thanksgiving to put up the Christmas decorations, but we must make sure the city knows our plans so they can invite the appropriate families. We know people have their pride and all, so we are always respectful. It's not a handout for them. We just give a little extra Christmas cheer," Chuck explained.

A light bulb went off in Charity's head. "Do you think we may be able to host an event for foster kids the weekend before Thanksgiving? It is a little more than two weeks away, but I think we can pull it off. They aren't fussy. They just want to know people care about them," she said excitedly.

"Well, I don't see why not. We could have lots of turkey-themed decorations and maybe have a surprise visit by Old Saint Nick himself," Chuck offered with a smile.

"That would be so exciting," boomed Charity.

"Well, I think it's time you gave your landlord a notice you plan to move. Let's get your belongings here and get you going in style," said Chuck as he pulled out his wallet and removed a debit card. "I should have done this before, but here is the debit card to your new bank. You have things to do, little lady. Let's hit it."

"But what do I do about Max? Can he live here in the house, or will he have to stay outside?" Charity wondered.

"It's your house, now. He comes with you and can go where you go," Chuck reassured her.

****

When he wasn't working, Henry usually spent his evenings relaxing with a book or watching a movie. But tonight, he opted to listen to music. Christmas music to be exact. He reclined on the couch as he queued up some of his favorite classic songs. He was halfway through the playlist when his thoughts turned to Charity Walters. He still really didn't know her…but he knew he wanted to know her better. He grabbed his cell phone and texted Erica.

"Hey, Erica, sorry to bother. How long does information on children who age-out of foster care stay in the Tennessee Family and Child Tracking System (TFACTS)?" Henry asked.

"IDK, once the case is concluded, we don't usually have any more contact. Hope that helps. What's up?" Erica typed back.

"Nothing in particular. Just wondering. TY," Henry replied.

"YW, have a great evening." Erica responded.

Henry went to the truck, retrieving his computer. He sat on the couch, opened the computer, and typed in "Charity Walters" in the TFACTS bar. It took a few minutes, but something finally came up. "Great," he said as he rubbed his hands together. "Let's take a look and see what we can find out."

Henry saw that Charity entered the system just before her fourth birthday. Her entry into the system occurred when the Walters couple who adopted her as a baby died in a car accident. It had been raining and they ran off the road and hit a tree. Luckily, Charity had not been in the car. It seemed the woman's maiden name had been Ledford. It took him through the placements she had lived. One by one, the placements had fallen apart on Charity. It said that at age fourteen, she decided she didn't want to get adopted. When she aged-out at eighteen, the Avery family was her foster family and Jennifer Ryan was her FSW. It was amazing that she had lived within a thirty-mile radius her entire life. He reread the file again and a name stuck out- Ledford. Wasn't there someone who died recently with that last name?

Henry opened another tab and searched for the last name Ledford. Ah, an obituary notice came up in *The Jefferson County Post*. It read:

Frank Ledford, real estate mogul and owner of the Silver Horseshoe

Ranch, died at the age of 76 from a brain tumor. His wife, Marion Ledford, preceded him in death. He was also preceded in death by their son, Jeremy Ledford, who died fifteen years prior. The estate is in the process of settling the accounts as a long, lost relative has been identified.

Henry couldn't believe it. How did *The Standard Banner* miss this? Henry guessed that Charity was the long, lost relative they were talking about. He wondered if she knew yet.

He had another idea. He typed in Jennifer Ryan. He didn't recognize the name although, he had been with the department for the last six years. There…maybe he could get a little background information that could help Charity get some closure.

Reading the notes out loud, Henry began, "Jennifer Ryan retired in 2013. After retirement, she moved to Texas to care for an ailing parent." Henry wondered if she made any notes on Charity's last court visit. It took him a little while, but he found Jennifer's notes on Charity dated November 2, 2012. They read:

Today was the last time I had contact with Charity Walters. I'm going to miss that kid. She is one of the bravest teens I have ever encountered. Though she decided to not seek adoption, she worked well with her foster family and has a good start for journalism school and making a future for herself. Though I have not always revealed it to her, I have loved Charity as if she was part of my own family. This is the last entry of case notes on Charity Walters.

Jennifer Ryan, DCS FSW

"Wow, it seems the answer to Charity's question of whether or not her worker cared as much was a definite YES. What do I do now?" Henry wondered. Henry could tell this news was going to keep him riled up until he had a chance to talk to Charity. The problem was, he didn't know when he would see her again.

****

When Charity arrived at work on Wednesday morning, Rachel, Marcus, and Mr. Cooper were all talking softly among themselves. When they saw

Charity come in, they scattered. She thought that a little odd, then realized why as she looked at the copy of the paper for today that was on her desk. It had a story that read…

The Standard Banner's very own Charity Walters has become the newest overnight sensation. She was recently named sole beneficiary to the Silver Horseshoe Ranch, right here in Jefferson County. Though she spent much of her life in the foster care system, she graduated from high school, then went on to journalism school. Working many jobs while taking classes for her major, Charity graduated early, in just two and a half years. She has been the Public Interest story writer for this paper for the last five years. She has also submitted a children's book to a publisher for consideration for publication. *The Standard Banner* is incredibly proud of her and all she has accomplished in her young life. We expect good things from our Charity Walters.

She couldn't believe what she was reading. Was she ready for the world to know about this? Would that mean that all the former foster parents she ever had would now come looking to her for a handout? "Buzz, did you write this?" Charity asked trying to recover from the shock.

"I did. I thought you deserved to have a bit of fame. You have worked so hard your entire life. Now you don't have to," Buzz said unapologetically.

Rachel butted in, "I tried to explain to him you may not want to have this out there, but well, it's done."

Marcus inquired, "Have you thought about how to invest the money yet? What do you plan on doing now that you have more money than you know what to do with? I'm always here for advice, you know."

"Look, um, I need to get some things done at the ranch. Can I take some time off?" Charity requested.

Buzz could see the blurb in the paper had upset her. He should have asked her before setting it to print. It was too late to change it now. Rachel was right, what's done is done. "Sure, kid, take as long as you need. There isn't much that happens this time of year anyway. And if it does, you can work remotely."

"Thanks, Mr. Cooper," Charity said as she retrieved her bag and purse and turned to head back out. "Thanks for understanding. I'm not mad. I just don't know what I am expected to do now. I have been used to working myself for the things I have. Now, I just need time to think."

By the time she got to her car, Rachel had texted her, "R U okay?"

"I'm fine. Going to start boxing up my apartment and give the complex my notice. They want me moved in at the ranch as soon as possible. I have to make sure I remember foster care review board is this afternoon at five o'clock," Charity returned text. "Thanks!"

Having a jeep is great when you need to haul things around. Right now, she needed moving boxes. She stopped at the home improvement store and bought as many as she could fit in the back of her jeep.

When she got to the apartment, she called Beverly in the office. "Hello, Beverly? This is Charity Walters. I need to give you a moving notice, effective immediately. I know there are three months left on my lease. I can pay you that amount when I turn in my keys. Thanks."

She carried the boxes inside and assembled them. Good thing she remembered the packaging tape. She had to keep getting Max out of the big boxes. She stood there for a moment and realized she really didn't feel like organizing things in boxes, so she stretched out across the couch. She knew she might fall asleep, so she set a timer for four o'clock. That way she would have plenty of time to get to the foster care review board. She grabbed her blanket and closed her eyes.

Next thing she knew, her timer was going off and Max was sleeping on her head. She pushed him off and went to check her hair and clothes. She had to look her best. She would sit in and ask questions on cases for this afternoon's review board. She wasn't presenting any information, just listening.

She drove to the juvenile courthouse. She went through the security section and back to the desk and checked in with Daniel, the court clerk.

"You're in Room Two this evening, Charity," Daniel relayed to her.

"Thanks, Daniel. Have a great night," Charity replied as she slipped over to Room Two.

The door was open, so she went inside and took her seat on the panel. She greeted the people on her left and right, then settled in.

Charity didn't pay attention as the first group of people came in and took their seats. This foster family had a baby, so the child didn't have to be present. Their Resource Parent Support Worker was present. The biological parents and their worker were also present. A Family Service Worker representing the baby was supposed to be there as well, but Charity didn't know who that was.

Charity and the other panel members listened as they heard good news of how the biological parents were doing everything on their permanency plan. The foster mom talked about how big the baby was getting and that she responded well after coming home from visitation. Charity's thoughts drifted from the present moment to things at the ranch. Then she heard the Family Service Worker speak and suddenly she snapped back to attention.

"Members of the panel, it is my recommendation that the child should return home after Thanksgiving. So much hard work had been done by Mr. and Mrs. Stewart that they need their little one back home," Henry said as neutrally as possible, as he looked Charity right in the eyes.

Charity felt heat flash to her face but returned his gaze and smiled. He took his seat and waited to hear from the panel.

The lead panel member cleared his throat and said, "It is always a good day to hear how hard a family works to ensure reunification with their children. It will be recommended to the judge to allow Breanna Stewart to return home as soon as possible, based on the court dates available. Thank you for being here today."

The foster parents and Mr. and Mrs. Stewart met in the aisle and talked about Breanna. Charity had to be in the room for the next two cases, so she stayed seated. Henry walked up to her and said, "Charity, I wasn't expecting to see you on this case this afternoon. How are you?"

"I've had a really interesting couple of weeks. But otherwise, I'm okay," she said, realizing it sounded kind of cryptic. "How's work been for you?"

"Well, luckily, this week has been uneventful. Did you do anything fun?' He hoped she would mention her new situation.

"Nothing I care to comment on. Just suffice it to say, it was remarkably interesting and educational," she replied.

Darn it, Henry thought, she wasn't spilling the beans. He had to go about this a different way. Henry put those thoughts on hold because the next case was coming in and he was not part of that one. "Oh, I have to go," Henry started, "I have nothing to do with this next case. See you later?" Before she could say it, he piped up, "I know, you never can tell." She blushed again that he remembered her saying that to him last week.

"You got it," Charity said pointing her thumb and index finger at him in a gun-like shape. "See you next time."

The case was finally finished and as she walked out of the doors, Henry met her with a Diet Mountain Dew in his hand. "Thought you could use a cold drink. Well, it was cold forty-five minutes ago. I didn't know when you were going to be finished."

"How did you? Oh, yeah. I said I liked them when you were glad you didn't spill coffee all over me," Charity said feeling suddenly timid as she took the drink from him. "Thank you very much. That was thoughtful."

Charity turned to head out to her car and Henry walked beside her. "You must be hungry," Henry started sheepishly, wondering if she would turn him down. "Want to grab a bite to eat?"

Charity stopped walking and thought for a moment, "Sure, but I get to pick the place."

"Okay," Henry agreed. "I'll just follow you. What kind of car do you have?"

"I have a blue Jeep Cherokee. No need to follow me. Just meet me at The Sandwich Shop. They have great soup and sandwiches. I got a chill in the courtroom and need to warm up," Charity explained as they parted ways in the parking lot.

Charity pulled into the parking lot at the Sandwich Shop. She got out of her jeep when she saw Henry walk up. He opened the door for her, and they walked inside. Charity had a standing order here, so she told Pablo, "I'll have the usual, please." Pablo nodded and sent the ticket to the cook. Henry needed a minute to look at the menu. Charity could see him struggling with what to order so she told Pablo, "Give him the number two, please."

Henry looked at her wondering, "Will it be good? I don't like food surprises."

"I promise you'll like it or your money back. Pablo makes the best sandwiches," she reassured him.

They found a seat at a table and only had to wait a few minutes when Jasmine, the server, brought out their food. Charity immediately started with the potato soup. She ate three spoonfuls in rapid succession, trying to make herself warm up. "Oh, that is so much better," she said before taking a bite of her sandwich.

Henry took a bite of his sandwich, toasted roast beef and provolone cheese, lettuce, tomatoes, and banana peppers. He was pleasantly surprised and declared, "Oh, this is good. Sorry I doubted you. And these huge chips are so crunchy."

"I'm glad you like it. Why did you wait around for me?" Charity asked cautiously.

He finished chewing the food in his mouth. He took a big sip of his tea, and said, "Well, I've been wanting to talk to you more than five minutes at a time since the day I almost flattened you in the courthouse lobby. You said some things that make me want to get to know you better."

Charity thought of herself as boring. How did she manage to intrigue him? "Oh, sorry. I must have sounded ridiculous." Taking the time to really look at Henry, Charity noticed he was good-looking. He was a bit taller than she was, slender but muscular, having brown hair and green eyes.

"On the contrary. You sounded fascinating," Henry said trying not to let his feelings gush out all over the table. He needed to maintain a little self-control.

"So, what do you want to know about me?" she continued.

"There are several things. Let's start from the top. Why do you attend the foster care review boards? What's in it for you?" Henry questioned.

Her expression changed to show a little sadness as soon as Henry posed that question. He almost regretted it. Charity began, "I guess I attend the foster care review boards as a way of giving back to the children in foster care. I spent most of my life in custody. I had a few chances for a permanent home, but they didn't work out. By the time I turned fourteen, I decided I was tired of the disappointments and aged-out at eighteen. I want children to know there is someone advocating for their success at going back home to their parents or getting to a 'forever family' and starting new."

"So that's what you meant at the Anderson party, during the interview. You said you wondered if the family service worker who worked your case cared as much as you think I do," Henry remembered feeling sad for her and wondered if he should mention what he found out about Jennifer Ryan. He opted to wait for another time.

"Wow, you remembered that?" Charity posed.

"Yeah, I remember all kinds of important information. Hard to believe though, right?" He joked.

Charity felt a little funny. He was trying hard to be attentive to her.

"Remembering facts must come in very handy in your line of work," she said sarcastically.

"Oh, I see how you are," he jabbed. "You won't get away with things that easily. Next question, how did you end up working at *The Standard Banner*?"

"Well, all through high school I wrote for the school paper. I entered writing contests and won first place once. I earn enough at the paper to be able to live on my own," Charity basked in confidence.

"That's great. There are not many foster children who age-out and make it on their own. You beat the odds," Henry said admiringly.

"I know," she replied.

"Then why do you look so unhappy?" Henry questioned.

"Well, the weirdest thing happened. I don't like to talk much about it. Two weeks ago, I received a letter saying that I was the sole beneficiary of a great uncle and aunt who have both died now. I have a horse ranch and I'm allergic to horses. And what's worse, I don't know what to do with it. I have never had more than a paycheck's worth of money saved at any given time," Charity concluded. She couldn't believe she told Henry all that, but somehow, she felt relieved that someone else knew besides her coworkers.

Henry already figured out she must have been the lost relative. He couldn't believe she told him all that she was feeling. "Wow, I don't know what to say. What can I do to help you?"

Charity had a hard time discerning if he really wanted to help her or if he felt obligated now that she got all moody on him. "I appreciate your thoughtfulness. There isn't anything to do for now. I have taken some time off from work and need to move from my apartment to the ranch. I started on that today, but just couldn't bring myself to pack any boxes. I think I will call a moving company tomorrow and let them do the heavy lifting…literally."

"If you could wait until the weekend, I can help move things with my truck," Henry offered. Before he could say anything else, she waved him off.

"No need for that. I can do it. It will help me process things as I work through it. Besides, I don't think Max would behave himself," she said taking a sip of her drink.

"Max?" Henry asked brow raised.

"My cat. It's been the two of us for four years now," Charity explained. Feeling a little overwhelmed, she exclaimed, "Oh, look at the time! It's eight o'clock. I have to leave. I have a lot of moving to get done." She gathered her belongings. "Catch you next time." She got up from the table and went out the door.

"Bye." He didn't realize she had written down her phone number on the sticky note she left for him. It said, *Text me when you can. I had fun. Thanks. C* He almost knocked the table over when he read that. He got in his truck and drove home.

CHAPTER 5

On Thursday, Charity moved her belongings to the ranch. She opened the gate, going through to the end of the driveway with the moving truck behind her.

Theresa popped out of the house and gave the men instructions, "Please put Charity's personal items in the master bedroom, here on the main floor. There's room in the office for the other boxes. Please put the big furniture pieces in the garage. It's empty."

"Thank you, Theresa," Charity uttered. "I had no clue what to tell them to do with everything."

"I must return to the kitchen. I have to keep an eye on a pot roast in the crockpot. Biscuits or cornbread?" Theresa probed.

"What would your guess be?" Charity tossed back seriously.

"Biscuits, definitely biscuits," Theresa replied.

"Oh, you're good," Charity responded with a huge grin. "I'm definitely going to like it here."

Theresa projected as big a smile as any one person could muster. Going back into the kitchen, she thought of how great it felt to be needed by someone again. She had never married and had children. And with the

Ledfords gone, there were just a few ranch hands to keep her company. Excitement bubbled up in her as she considered the impact she could make on Charity's life.

Charity watched as all the boxes were removed from the truck and placed in the house. Her phone buzzed. It was Henry.

"How are things going with the moving?" Henry texted.

"I'm here at the ranch getting the boxes off the truck. What are you doing?" She texted back.

"I took the day off to get work done on my truck. Just wanted to check on you. I know this is a big step for you," Henry admitted.

"Thanks for caring," Charity replied.

The movers finished unloading and headed out. "The gate will open by itself as you pull up to it," Charity called out. "Thanks!"

When she went back inside, Chuck sat at the bar drinking a cold glass of water. Sinbad had been difficult to coax to the stable to get new shoes put on. Charity realized she never asked Chuck why the house was so big, since it had just been Uncle Frank and Aunt Marion. She thought she would ask him now.

"Chuck," she began, "why is this such a big house when it was just Uncle Frank and Aunt Marion? What were they planning to do with the ranch?"

In his usual fashion when answering questions, Chuck pushed his hat back on his head, "Well, your folks wanted to have lots of children. They were fortunate to have Jeremy. It was too hard on your aunt to have any more children. When she had a miscarriage when Jeremy was two, they decided not to try anymore. Jeremy lived here until he went off to school. He became a big shot businessman in Nashville and didn't come home much. Then he was killed in that car accident. He never married because he was too busy chasing the next big deal. So, your folks decided on having the Christmas Eve parties for the hardship families and help support their children. It often takes two parents working hard to give children a good upbringing. They had other things they did to give back to people, but the Christmas Eve party was the one they loved best."

Charity was speechless, so she let silence hang in the air for a moment. Then she remembered the event she wanted to have in addition to the one on Christmas Eve. "Hey, what is the best way to start planning the Thanksgiving shindig for the foster kids? Oh, and could I possibly bring a couple children out here this Saturday? I promised them I would spend some time with them. They have a hard case right now. Mr. Whiskers may just be the thing to help the situation."

"Absolutely," Chuck said. "You can use this place however you feel like you ought to. Your folks would want you to make sure you did what made you happy. Just ask Theresa about the event planner for the Thanksgiving thing."

What made her happy…that would take some serious thinking to uncover. As she walked past the office and saw her boxes, she felt an idea start to bubble up. She wandered through the entire house again, looking carefully at the items in each room. She realized almost all the things she brought from her apartment were totally unnecessary. She decided to ask Theresa about this before texting Henry.

"Theresa, I looked through the entire house and realized I don't need most of the things I brought from my apartment. I wish I had thought to check before moving it all here. I know a guy who is a family service worker for DCS. Maybe I could ask him if he knows of any families who need these things so they can have their children come back home," Charity said proudly. This is one more way she wanted to give back to families in the system.

"Honey, that is a marvelous idea. But don't feel like you must give your things away. Keep what you want that belongs to you. If there are items here in the house you don't want, move those out, too," Theresa said with authority. "You are the mistress of the ranch now. Make this the home the way you want it."

Charity was a big hugger, so before she could help herself, she gave Theresa the biggest hug she had given anyone in a long time. "Thank you," she said happily and went off to text Henry.

She pulled out her phone and texted, "It's me, Charity. Have your truck back yet?"

A few seconds later Henry responded, "About to check out now. What's up?"

"Want to talk about it in person. Can you come to the Silver Horseshoe Ranch? When you get here, I will text you the gate code. We will feed you dinner…pot roast and biscuits," she sent back to Henry.

"I'll be there as soon as possible," Henry replied.

Charity had a feeling she forgot something. "Max!" she exclaimed. He was still in the kitty carrier in the jeep. She ran to her vehicle, opened the door, and pulled him out. "Are you okay? Let's get you inside." She had to make a second trip to grab the large bag that held all his food, the cat litter, and litter box. She went to her bedroom and shut the door. She put him in the bathroom and closed that door. She opened the flap to the carrier and Max flew out with a hiss. She filled his litter box. She put out a water bowl and his food bowl. He was a bit moody and didn't want anything to do with her. She completely understood and left the bathroom door open but shut the bedroom door as she went to the kitchen.

Charity opened the door of the refrigerator. Sometime when she wasn't aware, Theresa had put Diet Mountain Dew bottles in there, and they were ice cold. She grabbed one then pushed out the back door to stand by the pasture fence. She glimpsed the horses in the distance. They surely were beautiful animals. She felt the breeze blowing across her face. The fall air hung heavy with the aromas of hay, leaves, and Theresa's pot roast. She also smelled cinnamon…and apples. Theresa must have made a pie. She couldn't believe how Theresa knew so many of her favorite things without hardly knowing her at all.

Forty-five minutes later, Henry texted Charity, "I'm here at the gate. How do I get through?"

"Punch in 1103*," Charity texted back.

"Got it, on my way." He replied.

Charity went back through the kitchen and bolted out the front door to meet Henry. "I'm glad you're here. I need to pick your brain about something especially important. Come on inside," Charity began as they walked to the kitchen. Henry was awestruck as he viewed the things in the house. "What would you like to drink?"

Henry asked, "Do you have tea?"

Just then Theresa appeared responding, "Of course, we do, that's the best drink anyone could want," teasing Charity. Theresa poured a glass of tea for Henry.

"Theresa, how long until dinner is ready?" Charity pondered.

"Maybe thirty minutes," Theresa replied.

"Okay," Charity explained, "I just want to show Henry around out back."

She walked Henry out the back door toward the pasture fence. She pointed out the staff area built on the back. Henry felt the breeze on his face. "Wow," Henry started to say, "the view out here is so peaceful. The birds flying, the trees, one could get lost out here, just watching nature."

"I know, but nature and I have this love-hate thing going on. I want to enjoy it, but my face has other ideas," Charity said sarcastically.

"Come on, it can't be that bad," Henry said when Charity held her hand up to stop him.

"I sneezed all over Chuck the other day. It was awful. But Theresa came to my rescue with a spoonful of honey," Charity said thankfully. "I never would have made it without the honey."

Suddenly, Sinbad trotted over and stood in front of Charity and Henry. "Whoa, I never thought he'd do that," Charity said shocked. "After my sneezing fit, I figured he wouldn't want anything to do with me. Chuck said Sinbad has had a hard time since my Uncle Frank died. Apparently, they formed a bond."

Henry held his hand out, "Hey there, boy, nice fella."

Charity looked at Henry, "You like horses?"

"Oh, I love horses. I've been around them since before I can remember. We have pictures of me on horses with my dad. I took lessons when I was twelve. I always wanted one, but with our lifestyle, it didn't make sense," Henry replied. Sinbad let him pat him on the side of the face. Then Sinbad dashed off.

"Let me give you a walk-around tour before we are ready to eat. We still have a while," Charity uttered excitedly, grabbing Henry by the hand. She quickly let go of it as she used both hands to animatedly show him the rest of the ranch. "Over here is the arena," Charity started excitedly. "I'm not sure what Chuck does with the horses in here, maybe break them in." They walked a little further around the house. "This is the garage. Weirdly, there are no cars parked in it now. But I do have my furniture items out there."

Henry couldn't believe how large the ranch was and that this was now Charity's home. They came back around to the front of the house where Charity climbed the porch steps and sat on the swing. Henry took a seat beside her. Automatically, she started to move the swing back and forth, creating the creaky rhythm. Henry moved with her.

"I love sitting in the swing, hearing the creaky metal sound. I think better the noisier it gets," Charity confessed.

"With all the changes you have experienced, you must sit here quite a lot," Henry voiced logically. "Plus, the view is great here."

"Yeah, I have been here a few times, that's for certain. What do you do when you need to think?" Charity asked surprising Henry with the question.

"Oh, I go for a drive, or make a list or something," Henry answered.

"I go for drives, too!" Charity exclaimed. "We seem to have some things in common, huh?"

"Yes, I'd say quite a few," Henry declared, still moving to the swinging movement.

"Oh, I think we better go wash for dinner," Charity prompted. Henry followed her back into the house, and they washed up and asked Theresa where they needed to sit for dinner.

"We will be at the table here in the kitchen. We usually just use the formal dining room when we have special company or on special occasions," Theresa said as she was pulling the biscuits out of the oven. "Don't forget your drinks and go pick your spot. We don't have assigned seats around here," she winked at Charity. "Now, here are the plates. You can use a bowl if you want and the silverware is on the counter," Theresa told them. "Did you find what you wanted to drink, Henry?"

"I did, thanks. I found the tea jug and got a refill," answered Henry respectfully.

"Henry, I forgot to ask, are you right or left-handed?" Charity questioned.

"Left-handed, why?" Henry wondered.

"Well, then you need to either sit on the end or on my left side. That way you won't bump elbows," Charity said trying to be considerate.

Henry didn't know what to say. No one ever cared about that. It was weird that she would notice, "Oh, how thoughtful, I have bumped lots of elbows in my day."

Charity took a bite of the pot roast. She loved the celery and potatoes. "This is delicious, Theresa, thank you for cooking."

Henry was shoving another spoonful in his mouth as he nodded vigorously, "It is good."

Chuck and Theresa made their plates and took their seat at the table.

Everyone must have been hungry as no one said a word.

When the clanking of silverware stopped, Theresa asked, "Who wants hot apple pie?"

"With vanilla ice cream?" Henry asked.

"Of course, how else?" replied Theresa.

They finished dessert and Henry almost felt like he needed to loosen his belt. He had not eaten that good in a long time. He got up from the table and put his dishes in the sink. Charity got up and put her dishes in the sink as well.

"Okay, I'm dying from curiosity. What's the big thing you wanted to ask me about?" Henry probed about to burst.

Charity beckoned Henry to go back outside, this time to sit in the chairs. She started to explain, "I just packed up my apartment and realized that now that I live here, I have no need for most of it. Can you find families who are working their permanency plans, but may need things like furniture, and get these to them? I can pay for the deliveries and all."

"That's a wonderful idea, Charity. Many families will be able to benefit from your generosity," Henry stated enthusiastically. He was moved by her unselfish gesture.

"It is mostly big things like a full-sized bed, a couch, a dining room suite, and maybe some smaller things. Oh, like the dishes from my kitchen. All the rooms are decorated here, and it doesn't make sense to keep my old stuff," Charity trailed off. "These are all things that might make the difference for children to go home and all."

She wasn't wrong, Henry thought. He couldn't believe how deeply this all still affected her. She wasn't in foster care anymore, but it seemed to be always on her mind. "What are you going to do with all this?" Henry asked waving his hand toward the pasture.

"Oh, I have some ideas," Charity commenced. "In fact, this Saturday I've invited Amanda and Peter Ferguson over for a little while. Have you heard that their foster parents were transferred to Hawaii after the first of the year?"

"Yeah, I heard. It's stinks but does come with the territory," Henry remarked looking at a squirrel run across the driveway to the willow tree. "That's an awesome thing to do, but why these children?"

"Well, these are the children whose case I was attending when we first met. I promised myself I would advocate for children while they were in foster care. This way I can be a big sister, of sorts. Peter hasn't spoken to anyone since he and Amanda entered foster care. I'm hoping some one-on-one time might change that," Charity further explained.

Sitting erect in his chair, Henry proposed, "What time Saturday? I could come over, so you have an extra set of hands."

Confidence renewed by his offer, Charity placed her hand on his arm, "That would be so great! How about one o'clock? I think having a man here would be a good thing for Peter. He is close to his foster dad and isn't taking the upcoming move well at all."

Henry felt his skin tingle from her touch. He checked his watch then said, "I gotta get going. I actually have a little paperwork to do before tomorrow. I came straight here from the garage and totally forgot."

Charity responded, "I really appreciate you coming over…it means more than you know."

"Glad I could be of help. Your idea is perfect. You have a huge heart and that makes you so special," Henry remarked, trying not to sound insincere.

Charity walked with Henry to the truck and watched as he got in. "I'll text you the details before the thing on Saturday," she said putting her hands on the rolled-down window as he closed the door. "We will probably have pizza, so come hungry. Any special preferences for your pizza?"

"Nope, I love it all," Henry stated. "I will keep an eye out for your text. I'll be sure and check on the items you have available. I know you want to get those out of the way. How do I get out?"

"Oh, just ease up to the gate slowly and it will open," Charity directed.

Charity went back inside, and she realized she had not checked on Max all afternoon. She got to the bedroom and Max met her at the door. "Oh, Max," she said picking him up, hugging him for a moment, "I'm so sorry. Here, let's get you out of this room."

Charity walked to the kitchen and poured just a little milk in a bowl and set it on the floor. She then saw the dishes still in the sink and began putting them in the dishwasher. Theresa appeared and started putting the leftover food away.

"Things seemed to go pretty well," Theresa said probing just a little. "Did you get the answer you were hoping for?"

"Yes, Henry will help me find a family, or families, who can use the things I clearly no longer need. He volunteered to come over Saturday and help with the Ferguson children. You know, be an extra set of hands," Charity explained.

"What do you think of him?" pressed Theresa. "He's very likeable…and I think he likes you."

"Henry is a likeable person. He works hard to help children get back home to their families. What's not to like about that?" Charity asked defensively.

"You're afraid to like him, aren't you?" Theresa questioned point blank.

She wasn't sure she liked where this conversation was going. "How do I know he likes me for me, and not because I have this place?" she asked waving her hand around.

"Didn't you meet him before you knew about this place? From the way he looked at you today, I think he was thinking of you long before you got here," Theresa said reassuringly. The kitchen was almost completely cleaned.

"I've never worried about trying to meet anyone. I stay busy with my job and juvenile court…both of which I do well. It scares me to think of needing anyone, especially someone who might push me away," Charity said honestly.

"Honey, you have a lot to offer, and I am not talking about the money you just inherited. I can tell you're a person who feels everything deeply, thinking things through way too hard before taking any actions," Theresa diagnosed. It was like she could see right through Charity's heart and knew exactly how she felt.

"I have only known you a few days, and yet, you know me almost better than I know myself. How is that possible?" quizzed Charity.

"I was like you when I was younger. But I let fear take over when I had the opportunity to marry a wonderful man. I regret a lot of things in my life. I finally learned to get past it, but it changed the trajectory of my life forever," Theresa said sadly. "I was hired at the ranch as the house manager sixteen years ago. I worked along with your Aunt Marion. It was right before Jeremy was killed. Over time, she and I did many volunteer activities together. I just threw myself into caring for and serving others and never pursued romantic entanglements."

"Whoa, no one has even mentioned romantic entanglements. Except for meeting for a sandwich, today was the only other time we spent more than twenty minutes in the same room with each other. Are you sure you are thinking things through clearly?" Charity asked.

"Well, he may not have said it out right, but a lovely girl like you is bound to get some guy's attention…so why not him?" Theresa reasoned out.

Charity considered her words for a minute. She did like Henry that much was certain. But how much did Henry like her? She recalled all the times they had met. He offered her a soda. Then he bought her one that got hot while he was waiting on her. Theresa was right, the signs were there. Now what does she do?

Suddenly, Charity had a realization. "Where did Chuck run off to? I need to ask him a couple of business questions."

"He usually goes outside after dinner and sits in the fresh air. Check the front porch. He likes the view from the chairs out there," Theresa said as she put the last pan away.

Charity slipped down the hall and out the front door. She found Chuck right where Theresa said she would. "Chuck, can I ask you a couple of questions? They're really important."

"Sure, come on out here and sit down," Chuck said sliding over to the next chair. "What's on your mind?"

"I haven't quite gotten used to having this place. I realized I don't know how to pay you and Theresa and the others who work here. What do I do?" Charity asked with noted concern.

"I'm so sorry. I meant to explain that to you the other day," Chuck began. "When your Uncle Frank sold all his properties, he split some of the money off from what he planned to give you. Your part of the inheritance was thirty-five million dollars. He set another fifteen million dollars aside for salaries, household expenses and all the other things you would have to do for the ranch. Theresa takes care of running the house-the groceries, repairs, and the like. I take care of all the ranch hands, getting the horse supplies, vet expenses, and other outside things. Our salaries are paid all at once on our yearly anniversary. The only one that is paid monthly is Johnny. I'll give the invoice after I have signed the check each month. You just need to concentrate on what you need to do with your life. Your folks gave you the means to do whatever you dreamed of doing. The only limitations are what you place on yourself. What big dreams have you been carrying around all this time? When you have the answer to that question, then you'll know just what he left you this place to accomplish."

"Whoa," she said, "I guess I need to think things over very carefully. I don't want to let them down. They gave up a lot for me, huh?"

"Indeed, they did. Just follow your gut and you won't go wrong," Chuck said encouragingly. "Good night," he said as Charity got up to go back inside.

"Good night, Chuck, and thanks," Charity replied patting him on the shoulder.

CHAPTER 6

Friday morning Charity headed to *The Standard Banner* after she cleaned her apartment and turned in the keys. But she had one stop to make first. When she last left the gang, things were a bit tense. And how does someone signal everything was A-OK? With a huge selection of doughnuts, of course. The local donut shop had the best doughnuts in the area, with a slogan of "Our Jelly Will Fill Your Belly." The office had a coffee machine, so she got the doughnuts and drove on to work.

Rachel was the first to meet her, "Hey, kid, what have you done?"

"Oh, you know, a peace offering, I was rather difficult when I was here last. Besides, everyone loves a good doughnut," Charity rationalized. "Anyway, it will give everyone something to eat while I write up my next public interest story. It is a little weird, though, because it involves the Silver Horseshoe. This is what I want to do, tell me if it sounds okay."

Charity and Rachel sat down at Charity's desk and discussed her plans for the foster care party the weekend before Thanksgiving. "You know I've always wanted to give back. Now that I have all this space and money, I want to invite all the children in custody here in Jefferson County. I plan to have Santa Claus make a surprise appearance before it's over. I have some strategic details to work out, but between Theresa and Henry, I should be able to get things figured out."

"Henry?" Rachel summoned with a curious look. "Is there something you want to tell me?"

"Oh, he's the guy I met a few weeks ago. I interviewed him in my last public interest article about the Anderson family." Trying to be as normal as possible, Charity further said in a flat tone, "He can help me with the foster care connections, Rachel."

"Uh-huh, right. Well, I think what you are proposing is wonderful. You've always had a big heart. Where do you want to go for lunch?" Rachel inquired.

"You can pick," Charity said as she turned on her desk computer. "I feel strange writing a blurb about myself. Should I put my name on it? Is that a conflict of interest?"

"Just write the article and let Buzz handle that. He knows you want to be very neutral. This must be pretty strange for you," Rachel mused.

"That's for sure," Charity agreed turning back to her screen. She had a hard time getting started, but once she typed the first word, it came out very easily.

The Silver Horseshoe Ranch has extended an invitation to the Jefferson County Department of Children Services to participate in a Thanksgiving Shindig the Saturday before Thanksgiving. All children currently in care in Jefferson County and their foster families will enjoy a catered Thanksgiving meal, festive music, and a surprise visit from Santa Claus. The family support workers for the children will be notified directly as soon as the final details have been decided and then relayed to the foster families.

While Charity was typing her story, Buzz and Marcus came in and found the doughnuts. "Wow, who brought these in?" Marcus queried.

"Charity...I think she is trying to apologize for how she left the last time she was here," Rachel offered as an explanation.

"Thanks, Charity," Buzz said as he stuffed a Bavarian cream doughnut in his mouth. He waved to her as he went into his office and closed the door.

"How are things going at the Silver Horseshoe?" Marcus probed.

"Well, I'm still trying to wrap my brain around the idea that I now have a place of my own. I'm learning more about my family background and what they did to make sure I had a future. Chuck, the foreman who worked with my Uncle Frank, said my folks wanted to be involved with my life but they couldn't because of how old they were. They were already in their fifties when I was born. So, they made up for it by leaving me the ranch. Chuck keeps telling me I need to find out what my dreams are and then do that," she trailed off.

"Well, that's a logical bit of advice. If we don't know our dreams and what we want from life, then we aren't really living. We are just existing," Marcus pronounced wisely.

Charity internalized the words Marcus spoke just then. He was right. She had been just existing, to some degree. She did keep busy with foster care stuff, but was there more to her life than just that? She returned to her computer. She reread the article for the event again and when she was completely satisfied with it, she sent it to Buzz. She had a few minutes or so before lunch, so she went through her emails and caught up all her mail.

"Okay, kid. You ready?" Rachel asked sneaking up on Charity.

"I sure am. I'm totally caught up on everything. It will be at least a week before I need to stop back in the office," Charity said proudly. "What did you decide on for lunch?"

"How about burgers? You can follow me since you won't be coming back to the office," Rachel reasoned. "I'll meet you there."

Charity turned off her computer. She stuck her head into Buzz's office and told him she had sent him her article. He was deep in writing and just waved his hand. She headed out to meet Rachel at the best burger joint in town.

After ordering their food, they sat down in a booth. Rachel asked, "What did you do with all your stuff from your apartment?"

"Funny you bring that up," Charity began. "That is one of the things Henry is helping me with. I have a ranch house that is entirely furnished. I had just a little bit of stuff to begin with, so…"

"SO, you have decided to donate it? That's a very generous thing for you to do," Rachel said admiringly nodding her head. "The foster care connections you mentioned." It started to make sense now.

"Right. Henry knows which cases have families in need of furniture so they can have their children come back home to a safe environment," Charity explained. "He is a very thorough worker and is all about doing what is best for the children and their families."

Rachel raised her eyebrows, "Are you sure that's all there is to it?"

"Yeah, why?" Charity asked a bit confused. "Why does everyone think there is more going on here than two people working on the same problem? Children being reunited with their families."

Rachel looked at her. Charity knew that look all too well. Suddenly, her phone buzzed. It was Henry. Charity got an enormous grin on her face, prompting Rachel to ask, "Is that him? Go ahead, answer him."

Charity read his text message, "What are you doing?"

"Having lunch with Rachel at the burger joint. Are you okay?" Charity typed back.

"Can I stop by and see you for a few minutes before you leave? I need to tell you something, but not over the phone. Nothing is wrong, exactly. But we need to talk," Henry replied.

"Okay, we'll be done shortly. You can head this way," Charity offered.

"Everything okay?" Rachel observed the strange expression on Charity's face.

"I don't know. Henry said he needed to tell me something, but not over the phone. I hope he hasn't had to cancel Saturday," Charity frowned.

"What happens on Saturday?" Rachel demanded.

"You remember how I follow the case of the Ferguson children? Well, I invited the children over to the ranch as a diversion. Henry volunteered to come over to have a man around, so Peter wouldn't feel surrounded by girls," Charity explained.

"What a thoughtful thing to do, kid. I'm sure things will be okay," Rachel hoped.

"Peter still hasn't said a word. I hoped the horses, especially Mr. Whiskers, could break the barrier," Charity replied.

"Mr. Whiskers?" Rachel questioned with her head cocked.

"Yeah, he's a miniature pony. Comes complete with unruly hairs on his muzzle, earning him the name Mr. Whiskers," Charity explained excitedly.

"You know, this ranch may be of some use yet," Rachel said, frankly.

"What do you mean?" Charity asked, not quite understanding what Rachel meant.

"I'll let you come to your own conclusions. Just remember to take Chuck's words to heart," Rachel said mysteriously.

Just then, the bell on the door jingled and Charity saw Henry walk in. He looked around the restaurant, locating Charity and Rachel.

"Hello, Henry," Charity began. "This is my friend and coworker Rachel Peterson. She's the sports expert for *The Standard Banner*."

"Nice to meet you," Henry said as he shook Rachel's hand. "I didn't realize you weren't done. I can wait over there," Henry motioned to the seats at the counter.

"I have to get back to the paper." Rachel suggested, "You can have this seat. It was nice to meet you, Henry. See you later, kid."

Henry slid into the seat after Rachel had gone. "I'm so sorry to have bothered you like this, but I didn't know what to do without asking you first," Henry began frantically.

"Ask me what?"

"Well, it's my parents. They asked if my kid brother can spend the weekend with me *this* weekend. They decided to go away and do their annual leaf-looking drive. I'm supposed to be helping you on Saturday with the Ferguson children. What do I do?" Henry posed worriedly.

That's all? Charity felt relieved and assured Henry, "It's okay, your brother can come, too. We'll eat pizza and interact with the horses. I was hoping Mr. Whiskers could help Peter come out of his shell."

"Whew!" Henry exhaled. "I'm so glad you said he could come. His name is Brian and he's sixteen. He's a good kid. Our family adopted him when he was about two years old. I think he likes horses, so it will be a fun outing for him."

Charity thought Henry looked especially handsome today. She detected the faint smell of his cologne. He apparently liked to wear long-sleeved, flannel shirts and a sleeveless vest. The color in his shirt really made his green eyes stand out. She caught herself and snapped back to the other business Henry was helping her with, the furniture. "Have you found anyone who needs the items from my apartment?"

"As a matter of fact, Erica identified a family who needed just what you have to offer. All except for the entertainment center. They already had one of those. How should we handle picking those things up?" Henry asked.

"I can have them delivered. Just give me the address. When do they need the items?"

"Monday of next week. If that time will be okay with you," Henry responded.

"I will contact Jesse and get it ready. Just text me the most convenient time to have it delivered," Charity offered.

"That's great. What's wrong, though? You don't seem like yourself," Henry noticed.

Great, apparently even he could see that. "Well, people keep asking me how I'm doing since I have moved out to the ranch. Now that I don't have to worry about money, people keep telling me I need to figure out what my dreams are and bring them to reality. But I don't know what those are," Charity said, full of frustration.

"Hang on," Henry said putting his hands up. "Don't get so defensive." He paused for a moment then said, "Think of it this way. If you never had to worry about what you did to earn a living, and could do whatever you wanted, what would that be?"

With a tremble in her voice, Charity began, "Oh, Henry! I never thought about dreaming. I mean really dreaming like the dreams could come true. Marcus, a guy at the paper, said that people who don't try and live their dreams are not living. They are just existing. I don't want to just exist anymore. I want to know I am making a difference."

Feeling bold, Henry grabbed her hands and looked her in the eyes, "You are making a difference…every time you show up at the foster care review board and advocate for those children. But you also need to think about you. What do you want to do in this life? Didn't I read in the paper you sent a children's book off to get published? Isn't that why you became a journalist?"

"I've always wanted to write stories to make children feel better, so they understood there were others experiencing the same things they were going through. Hopefully, I will get good news. But what if they reject me?" Charity posed fearfully. "Like Marty McFly says, 'I just don't think I can take that kind of rejection.'"

"Just take things one step at a time. You don't have to hurry right now. Just get through this weekend with the Ferguson children and see where it goes from there," Henry said wisely.

Doing a one hundred eighty-degree mood change, Charity boomed, "Oh, I almost forgot. I need you to tell Erica about the Thanksgiving Shindig at the ranch on the Saturday before Thanksgiving. All the foster children and their foster families here in Jefferson County are invited. The paper states the details will come from DCS through their family service workers."

Henry sat there in shock. "Wow, Charity! I don't know what to say. You mentioned wanting to do something, but this…this is unbelievable!" She truly had the most unselfish nature of anyone he had ever met.

"There will be a catered Thanksgiving meal, music, fun and maybe a surprise visit from Santa. I originally thought of getting a gift for each child, but it may be easier to use one of the gifts on their Angel Tree list and just hand them out at the party. Depending on how many families are attending, the ranch will give each of the families a $100 gift card," Charity concluded.

"Are you sure?" Henry leaned in closer. "You are already being extremely generous just having an event at the ranch."

"Well, I wanted to have a Christmas party instead, but the ranch has a standing event every year for hardship families here in Jefferson County. Uncle Frank and Aunt Marion have done this for years. I didn't want to change anything that the ranch already had going on," Charity explained to Henry. All he could do was just stare at her in admiration. Or was it something else?

Charity felt a little unsure about Henry's gaze. Did she say something wrong? She saw the time on the clock behind the counter and abruptly said, "Oh, I have to go. I need to get with Theresa about catering the Thanksgiving Shindig. I certainly don't expect her to cook all that food."

As if coming out of a dense fog, Henry said, "Right, you go ahead. Thanks for letting Brian come on Saturday. It's nice of you to understand. I appreciate it more than you know. I will be sure and relay the message to Erica about the Thanksgiving Shindig."

"Of course. See you later," Charity replied as she slid out of the booth.

Henry sat there for a little while after she left. What was it about her that made him crazy? Her innocence? Her generous nature? He was brought back to the moment when his phone rang. It was his mother, calling to confirm the time to bring Brian for the weekend. He slowly got up from the booth and answered her call as he walked out of the restaurant.

****

Back home, Charity found Theresa in the kitchen trying to decide what to make for dinner.

"Hello, Theresa, what's for dinner?" Charity queried.

"Well, the options are a pot of chili and cornbread or potato soup and oyster crackers," Theresa voiced with exasperation. "I just can't decide. Which would you want?

Feeling terrible, Charity honestly stated, "I'm not a big fan of soup, but I do like potato soup. I am partial to chili but will eat whatever you make."

"Well, you are no help. And that was the same thing that Chuck said when I asked him what he wanted for dinner," Theresa retorted.

"Well, why don't we go out to eat for dinner. Where have you wanted to go but haven't been for a while?" Charity posed.

"It *has* been a long time," Theresa mused. "Let's see where Chuck wants to go eat. What time do you want to leave?"

"We can go around five o'clock. Unless that is too early. Since tonight is Thursday, the crowds won't be too bad," Charity reasoned.

Theresa texted Chuck about dinner since he was out back with the horses. An instant later she said he was about thirty minutes from being finished. He would take a shower and be ready to go by five o'clock. He was hankering for a steak.

"Theresa, do we have the number of a good caterer? I need to get the plans going for the Thanksgiving Shindig," Charity began.

"Your Uncle Frank and Aunt Marion always swore by a lady named Penelope Carter. She's a brilliant event planner, and she coordinates the food with all the best restaurants, depending on what you are serving," Theresa advised Charity.

"Thanks a million," Charity replied. "How was Max today?"

"Well, you won't believe it. He got out today and he headed to the barn. Chuck said he found Max sitting on Lightning's stall door. Lightning was sniffing him. They seem to be fast friends," Theresa said incredulously.

"Wow, I would never have imagined that. Amazing. Theresa? How hard would it be to put my entertainment center in the front living room?" Charity wondered.

"Not hard at all. There's an open space between the windows for something that size to slide into," Theresa replied. "Oh, speaking of furniture, did Henry find folks to use the things you're getting rid of?"

"He sure did," reported Charity proudly. "He will be sending me the address of the family and it will be delivered on Monday. That will clear out the garage nicely."

"It sure will. Henry's coming over Saturday, isn't he?" Theresa probed. She wondered if Charity had admitted the *thing* between them.

"He is. But now he must bring his younger brother, Brian. Apparently, his parents like to go out of town on leaf-looking expeditions and needed Brian looked after. We'll be eating pizza and just doing horse stuff," volunteered Charity.

"Anything after that?" Theresa pushed a little more.

"Well, Henry is relaying the information to his boss, Erica, about the Shindig. I'm sure I will see him again to work on that," Charity reasoned.

"Why don't you have him come over for dinner Sunday evening, after his brother goes home. You're running out of time. The Saturday before Thanksgiving isn't too far away," Theresa suggested.

"I will ask him when he gets here. Of course, it all hinges on if he gets called in to work," Charity reminded Theresa. "He's never really off duty.

Leaving Theresa in the kitchen, Charity went outside to sit on the swing and think until it was time to leave for dinner. She had a lot on her mind.

Henry had just pulled into his driveway when he received a text from his mother. Good thing he bought a two-bedroom house when he moved away from home. This way, he was equipped to cover Brian for his parents in situations just like this. His brother and sister were not always available, so covering Brian fell on him most of the time. He didn't mind. He loved being an active part of Brian's life.

He went inside and poured a glass of tea. He wasn't sure what to do with Brian tonight, maybe burgers and a movie. They both liked science fiction movies, and he had plenty to choose from.

Ten minutes later, Mike and Deborah Thompson pulled up with Brian. They got out of the car and went to the door. Henry opened the door as Mike's finger pressed the bell.

"Hello, Mom, Dad," greeted Henry hugging his mom. No matter how big a man gets, his mom always wants a hug. "Hey, Brian. How's it going?"

"Fine," Brian said excited to be there. He always looked forward to spending time with Henry.

"Listen, we have to get on the road. We'll pick Brian up on Sunday afternoon around three o'clock," Deborah told Henry. "You guys going to be okay this weekend?"

"We will be fine. We are actually going to the Silver Horseshoe and meet with a new friend, Charity Walters and some kids," Henry explained.

"Charity Walters, didn't she inherit the Silver Horseshoe?" Mike asked. "How do you know her?"

"Oh, you know about that. It's a funny story," Henry began embarrassed to tell the truth. "Let's just say I ran into her at juvenile court…literally."

"That's a likely story, Henry," Brian teased. Brothers had a way of starting things.

"Yeah, well, you'll meet her Saturday. So be on your best behavior," Henry scolded.

"We really do have to go, honey," Deborah said to Henry as she hugged him again. "She must be nice for you to get so defensive like this. Brian, we will see you Sunday at three o'clock"

"Okay, Mom, love you. Love you, Dad," Brian said as his parents walked out the door.

The parents had finally gone. Brian looked at Henry and said, "Okay, what gives?"

"What are you talking about?" Henry asked slightly annoyed.

"The girl," Brian said sarcastically. "What about the girl?"

"I'll let you see for yourself. You're going to like her," Henry grinned. "That's all you need to know." And Henry was right. Brian would like her. How could he not? "So, burgers?"

Brian was totally onboard with that idea. "Awesome, let's do it."

Henry and Brian went to the best burger joint in town. When they got back, they decided to watch movies about mummies and treasure. They watched two of the three movies before calling it a night. Henry tried to sleep but Charity kept coming to mind.

Theresa, Chuck, and Charity returned from dinner and Charity went straight to bed. She didn't realize how tired she had been adjusting to her new life. She said her good nights and found Max ready for bed, too.

She crawled into bed and pulled the covers around her. Max found his place on her right side around her hips on top of the covers. He didn't like being under the covers at all. She turned out her bedside lamp and just had the moonlight coming through her window. She was asleep in no time at all.

****

It was Saturday morning. Charity woke up the same way she did every morning, with the smell of coffee coming from the kitchen. Max sat in the window watching the birds out on the grass. She dressed and went to find Theresa, who had a nice plate of waffles waiting for her, with lots of bacon.

"Thank you, Theresa. This is great," Charity said about to stuff a bite of waffles in her mouth.

"You'll have an exciting day, won't you? With Henry and the children here today?" Theresa rattled off.

"Yeah, I just hope everyone has a good time and there are no accidents," Charity voiced. "Thanks for the waffles. You're the best. Need help with anything?"

"No, just get yourself centered and enjoy the day," Theresa advised.

She had some time before Amanda and Peter would be there, so after she finished eating, she went outside and looked around. All the horses were in the pasture close to the house. Charity walked to the fence and Sinbad walked over to her. This was really a shock, but she wasn't going to turn him away. She stood there for some time lost in thought, just caressing Sinbad's felty muzzle and neck. She wondered how Mr. Whiskers would do with Amanda and Peter. Chuck was going to put him on a harness and tie him to the corral post. They weren't riding any horses today, just petting them and brushing them.

Charity went back in the house and washed her hands so she wouldn't sneeze. She could feel her nose prickle from petting Sinbad. She grabbed her allergy medicine and headed to the living room. She picked out a random book from the bookshelf thinking of reading a while. She had grabbed *Black Beauty*. Of course, they would have this horse book. She put it back on the shelf. It was much too sad, and she didn't want to be moody before everyone arrived. So, she went out the front door and sat in the swing. She had a good, creaky rhythm going when her phone buzzed. It was Henry.

"Is it okay if we come on over?" Henry texted. "Brian is getting a little mouthy and I want him to see how nice it is there."

"Sure, come on over. See you in a bit. We could sit outside or something until the children get here," Charity replied. Well, now she really was getting nervous. Not because Henry was coming over, but it was how that thought made her feel. She was deep down excited, and it scared her. But what if he didn't feel the same about her?

Fifteen minutes later, Henry drove through the gate with Brian. Brian gasped as he saw how big the house was and the horses in the pasture. Henry parked his truck and they got out.

Coming down from the porch, Charity walked over and greeted them. "Hello, Henry. Thanks for coming over. Brian, I'm Charity," she said extending her hand to him. "Nice to meet you."

Shaking her hand, Brian said, "Thanks for letting me come with Henry today. This is some place! Do you like it here?"

"Thank you. It is a wonderful place. I'm still getting used to living here. I had a small one-bedroom apartment, so this feels like a mansion to me," Charity replied honestly.

"Well, how much time do we have before the children get here?" Henry wondered.

Checking her phone, she replied, "We have about an hour. What should we do?"

"Well, can we show Brian the horses?" Henry posed.

"Let's go around back, then. This way," Charity led them around the house.

Brian could only stare as he saw the arena, the pasture, and the horses off in the distance. "You get to see this every day?"

"Yeah, beautiful, isn't it? I wish I didn't have allergies to everything outdoors," Charity lamented. "I just took my allergy medicine a bit ago to keep from sneezing all over you guys."

Chuck had just ridden in on Ginger when he saw everyone at the fence. "You guys are early for the fun, aren't you?"

Henry replied, "We are. Sorry about that. My kid brother was getting a little mouthy, and I needed a distraction. Charity was kind enough to let us come early."

"Well, brothers can make you a little crazy, I guess," Chuck reasoned. "Charity, let me know when I need to have Mr. Whiskers ready."

"Thanks, Chuck. I will," Charity patted Chuck's jacket as he went on his way.

Charity stood there looking out at the pasture while Henry stayed with Brian as he stroked Ginger. Sinbad nickered and walked over to where she was standing. "Hello, big fella," she cooed. Suddenly, she felt her phone buzz. It was Melanie Henderson.

"Ooh, they're early, too. Be right back," Charity told Henry. "Just have to get the kids at the gate."

"Here, let me drive you down there. Brian, wait right here," Henry directed.

They walked around to the front of the house and Henry opened the door to his truck for Charity.

"Thanks," Charity said climbing in, "you didn't have to do this."

"I know," Henry replied.

They got to the gate and the kids jumped out of the car. Charity approached the gate and told Melanie, "I'll bring them home when we're finished. I'll text you when we head that way."

"That would be awesome," Melanie smiled. "I can't tell you how much we appreciate this. They've been looking forward to it ever since you first mentioned having them over."

"I'm so glad," Charity said. "All right, guys, hop in the truck. This is Henry. He and his brother, Brian, will be having pizza with us and play with the horses."

"Cool," Amanda said excitedly.

Henry drove the truck back slowly to the front of the house. Charity helped the children out of the truck.

"Okay, everyone, follow me." She led everyone through to the back of the house. They walked past Theresa, who mentioned she had the pizzas ordered and they would be delivered in forty-five minutes. "Thank you," Charity whispered putting her hands in a praying position. She led everyone out the door.

Brian had told Chuck the children were coming, so Chuck had put the harness on Mr. Whiskers and had sliced up two apples for the children to feed him. "He will be fine as long as no one steps behind him. So be sure to keep to the front of him. He does like to have his back brushed, but no further back on his body."

"Everyone got that?" Henry asked, trying to take a part in this activity. Brian and Amanda nodded and said, "Yes." Peter just nodded.

"Thanks, Chuck, I think I can handle things from here. I've taken my allergy medicine and Theresa has the honey on standby," Charity informed Chuck.

Slowly Amanda, Peter, and Brian all went up to Mr. Whiskers. Brian held his hand out and Mr. Whiskers put his hairy muzzle in his hand. Amanda grabbed a brush and started brushing his back. Peter grabbed an apple slice and jumped a little as Mr. Whiskers ate it rather quickly. Henry stood at the head of the pony and Charity took out her phone and snapped a picture. She took a few more as everyone switched around and did all the jobs. The pictures looked terrific. She had never seen a bigger smile on Peter's face.

It seemed no time at all when Theresa texted Charity to let her know the pizza was on the way and they needed to come in and wash up and get their drinks ready.

The children were not happy to leave Mr. Whiskers. Charity promised them they could come back out again before she took them home.

"Wow, pepperoni," Amanda said excitedly when Charity mentioned the pizza toppings. "I love pepperoni. Can I have a Coke, please?"

"Of course, you can. What does Peter like to drink?" Charity asked.

"He likes tea. Yuck," Amanda said. "You can't drink tea with pizza. That's gross."

Charity poured Peter a small glass of tea, and a tall one for Henry. "I know what you mean, Amanda, but some people like tea."

She handed Henry his glass of tea and he said, "We sure do, don't we, Brian?"

"Yeah, I want a glass of tea, too, please, Charity," Brian said jokingly.

Charity blushed. "Sure thing, Brian. Here you go," Charity said as she handed him his glass.

Charity stopped long enough to go get the pizzas from the driver who was waiting at the gate. Back inside, she set the pizzas out for everyone to serve themselves. She helped Amanda and Peter get their pizza.

Everyone was busy eating when Amanda asked, "How many horses do you have here, Charity?"

"Well, there are five. Maverick, Ginger, Sinbad, Lightning, and Mr. Whiskers," Charity named them off on her fingers. "Maybe next time, we can ride in a wagon."

Amanda cheered and said, "Yay! That would be so much fun."

"It would be fun, wouldn't it?" Henry repeated.

"Guys, it's time to finish your pizza. I have to take you home," Charity said sadly.

"Already? But the horses…" Amanda reminded. "You said we could see them one more time before we had to leave."

Peter walked up to Charity, poked her in the side and pointed out back towards Mr. Whiskers.

"Okay, okay," Charity said giving up. "Put your plates in the trash and we will go back outside for a while."

"Yay!" exclaimed Amanda.

"Cool," Brian said as he put his plate in the trash and his glass in the sink.

Charity just smiled at Henry and shrugged her shoulders as they all went out the back door.

Mr. Whiskers perked up as he heard them all walk over to him. He was hoping for one last apple slice.

Henry darted back inside and got a few extra apples and sliced them. Henry gave them to Amanda, Peter, and Brian. Mr. Whiskers chomped on them loudly. When all the slices were gone, Charity said it was time to leave. She couldn't believe that another hour had passed since they went back outside. She reminded Amanda and Peter, "Don't forget, you two will get to come back for the Thanksgiving Shindig."

"Aw, man. I could stay here all day," Brian said disappointedly.

"I'm so glad you had a good time today, Brian. Thanks for coming with Henry," Charity said sincerely.

"I had fun, too," Henry started to say. "Maybe one day, we can actually go for a ride. You can ride a horse, can't you?"

"Well, of course I can ride a horse," Charity said sarcastically.

Henry prodded Brian to the truck to hurry up and get in. Charity opened her car door and the kids got in and buckled up. Henry walked over to Charity and said, "This was a really nice thing you did today for these kids. They had a good time."

"Well, maybe, but Peter is still no closer to talking to anyone," Charity began sadly.

Henry grabbed Charity's hand and with his other hand brushed the hair out of her eyes, "You of all people know trauma doesn't just magically disappear. It must be worked through. And that's what Peter is going to have to do. It may take a considerable amount of time. But don't think for one minute you failed. He knows you are someone who cares about him."

Charity's eyes welled up with tears. Henry was right. All she could do was nod her head and with her free hand, she wiped the tears from her eyes.

Henry squeezed her hand and she let go, throwing her arms around him in a big hug. It completely took Henry by surprise. He hugged her back and just stood there until she let go.

"Thanks for a good time," recovered Charity.

"You're welcome," he smiled reassuringly.

"Oh, can you come over for dinner tomorrow around five-thirty? I need some help brainstorming this Thanksgiving Shindig," Charity asked, confidence restored.

"My parents are picking Brian up at three. I wouldn't miss it," Henry said a little cocky. "I hope you don't expect too much from my brain on the weekend. I don't usually think much unless it's really important" he joked.

"Oh, this is important, so you better come prepared," Charity smirked, pointing her index finger at him.

"Got it," Henry said playfully as he climbed in the truck, closing the door. "Okay, Brian, let's head home." Brian waved at Charity as they drove off.

"You were right, Henry. I do like Charity. Now I know why you like her, too," Brian confessed.

"Brian, you just can't imagine. Let's get back home," Henry said as they cleared the gate and drove on.

Charity got into her jeep and checked on Amanda and Peter. She texted Melanie they were on the way home. She put the jeep in reverse and headed back to their house.

Melanie came outside as she saw the jeep pull up. "How'd it go today?" Melanie asked curiously.

"Great, I think they had a little too much fun, they both conked out back there," Charity said apologetically. She nudged them both awake and helped Melanie get them inside. She said her good-byes and left for home. Only she didn't go home. She went for a drive, listening to her Christmas playlist. She had some thinking to do.

CHAPTER 7

On Sunday morning, Theresa made the house grocery list. Charity had lived at the house for almost two weeks now, so the house supplies were used up more quickly. Chuck was out in the barn with the horses. Today's weather would be stormy, and horses did not like thunderstorms. Chuck went horse by horse, making sure their doors were secured. Last thing he'd want to have happen was for one to get out and run off. They could hurt themselves, and others, that way. Charity found Chuck putting a big scoop of fruity- smelling oats in the buckets that hung on the side of the stalls.

"Wow, those smell really good. I almost want to eat them," Charity said as she inhaled the aroma. "Are the oats part of their diet or considered treats?"

"In small amounts, they make a great supplement to the hay. But if they eat too many, they could get a bellyache," Chuck explained.

"Theresa mentioned Max has taken up with Lightning. Isn't it a little strange for a cat to like a horse?" Charity asked curiously.

"You'd be surprised the kinds of animal friendships that develop on a ranch or farm. Dogs take up with a chicken and a bird might like to sit on the back of the goat," Chuck said humorously. "Animals are very smart."

"I guess the weather means taking Henry for a ride will have to wait," Charity said regretfully.

"Well, it is probably a good thing, because you haven't ridden any of the horses to see which one you need to ride," Chuck said wisely. "Maverick has the best temperament, but you may do better on Sinbad. He seems to be drawn to you."

"Oh, wow. I didn't think about riding the horses yet," Charity thought out loud.

Chuck wondered, "Can Henry ride horses?"

Charity shrugged her shoulders, "He said he grew up around horses. So, I guess he can."

Charity strolled back to the house and asked Theresa for the event planner's contact information.

"Go in the office and look in the right-hand drawer. Your Uncle Frank's list of business associates can be found in there. The woman's name is Penelope Carter. You are letting things get kind of close, aren't you?" Theresa questioned.

"Oh, yeah. Time is definitely sneaking up on me. It's not quite a week away. Good thing Thanksgiving comes late this year," Charity said thankfully. "Henry is supposed to get me the number of children in custody here in Jefferson County. We are going to work on that this afternoon while he is here. What's for dinner?" she asked as she moved toward the office.

Theresa thought for a moment and said, "How about spaghetti, garlic bread, and a big Caesar salad."

"That sounds great. What can I do to help?" Charity asked as she returned to the kitchen.

"Nothing. You need to make sure you have all the papers you need ready to discuss the Thanksgiving Shindig. Did you find the contact information for the event planner?" Theresa asked.

"Yes. Hopefully, she will be easy to work with, and very efficient." Charity posed thinking of the event.

With the weather being stormy, Charity decided to go upstairs and take a closer look at the bedrooms. It was hard to believe there were five of them. What in the world would she do with that many? The first room on the right side was colored in yellows and browns, perfect for a boy. It had a huge closet and a big window looking out to the pasture. The next room was colored in blues and greens. It would also be a good room for a boy. The first room on the left side was colored in purples and pinks. All these rooms had huge closets and looked much bigger inside than you would think from looking at the house from the outside. There was another room that was perfect for a girl. And the last, slightly larger room was colored in neutral colors of beige and gray. She truly had a beautiful home. There were also two full bathrooms, one on each side of the hall. She just needed to figure out the best way to use the house and make her uncle and aunt proud.

It was getting close to five o'clock and Charity assumed Henry would be a little early. Her phone buzzed at four thirty-five.

"Hey, I'm a little early. Can I come on through to the house? It's raining buckets out here," Henry texted.

"Sure. I'll meet you with an umbrella," Charity replied.

"No need, I have one in the truck. See you in a few minutes," Henry responded.

Avoiding the rain, Charity stood on the front porch to wait for Henry. He was dressed in red flannel today and looked like he had grown more handsome since yesterday. He had a huge umbrella that would have made him fly away like Mary Poppins if a big gust of wind had blown up. He crested the top of the steps, shook off the rain, closed the umbrella, and left it on the porch.

"Hey," Henry greeted with a smile.

"You almost had to swim in, didn't you?" Charity joked walking him to the couch to sit down. "We have a few minutes until dinner is ready. How do you feel about spaghetti?"

"It's great. Garlic bread and salad?" Henry asked hopefully.

"Yep, Caesar salad," Charity revealed. "But I am not sure if we have dessert. Oh, well. We don't always have to have a dessert, do we?"

"Well, I try and have them as often as possible," Henry said playfully. He returned to normal and said, "Let me tell you what I learned from Erica."

"Great!" Charity remarked grabbing the notepad from the coffee table. "So, how many children are we looking at for the event?"

"Well, I have good news and bad news. Which do you want first?" Henry asked biting his lip.

Charity shrugged her shoulders, "It doesn't matter, just hit me with the news."

"The good news is that there are only 75 children in custody here in Jefferson County, so we won't have to plan for an extremely large number of people. The bad news is that with it not even being Thanksgiving yet, most of the children have not had their Angel Tree tags put out for the public to help assist us with. Are you sure you want to give them all presents? That could be awfully expensive, you know, on top of the cost of the food and all," Henry said regretfully.

"So, 75 children plus at least three to four people per family as foster parents and bio children. That would be 225 to 300 people. That doesn't sound too bad. Do you think we should invite the DCS staff as well? That would push the number up to about 400," Charity said thinking out loud.

"Whoa, that would be a tremendous gesture. Most of the workers must stagger schedules to enjoy Thanksgiving. This would make them feel special." Henry declared, again amazed at Charity's generosity.

"Now, what food do we serve? And how do we do it? Do we have it served in a box and let people just grab and go? Or do we have about 75 tables set out with place settings and all?" Charity pondered, really getting into things.

"Have you actually spoken to the event planner to get their input or see what they have done in the past?" questioned Henry.

"Well, no. Not yet," Charity said, embarrassed. "I was just thinking out loud first. I guess I am getting carried away."

"Well, that's to be expected, considering all you have recently gone through. It will take you a while to get yourself going right," Henry mused.

Charity felt heat rush to her face, "Thanks. Oh, we better go and see if it is time to eat. Theresa made a fresh jug of tea this afternoon."

They walked into the kitchen as Theresa pulled the garlic bread out of the oven and set it on the stove. The salad was on the bar, as were the plates and silverware. It smelled amazing. She was still getting used to eating this kind of food on a regular basis. She used to just eat pot pies or lean meals.

"Where do you want us to sit, Theresa?" Charity asked as she held her plate.

"Well, it is really up to you. We can all sit here at the bar, or at either of the tables," Theresa replied as she was draining the noodles.

"Let's just eat here at the bar. There's enough room for everyone. Plus, it's close to the food for seconds," Charity reasoned out.

"I wouldn't have thought you to be the one making that excuse," Henry grinned. "How much spaghetti can you eat?"

"Well, truth be told, it's not about the spaghetti. It's the garlic bread. I can eat my weight in bread alone. I can't help it," Charity confessed.

"Okay, everyone. Plate up," Theresa directed.

Everyone made a plate of spaghetti, salad, and garlic bread. Charity savored a frosty cold bottle of Diet Mountain Dew. Theresa, Chuck, and Henry all sipped tall glasses of tea. Henry was the first one to say something.

"Theresa, this food is terrific. I haven't had good food this consistently since I lived at home," Henry said truthfully.

"Thank you, Henry," Theresa said shyly. She didn't like for people to make a fuss over her. She just really enjoyed cooking for others.

Chuck, who almost never had much to say, quickly responded, "Theresa hasn't come across too many foods she couldn't make. Isn't that right?" Chuck nudged Theresa with his elbow.

"Oh, come on. That's enough. I've just been doing this an awfully long time," Theresa said, closing the discussion.

"Well, it's perfect," Henry said as he finished his last bite. He sat there until everyone was finished.

The rain was really coming down and the lightning and thunder became more frequent as the storm grew worse. Now, it was really raining cats and dogs. Speaking of cats, Max pressed into the kitchen as the thunder was even too loud for him.

"Okay, just put your plates in the sink. We'll have to wait for the lightning to pass before cleaning up," Theresa instructed. "Why don't you two go back and finish working on the Shindig plans. Chuck can keep me company in here."

"Thank you. Come on, Henry. Let's get a few more things worked out this evening. It would be great if you could tell Erica and your team exactly what to plan for. Well, except for anything Penelope tells us to do," Charity said leading Henry back to the living room.

Charity pulled the curtains apart so they could see the flashes of lightning as they lit up the sky. They sat in silence for a few minutes and Charity finally said, "I can't get over how peaceful it is here. We are still close to the city, but I feel so relaxed here."

"I know what you mean. I think for you, it's the contrast of being on the go so much and having to look out for yourself all the time. Here you can take things slower. There are people who spend your days with you, doing things with you and for you," Henry explained logically. She did have someone other than Max to spend time with her. As if on cue, Max came and jumped on the couch beside her, trembled and dug in behind her arm.

"You know, the more I think about it, I'm not sure I can figure anything else out tonight. We need Penelope's advice before we can proceed. Do you want to listen to music or watch a movie?" posed Charity.

"What kind of music?" questioned Henry wondering if she would suggest Christmas music.

"Well, since it isn't even Thanksgiving yet, I won't play Christmas music. Though I listen to it frequently when I'm alone. So how about Mozart? He's my favorite composer," Charity announced proudly. She liked other composers, but in her mind, Mozart was the best.

"Sure, Mozart sounds good. Did you know he wrote a piece of music called something like *Variations on Twinkle, Twinkle Little Star*?" Henry asked trying to stump her. But it didn't work.

"I sure did, and it's a brilliant piece of music," Charity said putting the CD on through the DVD player. She sat back on the couch in between Henry and Max. Max didn't seem to mind Henry. Normally, Max didn't pay attention to anyone. He would just throw his nose in the air and walk off.

"This is very nice," Henry agreed.

They sat there for a while tossing back different bits of Mozart trivia. Henry wanted to know her favorite piece of music Mozart composed. It was Sonata No 11. Charity asked if he had ever been to any of Mozart's operas like *The Marriage of Figaro*. Henry said no. They laughed and joked, and Henry said he thought Beethoven was better.

The thunder subsided for the most part. It was still raining hard.

"Can we just sit here for a few minutes and listen to the rain?" Charity asked softly.

"Sure," he said, letting the silence hang between them for a moment. Then he started back, "I especially like to be in the truck when it's raining and watch the water roll down the windshield and hear it ping on the roof. What about you?" Henry realized Charity was leaning against him, her head on his shoulder and her arm tucked around his. When had she done that? He looked at her sideways and realized she had fallen asleep just that quickly. Henry struggled for a while about what to do. He didn't want to wake her up. But he couldn't sit there all night either.

Theresa walked into the living room to see if they wanted anything else from the kitchen. She smiled and quietly giggled when Henry looked at her and mouthed, "What do I do?" Max was asleep on the other side of Charity.

Theresa whispered, "Just get up slowly and she will naturally fall toward the side of the couch. Put her legs up and I will get a blanket. She'll be fine there. In fact, sometimes she and Max sleep there. It's been a big adjustment for her these past few weeks."

Henry stood up easy and got Charity positioned on the couch. Theresa gave him the blanket and he covered her up. The blanket covered Max a little, but he didn't stir. Theresa went back into the kitchen, but Henry stood there for a few minutes just watching Charity sleep. A warmness swelled up inside him he didn't expect. He bent down and kissed her tenderly on the forehead. He turned off the music and closed the curtains. He turned back around and whispered, "Good night."

Henry walked into the kitchen and awkwardly tried to thank Theresa for her assistance. "Can I help you finish these dishes now that the weather has eased up?" Henry asked quietly.

"Thank you. How good are you at drying dishes?" Theresa asked jokingly.

"Between my siblings and me, I had the best record of drying and breaking the least number of dishes," Henry said proudly and helped Theresa clean the kitchen.

As Henry was about to quietly slip out the front door, Theresa asked him, "Did you get the work done she needed to this evening?"

"Everything except what we need from the event planner. She is calling Penelope tomorrow. Don't make a big deal that she fell asleep. She'll probably feel bad enough on her own," Henry said letting himself out the front door.

Theresa locked the front door and left Charity to sleep through the night. Max had slipped out from under the blanket and was sleeping on top of it in the crook of Charity's knees.

While driving home, Henry's emotions were tied in knots. Using the voice command feature on his phone, he called his dad. "Hello, Dad?" Henry started. "How did you know you wanted to get married to mom?"

Mike replied, "Henry? Have you found a girl you are considering getting married to?"

Henry said, "Yes, Dad, I think I may have just found the one for me like mom is for you. I'll talk to you later, bye."

****

Charity awoke Monday morning as she nearly rolled off the couch. Had she slept there all night? What in the world happened? She went to her room and showered. She was mortified at what Henry must have thought about her falling asleep.

She dressed for a windy day. She dried her hair and pulled it back in a blue bow that matched her sweater. Hungry, she walked to the kitchen to look for Theresa.

Theresa had gone on an errand but left a note on the refrigerator. "Your waffles and bacon are in the refrigerator. Had to go take care of a few things. Be back by lunch time."

Charity pulled out the plate of waffles and bacon and warmed them up in the microwave. She didn't like hot syrup, so she put the syrup on after the waffles got hot.

She went to the table and sat down. She considered all she needed to get done today. She pulled out her notepad and read her list:

Call Penelope about Shindig details.
Email Erica about gift ideas for children.
Call Julie Patterson.

This was enough to keep her busy for a while. She put her plate in the dishwasher, trying to clean up after herself as much as possible.

Although she still felt unworthy to use the office, she decided to sit at the desk and make her calls. She opted to conform to her list and first called Penelope.

"Hello, may I speak with Penelope Carter, please?" Charity began. "This is Charity Walters from the Silver Horseshoe Ranch. Of course, I can hold a moment."

Charity was placed on hold while the phone service played a snoozak version of the song Mandy. A few minutes passed and a very polite woman began to speak.

"This is Penelope Carter. How may I assist you?"

"Great! Ms. Carter, this is Charity Walters from the Silver Horseshoe

Ranch. We require assistance in planning an event the Saturday before Thanksgiving, as in this coming Saturday. It will be for 300-400 people. I know the time is short, but can you assist us with the planning?" Charity petitioned hopefully.

"Let me check my calendar. We are almost always booked this time of year," Penelope began. "Oh, so this would be an additional event for the ranch? We also are scheduled to be out there on Christmas Eve for the party the Silver Horseshoe holds every year."

"Yes, that is correct. I am a former foster youth and wanted to plan an event for the children in custody here in Jefferson County and their foster families," Charity explained.

"You're in luck, Miss Walters. We had an event cancel for this Saturday and can pencil you in. What exactly did you have in mind?" Penelope asked, her pencil still in hand.

"Well," Charity explained excitedly, "I want to have a Thanksgiving meal for the number of people I indicated a moment ago. The extended forecast is calling for a warmer than usual day this Saturday. I thought perhaps we can have a large tent, maybe two, with 75 tables spaced out inside. I'm not sure whether to have the food in a box for ease of serving or have an actual buffet line at the back of the tent."

"I see what you are thinking. For this event, the idea of a boxed meal may be the better choice. I assume you want the usual Thanksgiving foods, turkey, stuffing, mashed potatoes, yams, and a dessert?" Penelope offered.

"Well, not exactly. As a child in foster care, I can tell you most of these children would not want the yams, and possibly the stuffing. What about just the turkey, mashed potatoes, green beans, a dinner roll, and apple pie?" Charity offered instead. "I would hate to waste lots of food."

"What kind of decorations do you want? Any other special things I need to plan for?" asked Penelope curiously.

"Well, as far as decorations, what about little vases with artificial, fall-type flowers in them? The families can take them home at the end of the event," Charity said as she envisioned the vases. "And I thought maybe we could have a surprise visit by Santa Claus. You know, to give every foster child a present."

"What about the decorations outside of the tents? Do I use the usual cornstalks, hay bales, and gourds?" Penelope considered.

"Sparingly, please. I'm allergic to hay, but I love the atmosphere it gives during the fall. Besides, it'll be less than a week before the ranch begins decorating for Christmas. That's it! I almost forgot. We will need a chair for Santa Claus to sit in when he hands out the presents. Does the Christmas Eve event do this, as well? If so, just plan to use those decorations for both events," Charity reasoned.

"The event does have a Santa Claus, as well. We will notify the man we use and make sure he is available. This is a thoughtful expression of love to the foster families. Is it because of your time in foster care?" Penelope asked bravely.

"Exactly. I want to give a little something back to the children. Something to make them realize they are important. I turned eighteen without a family of my own. It was my own choice. After several adoption opportunities fell through, I wanted to make it on my own. I just had no idea I had family here at the Silver Horseshoe Ranch. Uncle Frank and Aunt Marion left me the means to help others. And I'm going to make them proud," Charity concluded as she realized she probably told Penelope more than she wanted to know.

"Wow, you have a truly unselfish spirit. I'm glad I can assist you with this event," Penelope voiced sincerely.

"Oh, just so you understand, I will be making the vases for the table decorations," Charity told Penelope.

"Are you sure you can make 75 of them before Saturday?" Penelope was stunned.

"I can. I love making these things. They're good therapy for me. Oh, I think I forgot to tell you the time. It begins at two o'clock. We can have the grounds ready to set up at nine o'clock," Charity replied.

"Very good, then, Charity. We will get things rolling on this end. I will check back in with you a few times during the week. I text easier than making phone calls," Penelope disclosed truthfully.

"That will be great," Charity agreed. She was better at texting anyway. "One more thing. I am also giving away gift cards to each of the families. What is the best way to do that?

"Let me think on that one. I will get back to you about that by Wednesday," Penelope said, scribbling on her list.

"Well, I think that is everything, then. I can't tell you how much I appreciate your help. I'm extremely excited for the event and to meet you in person," Charity said. "Good-bye."

"Good-bye," Penelope said as she hung up the phone.

That went well. Charity thought striking that item off her list. "What's next?" She asked out loud. Email Erica about the gift ideas for the children. She looked through the texts from Henry and found the email address she needed.

Henry…she had been so busy she had forgotten all about how last night had ended. Before she emailed Erica, Charity texted just two words to Henry. "Thank you." She sent the message.

An instant later, Henry replied, "What for?"

"Tucking me in last night. I can't believe I fell asleep." Charity typed back.

"The weather was stacked against you. Besides, you just sat still too long." Henry explained.

"Busy day?"

"No more than usual," Henry relayed. "You?"

"Just about to email Erica about the gift ideas for the children for the Shindig. You can come, can't you?" Charity asked hopefully.

"I will be there. Always," was the last of Henry's replies. It made her smile.

Charity got her laptop computer out of her bag and set it up on the table. She opened the screen and went into her email. She typed in Erica's email address and began to type:

Hello Erica,

This is Charity Walters from the Silver Horseshoe Ranch, Henry's friend. I needed to ask you what gifts would be best to give the children on Saturday since the ability to use the Angel Tree gifts is not an option. Please let me know as soon as possible so I can purchase the appropriate gifts. I need time to buy them and have them wrapped. I thought it would be nice if each foster child had a gift to take home. The invitation is also extended to your entire DCS staff. The event begins at two o'clock this Saturday at the SHR.

Sincerely,
Charity Walters

"Okay, two items down," she congratulated herself. Max found her in the office and had jumped on the desk behind the computer. "Hey, Max," she said as she stroked him on the head.

She reviewed her list for the final time. "Call Julie Patterson." She looked up Julie's number. Julie had befriended Charity when they were journalism students. She and Julie had opposite personalities. Julie pushed her to think outside the box and get outside her comfort zone. Julie helped make her a stronger person.

"Hey, Julie, are you busy? I have something really cool to tell you about," began Charity.

"Hey there, what's up?" Julie inquired. Julie worked in production. After graduation from journalism school, Julie moved to Nashville. Within two years, Julie worked her way up to production manager.

"First, let me tell you what happened. Three weeks ago, I inherited a horse ranch here in Jefferson County. I had a great uncle and aunt, but they couldn't take me," Charity said bursting to tell the news.

"That's amazing!" Julie replied excitedly.

"I've also inherited thirty-five million dollars. People keep telling me I need to figure out what my dreams are and make them happen," Charity lamented.

"Wow! That's quite a sum. So, what's wrong, then?" Julie pressed.

"I don't know what to do with all this money. I'm having a Thanksgiving thing for the kids in care here in Jefferson County," Charity explained.

"Well, that's a start. Look. Think back to when you aged-out of custody. What were some things that prevented you from getting ahead?" Julie prompted.

"Well, I didn't have a car. If it weren't for meeting you, I wouldn't have had a ride to class most of the time," Charity said honestly and a little bit embarrassed. She hated depending on Julie during that time, but she desperately needed the help. And Julie was there.

"Sounds like you need to write down as many things that were barriers that you can think of and pick the one that can benefit the most children. You can't do them all, so pick the one that matters most to you," Julie suggested.

"Thanks, Julie. I can always depend on you to make me think things through," Charity finished truthfully.

Julie simply said, "Glad I could help. Talk to you later. Bye."

So, with all three things checked off her to-do list, Charity went to get a soda from the refrigerator. Theresa returned from her errands.

"Hi, Charity, how's your morning been?" Theresa posed with a smile.

"It's been very productive," Charity beamed. "I completed all three things on my list. However, I now have a new one. Where would you suggest I find materials for making table decorations?"

"I would try the craft supply store. What exactly are you making?" Theresa wondered.

"I'm assembling 75 table vases. They will be filled with artificial flowers and the families can take them home when the event is over," Charity said proudly.

"75?" Theresa exclaimed incredulously.

"I know, but I always feel better having something to work on," Charity explained. "I didn't want to depend on Penelope and her team to make them. I wanted to flex my creative muscles."

"Well, it's very thoughtful of you, but have you really thought this through?" Theresa asked respectfully, eyebrow raised.

"I have," Charity lied. Maybe she did overdo it. "Well, I need to go on to the store and get the materials. This will be fun."

As Charity left the kitchen, Theresa called out, "Enjoy! See you later."

"Bye," Charity yelled as she went out the front door. She clutched her list of the supplies she needed. "Let's see what deals we can come up with," she thought, pepping herself up for the trip to the store.

Henry sat at his desk at the office when Erica popped in and asked, "Got a minute?"

"Sure," Henry replied, moving his keyboard to the side, giving Erica his attention. "What's up?"

"Well, I received an email from Charity Walters at the Silver Horseshoe Ranch. Do you know her?" Erica asked curiously, remembering that Charity interviewed him for the story a week or so before.

Henry shuffled himself in his chair and cleared his throat. "I know her," Henry began. "She inherited the Silver Horseshoe Ranch. She's a former foster youth who aged-out. She spends her time, when she isn't working at *The Standard Banner,* going to foster care review boards."

"Well, no wonder she's being so generous by having the event and the gifts and all. She has been in the hard places these children are coming from," Erica said admiringly.

"It's amazing. There isn't a selfish bone in her body," Henry mentioned as he realized Erica took notice. "What?" Henry defended.

"Nothing. It is simply different seeing *this* side of you. Do you have feelings for her?" Erica asked with genuine concern.

"The more time I spend with her, the more I think I do," Henry admitted remembering how Charity looked last night when he left her asleep on the couch. "Say, Erica," Henry boldly began, "did you know a Jennifer Ryan here at the department? She was Charity's FSW."

Looking upward as if magically drawing information from the air, Erica replied, "I transferred from another region about the time Jennifer retired. I didn't get to know her. Why do ask?"

"Well, after seeing how much Charity struggles with the aging-out thing, I found her case notes from her last day in custody. Jennifer really did care for Charity. Should I tell her?"

"Henry, I don't know how to advise you on this one," Erica said regretfully. "Children…teens, can't always see the real picture because the trauma is in the way. She certainly had her walls way up to protect herself. Just proceed with caution. She may not be ready for what you have on your mind."

"So, what was your decision on the gifts? She mentioned she wanted your input before she could get the appropriate gifts," Henry redirected.

"I don't know what to tell her," Erica confessed.

"I got it! What about a board game for each of the families? That will encourage family interaction," Henry said triumphantly. "She could get a wide variety of games and it wouldn't matter if there were duplicates because the families will be scattered across the city."

"That's a great idea. Tell her to do that. Or am I supposed to relay that message?" Erica asked playfully.

"Hahaha," Henry laughed. "You relay that message. I don't want her to know I was involved."

"Okay, I'll go and email her with that information," Erica said leaving Henry's desk. "See you later."

"Bye," Henry said as he returned to his typing.

Erica sat at her desk and replied to Charity's email. "Hello Charity," Erica began. "After careful consideration, I suggest you purchase a variety of board games for the children. This will encourage family time over the holidays. We are truly thankful for your thoughtful gesture." Erica reread what she wrote and hit send. No mention of Henry anywhere. Promise kept. "He must really care for this girl," she thought to herself as she glanced his way.

Henry had several cases to work on today, so he didn't have time to think about texting Charity to see if she heard anything from Erica. He continued his work all afternoon until time to leave at five o'clock.

****

Charity brought in the bags of supplies and plopped down in the chair at the desk. The office would be the best place to assemble the vases. She was flexing her stiff fingers when her phone buzzed. Erica had responded to her earlier email.

"That's a great idea," she considered. "Board games aren't too expensive and would be easy to wrap," Charity said excitedly. "I can get the vases done by Wednesday, then shop for the games. I have plenty of time."

Charity worked straight through the afternoon into evening. She stopped only when Theresa brought her a sandwich, a bag of chips, and a drink. She completed twenty vases before she called it a night. She left all the materials where they were and closed the door to the office. She flopped down across her bed and crashed before she knew it.

CHAPTER 8

On Tuesday morning, Charity awoke to a commotion out behind the house with one of the horses. She dressed quickly and went outside to see if she could help.

"Chuck, what can I do to help you?" Charity asked with noted concern.

"Nothing presently. Ginger threw a shoe giving her a tender front foot. She reared back and knocked all the nails we had to reshoe her somewhere around here. It will take forever to try and find them all. Johnny Paulson, the other man who works with me here in the barn, had to go back and get an extra set of nails," Chuck recounted.

Johnny returned with the nails. "Johnny," Chuck started, "this is Charity Walters. She's the new owner of the ranch."

"Pleased to meet you, Miss Walters," Johnny smiled tipping his hat. "I have been on extended leave to take care of a family matter. I left just after we had the services for your Uncle Frank. He was a genuinely nice man," Johnny finished.

"Please, call me Charity," she said embarrassed. "I really appreciate your dedication to the ranch."

"Well, I've worked with Chuck and Frank many years. I was here before your Aunt Marion died. She was a very gentle woman, had a big heart," Johnny said fondly.

"Well, I'll let you get back to Ginger. I have 55 more vases to assemble before I move on to my next project," Charity said as she returned confidently into the house.

Theresa was searching cabinets to see what she was going to prepare for the day's dinner. "Are you hungry? Want some pancakes, or something? Theresa offered. "All you ate last night was a sandwich."

"I'm not very hungry right now. I need to get started on the vases that are left. I need to get them finished. I have presents to purchase and wrap," Charity said excitedly.

"Well, I'll check on you later to see what you need," Theresa offered thoughtfully.

"Thank you," Charity said hugging Theresa.

Charity went back into the office and readied her assembly line. The vases were lined up in rows of twos. The ribbon was measured and precut. The foam blocks were cut to the right sizes, and the potpourri divided into sections. She queued up her Christmas playlist, ensuring positivity and efficiency. She made herself comfortable and found her groove.

Charity worked smoothly when she heard her phone buzz. It was Henry. "Hey, what are you doing?" Henry texted.

"Finishing the vases for this weekend. You?" Charity replied.

"Thinking of taking some time off. Want some help?" Henry offered. "I know you have a lot of things coming due by Saturday."

"Are you sure? As a matter of fact, after I finish these vases, I need to purchase 75 board games. I can't manage the shopping carts myself," Charity replied embarrassed. "I'm not ready to shop today, so let's meet tomorrow. You can come here first if you like."

"I'm finishing up things here at the office. Alex and Randi will cover calls while I'm off," Henry replied. "What time tomorrow?"

"Let's start around nine-thirty. Will you need breakfast?" Charity wondered.

"See you at nine-thirty. No breakfast for me."

Wow, she thought. It was great he offered to help. But did he feel like he had to? Charity enjoyed spending time with Henry, to be sure. But she didn't want him to feel obligated to help with the party preparations.

She took a break. When she returned to the office, Theresa had put a cold drink on a coaster along with a blueberry muffin. "She is so thoughtful…and knows me too well," Charity smiled.

Max was courteous enough to *NOT* sit on the supplies, but he sprawled across the middle of the desk. It didn't slow her down. At her current rate of speed, she would finish in time to have a hearty dinner…

She worked steadily, enjoying the songs on her playlist, sometimes singing. Two hours later, she finally finished the last vase. Charity stood up and stretched her back. Sitting in a chair like that for so long made her back hurt. She bent over and touched her toes. Max eased over, rubbing against her leg. "I know, Max," she said. "I haven't paid much attention to you today. Thanks for being a good kitty."

Charity retrieved a trash bag from the kitchen so she could clean up her mess. Theresa stirred the beef stew in the crockpot as she asked, "Did you get them all done?"

"I sure did. All 75 of them. Come see how they look," Charity asked feeling proud of herself. Theresa walked in the office behind her. Charity got one of the vases off the desk and held it up for Theresa to inspect.

"Oh, honey, these will be so pretty on the tables. Now, what did you make these for?" Theresa wondered.

"Well, aside from being the centerpiece for the tables, the families will take them home as an extra gift from me," Charity explained.

"Well, I think they're a wonderful gift. I'm sure they will love them," Theresa voiced sincerely.

"Thank you," Charity beamed, proud of her hard work.

"Talked to Henry lately?" Theresa asked innocently.

"Oh, he's taking some time off and asked me if I needed any help with anything. Tomorrow he's helping me buy the board games for the children," Charity replied.

"Uh-huh," Theresa smirked. "Well, shopping is always fun."

"It was just a thoughtful gesture. I told him I wouldn't be able to steer both shopping carts myself. With all the rolls of wrapping paper and tape I must get…" Charity trailed off, though not convincing Theresa. Theresa knew exactly why Henry was taking the time off.

Theresa went back to her work. Charity picked up all the excess ribbon parts, potpourri shavings, and the bags that held all the supplies. She gathered the reusable pieces of materials in a plastic tote and stored them in the office closet. She vacuumed and made sure the room was in perfect condition.

Charity lined the vases up against the walls. She closed the door so Max wouldn't rip all the flowers out of the vases. Cats have been known to do such things.

After working on the vases, Charity went outside to sit in the swing. That had become her thinking place when she wasn't driving. The words Julie had said to her were running through her mind. "Think of all the barriers you had. Write them all down. Pick one," Charity voiced aloud. Though it was hard being alone when she aged-out, she managed to make new friends easily. But her closest friend was Julie. Julie had brothers and sisters and sometimes let her go to her house for holidays, especially when her family wasn't traveling. Charity had learned to be overly optimistic about everything, so she struggled with the list of barriers. The only barrier she really had was a lack of transportation right out of foster care. She could feel an idea bubbling in her mind. She decided to call Julie and tell her what she had thought up.

"Hey, Julie, can you talk a few minutes? I think I know what I want to do," Charity voiced excitedly.

"Hey there, what did you come up with?" Julie asked with enthusiasm.

"Transportation was my greatest barrier. Well, really my only barrier. I would have been all set had I had my own vehicle. I wouldn't have needed to depend on you so much and feel like a nuisance," Charity said. "What if I create a grant, or something, to give aging out foster youth money to get a car? Not an expensive one, but one that has been cleared by the mechanic and can get them where they need to go. Job interviews and doctor's appointments can be difficult if there isn't a bus route available."

"That's a great idea," Julie replied cheerily. "Do you have a price limit per youth?"

"Well, what about seven to ten thousand dollars?" Charity inquired. "The youth could pick out the car at whatever lot and the sales manager could contact me to transfer the money."

"What about insurance? The state says all drivers are supposed to be insured," Julie reminded Charity.

"Well, I could pay for it for the first six months, allowing them time to get a job and get settled," Charity voiced eagerly. "But what do I call it? Deals for Wheels? No, I don't think I like that. Wheels of Hope?"

"That name is already taken," Julie said regretfully as she keyed in other potential names in her computer. "How about Aspiration Station? Prosperity

Pedals?"

"Stop. I think I'm sold on Aspiration Station," Charity said animatedly. "You have the best ideas! THANK YOU, Julie."

"Thanks for including me in your brainstorming," Julie countered. "I need to go. I'll check on you later in the week."

"Okay," stated Charity. "I'll contact my coworker who is the financial expert at the paper and get his thoughts on this venture. Catch you later. Remind me to send you a 'thinker's fee'," Charity ended the call. "Aspiration Station. I really like that. It oozes the thought of having hope when you have no family of your own."

Feeling on top of the world, Charity went back inside. Theresa said it was almost time for dinner. Charity washed up and grabbed a drink from the refrigerator. Theresa, Chuck, and Charity poured their bowls of beef stew. Theresa had baked a yummy skillet of cornbread. They all sat at the bar and ate while Charity excitedly recounted her conversation with Julie and her decision about foster youth and cars.

"What a tremendous idea!" Chuck was awestruck. "I imagine that will be a big help to youth in regard to jobs and all."

"Definitely," Charity said quickly. "That kept me from being able to totally fend for myself. If it hadn't been for Julie and her family, I don't know what I would have done. I will consult with Marcus from the paper and get his advice on how he thinks I should set this up."

"Don't forget about Arthur Lovejoy from the law firm either," reminded Theresa. Charity had forgotten about him, oops.

After dinner, Charity helped Theresa clean the kitchen. "I think I'm going to take a bubble bath, then turn in early. I want to sleep in my bed tonight. I've made a habit of sleeping in strange places. Good night," Charity hugged Theresa. She gave a side hug to Chuck, "Good night, Chuck."

"Well, she seems a little off," Chuck said with his head cocked a little. "Is she okay besides figuring out what she finally wants to do?"

"Well, now that you mention it," Theresa started quietly, "Henry's going to help her buy the games for the children tomorrow. She said he told her he's taking a little time off," Theresa said shaking her head.

"Really?" Chuck scratched his head. "Why would he do that, I wonder?"

"Oh, come on, don't you see it?" Theresa asked incredulously, hand on one hip. "Henry is falling in love with that girl. I'm not sure she can see it yet."

"Well, we will just have to keep an eye on them, won't we? If what you say is true, I bet he'll propose to her before Christmas," Chuck added holding up his money clip.

"I would definitely take that bet," Theresa replied giving Chuck a wink.

****

Charity woke up fearful she had overslept. She had subconsciously turned off the alarm when it went off at eight fifteen. Now, it was eight thirty-five. She jumped out of bed. She thumbed through her clothes until she found the right outfit-her dark, blue jeans and a plum-colored sweater. She decided to wear her blue ankle boots. She kept her hair straight today but placed her sunglasses on her head as a headband. Normal headbands made her head hurt. She grabbed a short brown jacket. She seized a leftover blueberry muffin that Theresa had made yesterday. She thought she looked rather good and would be ready to go when Henry arrived. And right on cue, her phone buzzed.

"I'm here, can I come on up?" Henry asked.

"Sure. I'll meet you outside. Do you want to drive, or do you want me to?" Charity asked trying not to be a bother.

"I don't mind driving," Henry texted.

"I will be right there," Charity replied, heading out the door.

Henry caught a whiff of the Christmas scent on her as she climbed in the truck. "Where are we going to get the board games?"

"Well, what about the game store? We will also need a ton of wrapping paper, bows, and tape," Charity figured.

"Well, then let's hit it," Henry uttered all macho-like.

Charity was a little surprised to hear him listening to Christmas music. "You're already listening to Christmas music?" she queried.

"Of course. What better way to make yourself feel happy? Besides, aren't we buying presents today? Don't you want to be in the Christmas spirit?" He tested, hoping she wasn't going to be a scrooge.

"No, it's fine. Truth is, I've also been listening to Christmas music for that same reason. I just didn't know there were others who did that. Guess that is another thing we have in common, huh?" Charity stated honestly.

"Yeah. So, what is your favorite Christmas song, then?" Henry probed.

"Well, I would have to say *The Train* by Celestial Navigations," Charity considered thoughtfully.

"But that really isn't a song. It's more of a story," Henry rebutted.

"I know, but I always felt like I could identify with the woman on the train. Well, except for not having a baby. I could understand her loneliness and feeling of despair. I loved that contrast to the man who was telling the story of his family. I felt like I could fall right into that memory," Charity told Henry.

Henry sensed her sadness. To have been all alone the way she had been, she was still so optimistic. How could she do that?

"Well, I told you mine. What's yours?" Charity asked, snapping Henry back to the moment.

"It's so hard to pick just one song," Henry thought for a few moments. "I think my favorite song would have to be *The Christmas Song* by Nat King Cole."

"That is a good song," Charity said patting Henry on the arm.

They arrived the game store. Henry parked, and they went inside. They each got a shopping cart. "Do we really need both of these?" Henry asked feeling silly.

"Yes, I told you I can't drive two of them filled with all the things we need. Let's go," Charity commanded.

They walked to the board game aisle and reconnoitered the selection. It was remarkably diverse. Charity had her game on…no pun intended, and advised Henry, "There are many different games here. Let's just get five of the 15 best ones."

"That's a good idea," Henry considered.

"Don't forget we still need to get the wrapping paper. I'll get five of these eight games and you get five of those seven," Charity pointed to the games next to Henry. "This is going to be so fun…watching the children open the presents."

"Okay, we have the games. Didn't we pass the wrapping paper on our way back here?" Henry asked thinking out loud.

"We did," Charity remembered as they were leaving the game aisle. "This way, oh, grab the tape right there, please," Charity nudged Henry as they went onto the wrapping paper aisle.

"How many rolls should I grab?" Henry asked. She couldn't hear him, so he grabbed three rolls of tape.

"Okay, we should figure maybe seven to eight normal sized gifts per roll. We should get probably ten rolls total, just to be on the safe side," Henry concluded as he calculated the paper.

"We will need just two bags of the bows. They come in a package of 45," Charity said quickly.

They gathered many beautiful rolls of paper, then headed to the checkout lines. This would take a little while. They patiently waited in line and twenty minutes later wheeled the items out to the truck. They went through the donut shop drive thru so Henry could get a coffee and Charity, a hot chocolate.

As they ventured back to the ranch, the smell of Charity's hot chocolate brought back a childhood memory. Henry had a huge smile on his face as he relived it for Charity.

"Your hot chocolate just made me remember one of the times my family went to church on Christmas Eve. I was about seven. After the service, the church gave out hot chocolate and cookies. We all grabbed a cup and a cookie before heading home. When we arrived back at our house, all the presents had been placed under the tree. Santa left a note saying that he had to get an earlier start than he expected, so he left our presents while we were gone. It was only when I became an adult that my parents told me our neighbor put them out for us," Henry recalled fondly.

"Wow, that must've been exciting. Did you get to open them all on Christmas Eve, or did you have to wait until morning?" Charity wondered curiously.

"Oh, we opened a couple of them. But Mom and Dad were strict about doing the rest *on* Christmas morning," Henry regaled. "Do you have any happy Christmas memories?"

Charity thought for a few minutes, then finally spoke, "I think the happiest Christmas I can remember was when I was 15. I knew that adoption was out of the question by then. It was by my own choice. My foster family took really good care of me. I was getting particularly good with my writing and I was given a journal, some great pens, and a camera for Christmas. They encouraged me to take pictures and write about things in my journal. I guess that is how I decided to pursue journalism after high school."

Once they got back to the ranch, they lugged all the bags into the house. Charity led Henry through to the kitchen because a job like this would need the big table in the formal dining room. They passed Theresa on the way through, and she just stared at all the bags.

"You have to do all that?" Theresa gasped.

"Yes, but we can do it. There are two of us working on it," Henry confirmed.

Theresa had her doubts, but she believed it would make for an interesting afternoon.

They piled the bags with the games in a corner. Charity pulled out the rolls of wrapping paper and set them at one end of the table. She staged the tape and one roll of wrap for Henry and one for her. She set the bows at the other end as they would be the last things to go on the presents. She remembered the scissors and ran to the office and brought two pairs back, walking gingerly, of course. Henry helped her stack the games in piles to make it easy to grab and wrap. Everything was in place. Charity put on Christmas music to give the experience the perfect atmosphere.

"Before we get started, I have to confess I'm not the best present wrapper in the world," Henry confessed. "I hope you don't expect perfection."

"Surely it can't be as bad as all that," Charity doubted, thinking he was overreacting. "Here, you work here, and I'll work over here," she said as she walked around to the other side of the table. Do we want to wrap the same game with the same paper?"

"Why don't we grab one of each kind and wrap until we run out of this paper?" Henry suggested.

Seeing how that made sense, Charity replied, "Good idea. Ready? Here we go!"

They both pulled a game from the pile and began wrapping. Henry was the kind of wrapper who cut the paper almost too short and had to really work to avoid any gaps that would show what was inside. Charity took the gift, centered it in the middle of the paper, leaving about two to three inches on each side. She cut one long sheet. She placed the gift face down, orienting the front of the game in correspondence to the print on the paper. She secured it with tape, then rolled it up until the paper got to the end. She folded the paper to make sure it ended on the bottom of the gift. She cut any excess paper from either side, then taped it into a perfect square, or rectangle, depending on the shape. It was impressive.

"How do you expect me to compete with that?" Henry protested, observing how quickly and precisely Charity wrapped the gift.

"Oh, sorry. I just really get into wrapping. Just do it as close to this way as possible and you will be fine," Charity smirked.

Charity and Henry dug in and wrapped all 75 gifts in a little over three and a half hours. Henry marveled at how Charity moved so quickly and made the gifts look so good.

Theresa had Chinese food sitting on the bar in the kitchen. She met Henry in the dining room, "You guys need a break. Come get some Chinese food while it's hot. I'll save some food for Chuck. He is occupied with the horses."

Suddenly Henry perked up, "Is that soy and cabbage I smell?" He drifted toward the kitchen. "Theresa, thank you for this delicious-smelling cuisine."

"I didn't realize how hungry I was," Charity said. "I just had a muffin this morning."

"You're welcome. You haven't stopped all afternoon," Theresa said, making a fuss.

"You're a saint. Thank you!" Charity declared as she gave Theresa a hug. "Theresa, what is your favorite Chinese food?"

"I like the orange chicken and fried rice," Theresa declared. "Henry, what about you?"

"Oh, I like just about everything, even the spicier food. I can't decide if I like the rice better or the noodles," Henry floundered. "Charity, I bet you just like the fortune cookies, right?"

"Oh, I do like the cookies, and the Chinese donuts. I discovered I have an affinity for egg rolls and wonton soup. And I don't usually like soup, but this soup is great," Charity said definitively.

"Yeah, this Chinese food was great. Want me to help you clean up the dining room and put the bows on the presents?" Henry asked.

"Sure, that would be nice," Charity said thankfully. They returned to the dining room and got back to work.

"What do you have left to do before Saturday?" Henry asked as they worked to attach the bows. "The vases are done and now the presents are almost finished, as well."

"I'll check in with Penelope tomorrow. We have the outside decorations and I think that is it," Charity added. It took only ten minutes to put the bows on all the gifts. They gathered up all the paper shrapnel and returned the room to its normal appearance. Henry helped Charity put the presents in the office along with the vases.

"Well, I will head out and check in with you tomorrow," Henry gifted the bag of trash to Charity. "No need to walk me out. See you later."

CHAPTER 9

Charity felt rather good about her accomplishments. She created beautiful vases. She and Henry also secured and wrapped all the presents for the children for Saturday. All that was left was the check-in with Penelope Carter ensuring all the details were handled. It was Thursday and she sat at the bar planning the best way to spend the next two days before the party on Saturday. Her phone buzzed. It was Henry.

"Can you talk for a few minutes? Henry asked.

"Okay, you can call me," Charity replied. An instant later Henry called her. "Hello?"

"Hey," Henry began slowly. "I don't know how to tell you this so I will just come out and say it. Erica had the wrong number of children in custody here in Jefferson County. It isn't 75 children. It's 106."

Charity almost fell off the stool. "106 children?" Charity questioned as she ran her hand through her hair in disbelief, but her voice showed no emotion.

"Yes, are you okay?" Henry asked worriedly. "Have you called Penelope yet?"

"Not yet," Charity said trying to sound positive, "I was just about to call her."

"What are you going to do?" Henry probed poised to scribble notes on a pad.

"Well, the easiest thing is to just ask her to add 31 tables to the 75. That means we need to add another 124 people to the food list," Charity said as if it was no big deal.

"But the presents and the vases? Now you don't have enough," Henry reminded her.

"Well, luckily the store had plenty of games when we were there before. I can get enough materials to make the rest of the vases. Tell you what, why don't I go shopping and get the stuff we need. You plan to be here in about two hours. Then, we can divide and conquer. I'll make the vases and you can wrap the presents. But first, I need to contact Penelope. This is a big change. If you get here and I'm not back yet just come on inside. I will tell Theresa to expect you. Bye," Charity said hanging up.

"Okay, bye," Henry said before he heard her end the call. "She took that better than I expected," Henry exhaled as he glanced upward.

Charity called Penelope. "Hello Penelope? It's Charity Walters. I need to tell you of a development that has arisen."

"Okay, shoot," Penelope uttered.

"It appears that we have an incorrect number of people for the event on Saturday. We need to add 31 more tables and food for 124 people," Charity paused, bracing for impact. "Can we accommodate that change?" her voice trailed off.

"We can make that change, not a problem at all. Is there anything else I need to do?" Penelope asked.

"No, just add the tables and people to the list. I'll handle the 31 additional gifts for the children and the vases for the tables. They will be ready in time," Charity affirmed.

"You must be a marvel to get this done so quickly," Penelope said in awe, eyebrow raised and shaking her head.

"No, I just have a right-hand man who just happens to be available to assist me. Not to worry. See you bright and early Saturday morning for the set up," Charity concluded.

Charity messaged Theresa about Henry. Charity snatched her keys and trekked to the game store and craft supply store. She and Henry had a *lot* of work to do.

Henry did, in fact, get to the ranch before Charity returned from the stores. As he reached for the doorbell, Theresa opened the door and let him in.

"Hello, Henry," Theresa began, "how are you?" Theresa walked back down the hall to the kitchen with Henry in tow.

"Well, honestly, I feel like I dropped a ten-ton boulder on Charity. We had the numbers wrong on how many children were in custody here in Jefferson County. It is 106 children, not 75. Now she must do this extra work in a hurry," Henry furrowed his eyebrows.

"I'm sure she is fine," Theresa consoled. She could see why he felt badly. "That's a lot of unexpected work. But Charity has a gracious nature. Deep down, she loves a challenge. Well, you can't change things by worrying. Here, grab yourself a glass of tea. She should be home momentarily."

"How can she just be so accommodating like that?" Henry mused.

"Henry, she has a heart of gold and would give folks anything they needed. You know that. When she gets here, just do whatever she needs you to and get the things taken care of," Theresa coached.

"You're right. I'll do whatever she tells me and get these things done," Henry pounded the bar.

Henry was about to sip his glass of tea when he heard a car door close outside. He sat his drink down and went to open the front door.

"Oh, thank you very much. I can get these but there are more bags out there. Can you get them and take them to the formal dining room?" Charity bounded through the doorway.

"Sure," Henry declared as he moved toward the car, skipping two steps in stride.

Charity had the materials for the vases, so she put them in the office. Henry came back in the house carrying the rest of the bags and went to the dining room as instructed. Charity got a drink from the refrigerator and met up with Henry to form their game plan.

"Okay," she began, "we can finish these one of two ways. You can wrap the presents in here and I can finish the vases in the office. Or we can work together on each project. Which would you rather do?"

Honestly, the second option would be better...then he could spend more time with Charity. But he could see the benefit of the first option. Knowing time was of the essence he went for option number one. "Why don't we split these up. If I get finished with the presents before you are finished with the vases, I'll come help you," Henry offered reluctantly.

"Right. All the things you need are in the bags. Oh, let me get the tape and scissors, hang on," Charity said as she dashed to the office and back to the dining room. "I'll settle in the office. Yell if you get into trouble."

Henry piled the games on the end of the table. He had the rolls of paper ready to go. He split the paper up between the games and started wrapping. He tried to recall how Charity showed him so he could save more time. He went straight to work.

Charity stepped into the office and looked around. She had forgotten how full the room already was with all the other vases. Plus, they had put the games in there, too. "This won't work," she said to herself going back to the dining room to help Henry.

Henry was surprised to see her back already and asked, "What gives? I thought you were doing your job and I was doing this one," he joked.

"Well, I forgot how crowded the office is with all the vases and presents that are already in there. It makes more sense for me to help you with wrapping so I can use the table for the vases," Charity confessed. "Here, give me some of those games. Put on your Christmas playlist this time."

In no time at all, they wrapped the rest of the presents and carried them to the office with the others. Henry helped Charity carry the materials for the vases to the dining room. It was unbelievable how heavy glass vases can be.

Charity placed the wrapping paper in the corner and began organizing the vases at the end of the table.

Henry pointed to the vases, "Okay, so what do we do with these?"

"Well, you can take this piece of ribbon and cut 31 strips all the same size. I'm going to divide the potpourri for when we put it in the vases. I'll cut the foam into the number of pieces we need. Then, we just put it all together," Charity detailed as if it was the easiest thing in the world.

"That sounds confusing," Henry confessed.

"You just cut the ribbon and I will show you what to do," Charity reassured. Henry worked to cut the pieces of ribbon, being sure to match the length exactly.

Charity put the foam block in a vase. Then she pushed the artificial flowers into the foam. She then covered the foam with the potpourri. The ribbon was tied around the neck of the vase, which made it very festive.

Henry finished cutting all 31 pieces of the ribbon. After seeing how she did the first vase, he said, "This actually looks like something I can do." He took the vase, flowers, block, potpourri, and ribbon and did exactly what Charity did. It looked surprisingly good.

"Wow, most impressive," Charity said channeling her best Darth Vader impression through an empty wrapping paper tube. "Even your bow looks great. Now, we just do them one at a time until we get them all done."

They worked silently and concertedly as they listened to Henry's Christmas playlist. Henry observed Charity deep in concentration. He saw that she sometimes wrinkled her forehead when she is doing something that was a little complicated. He marveled at how fast she could assemble these vases. He guessed that when you have done so many, you find ways to speed things up.

Theresa stopped by to check on them and nodded in agreement when Charity asked if they looked as good as the last ones. Theresa left them some cookies and refreshed their drinks.

"Wow, Theresa thinks of everything at the right time, doesn't she?" asked Henry.

"You'd be surprised," Charity started, "I was in the office working. I came back from the bathroom and she left me a muffin and a Diet Mountain Dew."

"Hey," Henry asked slyly, "Since you had all this extra work to do, why don't I take you out for dinner. It's the least I could do."

She would normally say it wasn't necessary, but she thought it would be fun. Charity replied, "What a thoughtful thing to do. But remember, you helped *me* this afternoon."

"Great, where should we go?" Henry asked curiously.

"I'll let you pick," Charity said wondering what he would choose. "But we can't go until all this is finished."

"Well, let's finish it then," Henry smiled. It took them another forty-five minutes to finish the last ones. They moved the vases to the office. Henry collected what he knew was trash.

Charity put the supplies back in the plastic tote and took a washcloth from the kitchen and wiped off the table. She informed Henry, "Okay, let's go eat. I'm famished." Charity grabbed her purse and jacket, and they went out to dinner.

Henry wanted to take Charity to a semi-romantic, but not trying to be romantic kind of place. He decided on the local Italian restaurant. The lighting was dimmed, and they played beautiful Italian music. They were seated in a corner booth and given menus.

"I hope they have manicotti," Charity remarked excitedly as she scanned the menu. "What do you order here?"

"Oh, I like the fettuccini alfredo. And lots of garlic bread…I'm talking I could kill a vampire if I breathed on him," Henry offered without hesitation.

"I can't tell you how much I appreciate you assisting me with the vases and presents. Sometimes it's hard for me to admit when I need help. I don't want to appear weak," Charity explained, letting her guard down.

"Why would I think you are weak? That was a considerable jump in number. The vases and the presents look wonderful. The families and the children will be thrilled to receive them," Henry replied, not understanding her thought process.

"I don't know…I guess it was a silly notion. Everyone needs help sometimes, right?" Charity questioned insecurely.

"Of course, they do. Let's not think about that anymore. I'm ready for an enjoyable dinner," Henry put forward. They had a good time and Henry had Charity back home at a respectable time.

****

Saturday morning finally arrived. The Thanksgiving Shindig was the first event Charity had ever planned so she was up, dressed, and ready when Penelope and her crew arrived to set up the tents and tables.

"Good morning, Penelope," Charity greeted. "What do I need to do?"

"Good morning, Charity," Penelope said cordially, "we're just about to get the tent set up. Once the tables are set up, you can bring out the centerpieces."

"Great, then I just need to know where Santa will be staged so I can leave the presents with him," Charity grinned.

Charity watched as the workers raised the support beams for the tent. Then it went up quickly. The men moved the tables from the trucks and staged them along with the chairs in no time. The tables were numbered to make seeing Santa Claus much more orderly. The outdoor decorations were beautiful. The cornstalks, hay bales, and gourds were placed near the entrance of the tent on both sides. Small cornucopias, pilgrims, Native Americans, and turkey decorations were placed inside to give it that Thanksgiving atmosphere. Confident she wouldn't be in the way of the workers Charity began ferrying the vases from the office. After two trips, she realized it would take forever and asked if she could borrow a trolley cart. It had two tiers and would hold many vases. She parked it at the back door and loaded as many vases as she could without the risk of them falling off. She was on her way back to the tables when Henry appeared and buffered the trolley.

"What are you doing here so early?" Charity queried, thankful that he was protecting the vases from the edge of the cart.

"I came to be an extra set of hands in case you needed anything," Henry explained. "So, what do you still need to do?"

"Well, I need to find the area the gifts need to be stashed so Santa can give them out when he sees the children later," Charity said looking around with no luck.

"You put the vases on the tables, and I will look for Santa's table," Henry offered.

"Thanks," Charity yelled as Henry dashed away. She had quite a few more tables to do when Henry came back a little out of breath.

"I finally found it," he said a touch out of breath, "it's over there," Henry pointed toward the back of the tent.

"Great, I can get these out, hopefully before the families start arriving," Charity remarked calmly. She drove the trolley cart back to the house. It took two more trips with the vases. Next, she hauled out the games. Henry stacked the gifts in an orderly way on the table. Finally, Charity returned the trolley.

It was time for all the families to begin arriving. Chuck and Theresa wandered outside and strolled around looking at the tables. They were impressed at how lovely the vases were on the tables. Charity had done a tremendous job. Penelope and her assistant guided people to their seats. Charity hadn't told anyone, but she was going to say a little something before everyone was served.

Penelope directed, "Charity, it is almost time for you to address to the guests."

"Right, I am prepared," Charity replied. "Have all the DCS employees been seated as well? I just realized I didn't get the family gift cards. Let me check with Henry if DCS relayed that message to the foster families."

Charity had a few minutes, so she wandered around until she found Henry. She beckoned him to come to her and whispered, "I completely forgot the $100 gift cards. Do you know if Erica told the foster parents whether or not they would be getting them?"

"I'm not sure," Henry expressed, "let me go find her." Henry rushed off and found Erica. Charity could see Erica shake her head "NO," so she may have been in the clear.

Henry relayed happily, "Erica said she did not tell the families about the gift card. She figured if they received one it would be an extra bonus. We think the food for the children and DCS staff plus the presents for the children are enough."

Charity blushed at his words, "It's the least I can do." She looked at her watch and it was two o'clock on the dot. She made her way to the front of the tent.

"Hello everyone. I'm Charity Walters. I live here at the Silver Horseshoe Ranch. I wanted to take a moment and show appreciation to you as foster parents and DCS staff for working with the children we have in custody here in Jefferson County. You may not know it, but I'm a former foster youth. Just eight years ago I aged-out of state custody. I just recently found out I had relatives here in this area. Please enjoy the delicious Thanksgiving meal that will be delivered to your tables momentarily. All current foster children will receive a gift from a special visitor before the conclusion of the festivities. Enjoy your food and thank you very much for attending. Families, be sure to take the table decoration with you as you leave." Though nervous, Charity sounded like a pro. She stepped away and the servers began distributing the boxed meals and drinks.

Charity took her place at the table with Chuck, Theresa, and the Hendersons. Across from Chuck and Theresa were Jeff and Melanie, who had book-ended their three-year-old son, Zach. Amanda and Peter were on either side of Charity.

"Melanie, Jeff, this is Chuck Hobby and Theresa Wilson. They live with me here at the ranch," Charity said proudly as she introduced them.

"Wonderful to meet you. Thank you for having this lovely event. We're so excited to be here. Amanda and Peter had such a great time here," Melanie spoke first.

"We have always enjoyed entertaining here at the Silver Horseshoe. The children seem like good kids," Theresa complimented.

"You enjoy the meal. I need to make sure everything is going okay," Charity stated as she got up from the table.

Hearing the laughter, Charity could tell the families were having an excellent time. She noticed she had correctly advised Penelope about the food as the turkey, potatoes, green beans, dinner roll, and pie were quickly consumed. Foster moms picked up the vases and looked at them with smiles on their faces. Soon, the special guest would be arriving, and the children would receive their presents. Charity was overcome with emotion knowing she could give a little appreciation and kindness to people.

Henry ate lunch at the table with Erica. Erica couldn't believe all the vases Charity had made. They were beautiful.

"We had craft supply stuff all over the place. But it was fun," Henry narrated how he helped Charity do the last 31 vases. He detailed how they had gone shopping for the board games and had such a good time wrapping them.

"Well, they turned out great," Erica assured Henry. Erica hadn't spent any time with Charity but could see why Henry held her in such high regard. Erica detected the twinkle in Henry's eyes when he talked about her. Henry disappeared to find Charity.

Henry casually walked the back half of the tent when he found Charity. "How much longer until Santa visits?" Henry asked.

"Let me go check with Penelope," Charity said as she disappeared. After a few minutes she came back and said, "Santa will be ready to see visitors in ten minutes."

"Good, then I want to introduce you to Erica," Henry said as he clasped Charity's hand and pulled her along.

"Charity, this is Erica, Randi, and Alex. They work with me at DCS," Henry said proudly. Alex stood up and shook Charity's hand while Randi and Erica just waved hello.

"A pleasure to finally meet you in person," Charity began, "I really appreciate the work you do with the children in our county."

"We are grateful for this exciting event," Erica offered, thankfully looking around. "This is a beautiful place. Have you gotten used to living here yet?"

"I have now, but it was hard at first. I have family that lives here and remembers my uncle and aunt! I have heard a few stories," Charity recalled. "Though they couldn't have me live with them, they *were* thinking of me. But still…sometimes I wonder what it would have been like if I could have lived with them." Charity realized they were empathizing, so she said, "Enough of that. It's time for Santa!" She dashed off.

"She still has really deep emotions about all of this, doesn't she?" Alex observed.

Henry nodded in agreement as Erica remarked, "I can understand why. She lived all that time thinking she was alone only to find she had people here so close."

"She's trying to find her path and figure out what she's supposed to do with her life," Henry explained. "She's been a little tight-lipped and I don't have a clue what she's thinking."

"She seems to have a good head on her shoulders and a generous nature," Randi praised.

Henry added, "I felt really bad that we didn't figure siblings into the number of children we told Charity. But with all the DCS staff she invited, the tables were just enough."

"Yeah, they were, weren't they?" Erica replied. "It's been a special day for us, too."

Charity addressed the microphone, "At this time, Santa will begin seeing the children who are the special guests today. We will proceed numerically with tables one through ten. After your child has received their gift, feel free to stay if you like. Please take your vase with you when you leave. Children, please follow me, as Santa is waiting to see you," Charity moved to the aisle and the children followed her to Santa's table.

The tent swelled with the noise of children excited to get their gifts from Santa. The rest of the tables moved quickly and orderly. There was still a lot of Saturday left to enjoy, so most families left after their children received their gift. Some families stayed behind to see their workers for a few minutes. They used the event as an opportunity to complete a monthly face to face visit. Charity thanked Santa Claus and complimented him on his magnificent job. She couldn't have imagined it going more smoothly.

Jeff and Melanie Henderson were still talking with Barbara Frederickson. They didn't realize it, but Peter had wandered away from the table and drifted over to the pasture fence. Chuck pressed out the back door, trash bags in hand, when he noticed Peter's eyes fixed on the horses.

"Hello, Peter," Chuck said softly as he shoved the bags in his back pocket. "Beauties, aren't they?" He knew Peter wouldn't say anything. "Let's see if we can get one to come over here." Chuck lifted Peter up and stood him on the bottom rung of the fence to be eye level with the horses. Chuck whistled and a few seconds later, Maverick trotted over. "Hold out your hand and let him sniff you," Chuck nodded encouragingly as he held his hand out. Peter mimicked his movement. "That's it," Chuck soothed. Maverick let Peter rub the velvety part of his muzzle. Suddenly, Peter released a soft giggle. They stood there for quite a while, just petting Maverick, who nickered rhythmically in the soft glow of the afternoon light.

Charity was making the rounds when she spotted Chuck nestling Peter at the fence. She walked over slowly and listened to Chuck encourage Peter.

"When a horse lets you pet them like this, it means they feel safe with you. They know you won't hurt them," Chuck grinned as he saw Charity approach and beckoned her to come over. "He was looking at the horses, so we called Maverick."

"Hey, Peter. Maverick has a soft face, doesn't he?" Charity asked. Peter again let out a soft giggle. Charity couldn't believe it. She looked at Chuck incredulously.

"That's the second time he's done that," Chuck whispered. "I have always heard the outside of a horse is good for the inside of a man." Peter gazed up toward Chuck.

"Okay, Peter, we better get you back to Jeff and Melanie. Did you like Maverick?" Charity asked hoping for more than just a giggle. Peter simply flashed a big, teethy grin. "Thanks, Chuck," Charity brushed Chuck's blue jean jacket.

Taking his hand, Charity routed Peter back over to Jeff and Melanie. They were wrapping up with Barbara and had to get home. Zach was not cooperating. Amanda gave Charity a tight squeeze and waved good-bye.

Charity floated back around to Erica's table. Erica gave Charity a quick hug, as some DCS workers were huggers, and thanked Charity for the wonderful time. She and Randi did rock, paper, scissors to decide who took the vase from their table. Randi screamed excitedly.

It took about an hour and thirty minutes to clean up. Though Penelope told Charity there were people to cover the clean-up, Charity helped to make their jobs easier. Henry stayed out of the way. When it was almost clear, he went up to Charity to see how things went from her perspective. "Hey, how do you think it went today?"

"What are you still doing here?" Charity asked, taken aback, then answered his question, "I thought it was awesome. Except for totally forgetting to buy gift cards, it went off without a hitch."

"Well, Jefferson City doesn't have Christmas events begin until after December 1st. Want to go up to Gatlinburg and visit the Crafts Fair, then drive back through Pigeon Forge and see the Christmas lights?" Henry motioned to his truck.

Charity's eyes lit up with excitement. "I have never had a chance to really do Christmas shopping in a place like Gatlinburg," she said, hardly able to contain herself.

"Great," Henry replied with a smile, "we can leave as soon as you check off with Penelope."

Charity and Penelope reviewed the event and spoke quickly about the event on Christmas Eve. Charity shook Penelope's hand and they parted ways.

"I'm almost ready to go. Let me get my stuff and tell Theresa and Chuck I'm leaving with you," she called over her shoulder.

Henry opened the door to his truck for her and they set out for craft fair shopping in Gatlinburg.

Charity and Henry had an entertaining evening. Before the craft fair, they ambled through parts of Gatlinburg, specifically the Village Mall. They visited many shops, but Charity decided her favorite was the cheese shop. She bought several slabs of cheese, including a seven-year-old slice of Irish cheddar. She secured a few Christmas gifts for the guys at the paper. She also savored a chocolate-covered caramel apple that made her mouth water just thinking about it. Henry watched in amazement as she experienced the shopping adventure.

Henry had a difficult time keeping up with Charity as she dashed from table to table at the craft fair. He marveled how something like a craft fair fascinated her so much. He had to show great restraint to keep from compulsively buying all the items she picked up when she asked him, "Aren't these the cutest things?"

They finished shopping and headed back to the ranch. Since it was Saturday night, the roads were somewhat crowded, allowing for close observation of the Christmas decorations on the streets.

"I can't believe they put up all these decorations every year," Charity marveled. "I love the colored lights on the trees."

"I always like the Incredible Christmas Place. It stays open ALL year. You could get a Christmas fix in February, if you needed to," Henry countered.

They enjoyed all the Christmas lights between Pigeon Forge and the ranch. Inside his head, Henry was having a war with his emotions. His attraction to Charity was unmistakable. Henry pulled up to the house and walked Charity to the door, carrying her shopping bags.

Taking the bags from Henry, Charity confessed, "I had a terrific time with you today. It was the perfect ending to an already exciting day."

"It was a full day, that's for certain. I had a great time, as well," Henry recalled. He wanted to kiss her, to feel her lips on his. Panicking, he whispered, "Good night," as he leaned in and kissed her on the cheek.

"Good night," Charity replied. She watched him leave, then turned and went inside. It had been a fun-filled day. She dressed for bed and was asleep before her head hit the pillow.

CHAPTER 10

It was Sunday. Charity was behind with establishing the criteria for her Aspiration Station grant program. She needed to have a conversation with Marcus. She decided to text him. "Hey, it's Charity. Sorry to bother. Need financial advice for a new idea. Lunch tomorrow? I'm buying."

"Sure, what time?" Marcus replied.

"Noon?" Charity asked. "At the pizza place?"

"Done. See you then," Marcus ended the text.

Now that she had that out of the way, she consulted her calendar to view the foster care review board dates she had coming up. She also surveyed her emails when she noticed she had a message about the Ferguson children. She opened the email and read:

Due to an unexpected change, the Henderson family caring for the Ferguson children will be in court on Tuesday, November 24th to determine next steps due to military transfer earlier than originally expected. Please be present if possible.

"Why didn't they mention this yesterday?" wondered Charity.

That was just two days away. The children's parents' rights were terminated, and they were almost through the appeal period. Now, their foster family was leaving sooner than originally planned. Obviously, it wouldn't be great for Amanda or Peter. She texted Melanie saying she would be in attendance on Tuesday.

Now, her head was spinning. She went outside and walked to the fence. Before long, Sinbad came trotting up. He stopped and stood there, waiting for Charity to rub his muzzle. Charity loved the velvety feel of his lips. She marveled at how horses drink. The horse places its lips on the surface of the water and acts as if drinking from a straw.

"That's a good boy," she soothed. She stood there for several minutes just stroking Sinbad. Then the notion hit her. What if she petitioned the court to become a kinship placement for Amanda and Peter? Of course, she would run that by Theresa and Chuck first. They may not want to have small children around all the time. She decided she would ask them in a while. She said bye to Sinbad, and he trotted off. She went inside to wash her hands so she wouldn't sneeze too much and dashed off to do some thinking driving.

Instead of putting on her Christmas playlist, she went to her 80s playlist. Even though she was born later, let's face it, the 80s had the best music. She started with Don't Stop Believin' and left the grounds and got on the highway. She didn't have a particular place in mind to go, so she just drove on.

All she kept thinking about was how could she make a difference in this world. She was working on the Aspiration Station thing. But that would just benefit older youth. Here she had two young children who needed stability. Before she realized it, she was at Rachel's house. She grabbed her phone and texted Rachel.

"Hey, I need some advice. Actually…I'm outside your house right now. Can you talk a few minutes?" Charity pleaded.

"Sure, I can come out and sit in your car, if that's okay?" Rachel replied.

"Definitely, I don't want to disturb your entire house," Charity declared thoughtfully. A few seconds later, Rachel came out and climbed in the jeep.

"You look terrible. What's going on?" Rachel asked with concern.

"The Ferguson children, the case I have been following. They are going to be moved again. The foster dad's transfer orders have been moved to an earlier date than originally expected. Parental rights have been terminated and the appeal period is almost over. The little boy doesn't speak already, and I am just afraid of what this news will do to him," Charity wiped her eyes.

"Hey, it's okay," Rachel voiced soothingly. "You know this is how things go sometimes. It stinks, but it happens. What's on your mind? I know you are thinking something or else you wouldn't be here now."

"You know me too well," Charity retorted as she sniffled. "What if I petitioned the court to be a kinship placement for the children? I have the room. I have the means to support them. And I certainly understand what it's like to be in the system," Charity said almost bitterly.

"Well, I think that could be an incredibly good idea. You need to be sure of one thing first," Rachel warned. "You need to be sure that if you do ask to be a home for these children, you back off on the foster care review boards and concentrate on only these two for a while. It'll take you some time to get used to them…and they to you. What do your folks at the ranch think of this idea?"

"I was planning to discuss it with them this afternoon. I just needed to think about things first," Charity said honestly. "Oh, let me tell you my other idea. Remember I told you that if it weren't for my friend, Julie, I never would have made it through journalism school because I didn't have transportation?"

"Yeah, I remember," Rachel agreed.

"Well, I am going to create a grant program called Aspiration Station to give aging out foster youth seven to ten thousand dollars for a used car to get them to school or job interviews," Charity finished proudly.

"Honey, it sounds like you have found the two things you need to do with your life. Take care of the Ferguson children and give away cars." Rachel paused a few moments. It started raining, the plinking rain on the windshield filled the silence. "How are things going with Henry?" Rachel asked curiously.

"Henry is the sweetest thing. He took me Christmas light-looking in Pigeon Forge and craft-fair shopping in Gatlinburg," Charity said with a huge smile on her face.

"So, it's getting serious, then?" Rachel asked bluntly.

"What do you mean serious?" Charity questioned.

"Charity, you have to see by now that Henry has feelings for you. How do you feel about him?" Rachel pressed in.

"Well, he makes me laugh. We both play Christmas music way before Christmas. He literally dropped everything to help me with the Shindig yesterday. I guess I like him, too," Charity admitted honestly for the first time. "I don't feel so alone when he is at the ranch. Is that silly?"

"Of course not! Special relationships often help complete us. Not that we aren't good enough by ourselves, but they fill the part of us that we need filled," Rachel tried to explain but felt she failed miserably.

"You mean, like teammates? If you aren't good at hitting but good at catching, you find someone that can hit better than you?" Charity asked innocently.

Rachel smiled, "Yes, something like that. I think you'll be okay now. I need to go. Hopefully, I won't get soaked."

"Thank you for talking with me," Charity said gratefully as she hugged Rachel before she went back inside. "I feel much better."

Charity pulled out of Rachel's driveway, and turned back for home. When she got there, she dashed to the porch. Theresa and Chuck were sitting in the chairs strategically avoiding the rain.

"Where did you run off to?" Theresa asked with an air of concern. She and Chuck stood up and they all went into the house and sat in the living room.

"Oh, I needed some time to think. The Ferguson children will most likely be moved to a new home right after Thanksgiving since the foster dad had his transfer date moved up. Their parents have just lost their rights to them and I just don't think little Peter can take a blow like this," Charity recalled sadly. "What if I petitioned the court to be a kinship placement for them?"

"Well, you really like them, and they respond well to you. Do you think you could handle two children all the time?" Theresa asked honestly. "Maybe you should just take them on a temporary basis. What's that called?"

"Respite. That's what you are talking about. I could do a trial visit and see if they can adjust well here. That is a more logical solution. Thanks for being open to this," Charity declared, as their desires mattered, as well. "You and Chuck wouldn't mind the extra people here?"

"I think it would be fine," Theresa said truthfully.

"I think being here may just be a good thing for that boy. Did you hear him giggle when he was petting Maverick? You said he hasn't spoken in a long time. A giggle is a good beginning," Chuck discerned, running his fingers in circles around the brim of his hat.

"What are your plans for the rest of the day?" Theresa inquired.

"Well, I need to get the Aspiration Station idea down on paper for when I talk with Marcus tomorrow. Then I need to articulate what I want to say to the judge on Tuesday. Oh, I have not thought to ask before, but what happens at the ranch on Thanksgiving Day?" Charity wondered.

"Well, we usually have the typical turkey dinner. This is the first year your uncle Frank isn't here. He liked to go all out. We will eat around noon. Then, after cleanup, we get the Christmas decorations out and start getting in the Christmas spirit. The tree goes up first. Then the lights on the grounds. But you can do it however you want," Theresa explained.

"Oh, I think that sounds perfect. Max and I usually just had a turkey tv dinner or something. No muss, no fuss. Just let me know what I need to help with. I don't want you and Chuck to take care of it all on your own," Charity said, being profoundly serious.

"I will be sure and keep you updated," Theresa smiled, truthfully hand up in oath.

Charity went to the office and sat down. She got out her notepad and tried to write down the points she wanted to ask Marcus about. She listed insurance. How would the youth get the cars if they lived all over the state? Should she just use certain dealerships? Should there be an overall limit of how much money she spent? She didn't want to deplete all the funds she was given and cause the ranch to close. The last thing she needed to know was the average number of children that age-out each year, so she would know what type of budget to create.

She tossed list aside and started to think of what she wanted to say at the case for the Ferguson children on Tuesday. Her eyes welled up with tears every time she thought about the pending move. She remembered how hard it was for her to get settled in a foster home only to be moved some six months later. Maybe that was why she had a hard time seeing just how much Henry liked her. She put up a safety barrier that kept her emotions guarded all the time. She didn't feel like dwelling on the sad topic of moves, so she closed the office door and trudged back to her room.

Max followed her in, and she closed the door. With the rainy weather, it was a nap kind of afternoon. She grabbed her blanket and stretched out across her bed. Max found a corner of the blanket and curled up in a ball and they fell asleep.

It had been some time and Theresa had not seen Charity. She looked in the office. She wasn't there. She saw that Charity's door was closed. She opened it quietly and saw Charity and Max sleeping. Max lifted his head and looked at Theresa, but he didn't get up. Theresa shut the door and disappeared.

The silence and deep darkness awakened Charity. It was ten o'clock when she woke up. Hair matted, she opened her door and walked through the house. The overhead stove light was on and a note was on the refrigerator.

"You must've needed the rest. There's food in the fridge. See you tomorrow. T"

Charity got the plate out of the refrigerator. It was meatloaf, mashed potatoes, peas, and a huge biscuit. She didn't have to worry about the noise, so she microwaved the food to make it just a little warm. She ate at the bar. She washed her dishes and went to the living room. She was very alert after sleeping for so long. She decided to play her favorite 'pick me up' Christmas movie, *The Polar Express*. She grabbed the blanket and settled in. She wasn't sure what it was about *The Polar Express* that made her watch it so many times. Maybe it was the hero boy really struggling to believe there was a Santa Claus. She could relate because she had always wanted to believe she was worthy to have her own family. And besides, experts say that "watching your favorite movies over and over is good for you. The repetition calms you because knowing the outcome of a story helps you feel safe in an unpredictable world, and it comforts you by recapturing lost feelings."

She sat hypnotized through the movie at least twice before falling asleep. The movie restarted by itself. When Theresa went in the living room at seven o'clock, it was still playing and startled Theresa. She saw Charity still asleep on the couch and nudged her awake.

"Good morning," Theresa said cheerfully.

"Oh, good morning, Theresa," Charity said, embarrassed that she slept on the couch again. She got up, folded the blanket, and turned off the tv.

"What can I make you for breakfast?" Theresa asked.

"What were you going to eat?" Charity wondered. She hated making breakfast food decisions.

"Chuck usually likes biscuits and gravy every Monday," Theresa said plainly.

"Okay, I will just have some of that. No need to make anything else," Charity replied.

"What's on your agenda today?" Theresa questioned.

"Oh, the only big thing is to meet with Marcus for lunch and talk about the grant for cars," Charity said excitedly. "I may do some Christmas shopping either before or after, I'm not sure. Do you need anything from town?" Charity offered.

"No, thank you. I'm having a lazy day today. All the work is caught up. We won't think of food prep for Thanksgiving until Wednesday. Speaking of, were you inviting Henry over for Thanksgiving?" Theresa asked sneakily.

"Oh, I'm not sure if he'll be home. His family doesn't live too far from here," Charity replied. "I can see if he is available. It would be nice if he could be here."

Theresa whipped up breakfast while Charity walked to the pasture fence. Sticking to the usual pattern, Sinbad appeared within a few minutes. Charity had no idea how horses knew people were standing at fences. They are so mysterious. Can you call a horse like a dog? Do you whistle for them? She thought she had heard Chuck whistle before.

Chuck came out of the barn just as Sinbad met Charity at the fence. "That's amazing," he said in disbelief. "I can't get him to come when I want him. What did you do?"

"I just came and stood here. This is the third time he has just appeared out of nowhere. I don't understand it. How do you even call a horse? I thought I've heard you whistle for them before," Charity posed.

"Horses are curious animals. They are unpredictable and don't always come if they hear a whistle. People disagree about whether they miss humans, how much they feel and all that. But one thing is certain. The fact he comes up to you like this means he likes you and trusts you. He may be telling you to pick him as your horse." Chuck said amazed, zipping his jacket.

"Wow, he likes me. We better go inside. Theresa was making biscuits and gravy. You know how she feels about food getting cold," Charity reminded Chuck.

"Let's go wash up. I'm hungry," Chuck replied, scraping the muck off his boots before going inside.

As they entered the kitchen, the smell of fresh, hot biscuits and sausage gravy filled their senses. They ate breakfast and chatted happily. Charity noticed the time and made off to her room. She inspected her clothes, gathered her notes, and struck out for more shopping before meeting Marcus.

Charity bounced from store to store unsuccessfully. She eyed her phone and found it close to eleven-thirty. She figured she should head to the restaurant and wait for Marcus. She pulled into the parking lot. Her phone buzzed.

"What are you doing today?" Henry typed.

"Meeting a coworker for lunch to ask about a project. How about you?"

"Not sure yet. Plans for dinner?" Henry asked.

"Not yet. After lunch, thought about going shopping. Didn't find what I wanted earlier." She replied.

"Want company?" Henry suggested.

"Well, if you want to. I gotta ask you about Thanksgiving. And I want to tell you my latest idea," Charity texted.

"Great, want me to meet you at the ranch so we can take one vehicle, or just meet you at a store?" Henry positioned strategically.

"The ranch. Makes more sense to take one car. Text you when I'm on my way home."

"Okay."

Charity wandered into the pizza place and found a seat. She was lost inside a picture of a picturesque Italian port city when Marcus came in a few minutes later.

"Hello, Charity. Nice to see you. Thanks for treating me to lunch in exchange for my brain," Marcus said jokingly.

"Well, it will definitely be worth it if you can help me with what I want to do," Charity replied.

After ordering their food, Charity laid out the details of the Aspiration Station plan.

"As a former foster youth, I faced a major transportation barrier. It impacted everything I wanted to do. I want to create a foundation that gives grants to aging out foster youth to get a sturdy, reliable vehicle. Maybe spend between seven to ten thousand dollars max. What do you think?" Charity asked hoping for an honest answer.

"This is tremendous. Do you know the number of youths who age-out each year?" Marcus wondered.

"I don't have that number yet. I know that will determine how many I can assist each year. I want to set a cap of eight million dollars on this project. I don't want to use up all the money I was gifted and cause financial hardships on the ranch," Charity offered.

"It is important to be fiscally responsible. Now, what about car insurance?" Marcus wondered as he crunched some numbers.

"My thought was to pay it for the first six months to give the youth time to get a job and all," Charity confessed.

"Okay, say we set the limit of the total amount to spend at eight million. If you set a limit of eight thousand dollars per youth, you could help about one thousand youth get cars. The insurance may be a little trickier, but we will see what kind of rates we can get. I just happen to know a guy in the business. This is definitely doable," Marcus said, excited for Charity. "Looks like you have found your 'Why' and you're acting on it."

"I'm calling it Aspiration Station," Charity announced proudly.

"Well, that sounds appropriate. You will be giving these youth hope they can actually make it on their own- like you did," Marcus nodded as he snapped the buckle on his leather folio and headed back to the office.

Charity dodged his glance. "Thank you," she cleared her throat. "See you later."

Charity texted Henry that she was finished with her lunch with Marcus and was heading back home. He was waiting for her as she drove up. Henry smoothed his clothes as she approached him.

"Hey," Henry grinned.

"Hey," Charity countered. "How long have you been here? You could have gone into the house."

"I just got here literally two minutes before you. Are you ready to go shopping or do you need to go into the house first?" Henry asked considerately.

"We can go. My briefcase can wait until later. Besides, daylight's burning," Charity uttered animatedly as she climbed in the truck.

"Well, you seem happy today. What's going on? What are you wanting to shop for? And what did you need to ask me about Thanksgiving?" Henry fired off quickly.

Charity shut the door. "Firstly, I don't care where we go shopping. Secondly, I have figured out one of the things I want to do to keep giving back to foster kids." She snagged the seatbelt, "I'm starting a short-term foundation to give free vehicles to aging out foster youth. It was a huge thing for me to not have my own transportation. Marcus is helping me with the details. I want to call it Aspiration Station," Charity said proudly. As she buckled, she concluded, "And lastly, were you going to be home for Thanksgiving this week or going out of town? It would be nice if you could have dinner here."

Henry was blown away, "You really want to give away cars? That's fantastic." He started the truck and they headed out.

"I am excited. But one of the variables I don't know is the average number of youths who age-out every year. I'm planning to spend enough money to help about one thousand youth get cars," Charity said.

"Don't worry. I'm sure Erica can get this information for you pretty quickly," Henry said reassuringly. "As far as Thanksgiving, I had planned to go home, but I can come over if you want me to."

Charity hadn't considered Henry's family until Theresa suggested he come over for Thanksgiving. She countered, "Don't change your plans. Your family is looking forward to seeing you."

Henry could tell she was disappointed, so he changed the subject back to shopping. "What exactly are you looking for with this shopping adventure?"

"I'm not sure. I'll know it when I find it," Charity said. Henry didn't know much about women and shopping, but he knew enough that this comment was dangerous. Especially after their trip to the craft fair.

They covered several different places. The craft supply store, the home décor store, and the candle and hand sanitizer store. Charity bought several things there. She needed refills of hand sanitizers for her purse. She always relished the candle store. Though she was allergic, she still purchased candles that smacked of Christmas trees.

Henry could tell she still wasn't completely happy with the shopping results and asked, "What is it that you haven't found that's making you so crazy?"

Charity almost burst into tears. "I just don't know what to get Theresa and Chuck for Christmas. They are being so good to me. They've taken care of the ranch all this time. It's the first Christmas for them since my Uncle Frank died and I just want to show them how much I appreciate them."

Henry marveled at how such a small person could have such enormous feelings about everything. "Has anyone ever told you that you worry too much?"

"Yeah, maybe one or two," Charity said trying not to laugh. "And on top of that, the Ferguson children have court tomorrow to discuss a possible move. The foster dad's orders have moved up his transfer date. I'm going to request taking them for respite after Thanksgiving. If they adjust okay, I'm going to petition the court to be considered as a kinship placement for them."

"Wow, it's only Monday, and you've been on an emotional roller coaster," Henry consoled affectionately.

Suddenly Charity had a great idea. "I know what we can do," she started saying, "we can eat dinner and then sit in the living room and watch that Thanksgiving Christmas movie and assemble the crafts at the coffee table."

"Are you sure?" Henry questioned.

"Absolutely. I manage emotions better when I keep my hands busy. Did you have any gifts you were planning on giving your coworkers? We can make them something instead," Charity commanded, her mood shifting immediately.

"Uh, no. I usually just give them a gift card to their favorite restaurants," Henry confessed.

"That's taking the easy way out. What things do they like?" Charity pressed. "Here, let's go back to the craft store. I have a great idea. Then we need to get home."

They went back to the craft store and Charity helped Henry pick out enough materials to make three sets of coasters for coffee tables. She got an extra set, just in case of accidents. They made it back to the ranch. Charity put the materials in the living room. Then she and Henry walked back to the kitchen and sat at the bar.

"Hey, you two!" Theresa said as she pushed back from the oven's heat blast. She wiped her forehead. She gave Charity a Diet Mountain Dew and poured a glass of tea for Henry.

"Thank you," Charity and Henry chimed.

"That smells delicious," Henry's stomach growled audibly.

"It's oven fried chicken, potatoes and onions, corn on the cob, asparagus, and of course, biscuits," Theresa said recounting the menu. And before either of them could ask she added, "And we have peanut butter cookies for dessert."

"Remind me to tip the wait staff," Henry winked.

"You think of everything, Theresa. I always prefer a potato to pasta or rice anytime," Charity said honestly.

"What? Are you crazy?" Henry asked in disbelief.

"Not crazy. I just like taters more, precious," Charity quoted, seeing if Henry would catch the reference.

Henry had a very confused look on his face. "It's a movie quote, Henry," Theresa explained.

"Oh. Right. A movie quote," Henry glanced up and away. "Another Christmas movie?"

"If you consider orcs and wizards marks of Christmas. Okay, we will have to get you caught up with that series. Maybe we should watch that instead," Charity said excitedly. "The second movie in that series is my favorite of the trilogy."

"Right," Henry offered weakly.

Dinner was ready and they ate at the table in the kitchen. They laughed and joked about things that had happened today.

"Theresa, what exactly does a lazy day look like for you?" Charity inquired.

"Well, just like it sounds. I do as little as possible. I'm not a nap taker like you. I enjoy reading an interesting book. Sometimes, I go for a walk on the property," Theresa expounded. "I have a favorite spot I like to walk to and then back to the house."

Chuck interjected, "I spent a good part of the day checking the equipment for need of repairs. Also, it has been fascinating that Sinbad seems to know when Charity stands by the fence. He has found her three times now."

"That's remarkable," Theresa put her hands to her face. "That horse hadn't paid much attention to anyone except Frank."

"Well, I had to drive Charity all over town because she couldn't make up her mind what she was shopping for," Henry jested.

"Oh, it wasn't that bad," Charity corrected. "Besides, we finally found something. Oh, I met with Marcus about Aspiration Station. We will get the plans finished soon."

"Theresa, you keep relaxing tonight. Henry and I will clean the kitchen," Charity insisted.

They put the few leftover things in containers and put them in the refrigerator. Theresa was very nearly perfect cooking food down to the last bean, spoonful of rice, etc. Thirty minutes later, Henry and Charity were done with the dishes and they collapsed in the living room.

Charity started at the beginning and put on *The Fellowship of the Ring*. It would be *The Two Towers* before Henry would understand the "taters, precious" reference. Charity arranged the order for making the coasters. Henry helped her slide the coffee table more toward the tv so they could sit on the floor.

Max loved to see what was inside of bags, so he tiptoed through their stuff until he was sure there was nothing exciting to play with.

Charity had to explain the beginning part of the movie. Henry seemed to grasp the premise and watched with interest.

Charity collected the four squares for the coasters for Henry and four for herself. She gave him the adhesive and the pictures to put on the squares. After they placed them exactly right and applied the adhesive, it was time to put on the sealant. The room was overcome with fumes as the odors of the adhesive and sealant clashed. They opened the window to let in some fresh air. They had two more sets to make. They repeated the process and finished quicker.

After applying the sealant to the last of the coasters, they moved up on the couch so their legs could stretch out. They fought the burning sensation of pins and needles. Several minutes later, they sat peacefully. The movie was at the part where the fellowship set out on the dangerous journey.

Theresa brought in the plate of peanut butter cookies. She came back a minute later with a drink for each of them. Charity and Henry watched the rest of the movie, with Charity having to explain just a little of it to Henry.

Charity had forgotten the movie was so long and Henry struggled to stay awake. When it was over, Charity remarked, "I'm sorry. I forgot it was so long. Will you be okay to drive home?"

"Yes, I'll just drive with the window down. Let me know how court goes tomorrow," Henry stated as he tried to shake himself awake.

Henry left and Charity closed the door. She watched him wave to her as he pulled away and waved back. She cleaned up the mess and set the coasters in the office on the floor against the wall. They had to dry out a while. She closed the window and turned everything off.

Charity went to the kitchen, put the glasses and plate in the sink, and stared out the window in deep thought. She floated to her room and changed into her pajamas. She remembered the feeling of Henry's companionship. It made her feel warm all over, like being wrapped in a warm blanket.

She set her clock on her phone and put on the rain. She fell asleep and had pleasant dreams.

CHAPTER 11

Charity arrived at the juvenile courthouse when the doors opened. She went through security.

"Hello, Daniel, it's been a while. How are you?" Charity greeted Daniel.

"Hello, Charity. I'm fine. I don't have the room yet for the Ferguson case. Just listen to the overhead announcements," Daniel advised.

"Okay, and have a Happy Thanksgiving," Charity replied.

"Happy Thanksgiving to you, too," Daniel said as Charity walked away.

Charity walked over and took a seat in a chair and waited for the case to begin. Her pocket vibrated. It was Henry, "Thinking of you. Hope it goes well. See you later."

Charity responded, "TY. Don't know why I'm so nervous."

"Just be yourself," Henry texted, adding a smiley emoji.

The Hendersons came in with Amanda and Peter. Jeff and Melanie sat beside Charity and the kids sat to the side.

"How are they doing knowing you will be moving soon?" Charity asked quietly.

"Well, they're both trying to be strong, but Peter has retreated deeper into himself and doesn't want to do much with us," Melanie spoke woefully.

"If it's okay with you, I'm going to ask the judge to let me take them for respite after Thanksgiving. That way, you can begin the moving process. I imagine military moving is a little more complex than what I just went through moving to the ranch," Charity said trying to be encouraging.

Jeff's eyes moistened, "I think the kids would do well with that change. They had a great time with you that day and at the Shindig. We have played that game twice now," Jeff said thinking how much he was going to miss these children.

Charity needed to catch Barbara Frederickson before going in to see the judge. After Barbara checked in with the clerk, Charity caught her attention, "Barbara, I need to talk to you for a minute."

Seeing Charity sitting in a chair, Barbara took the seat next to her, "Hello, Charity. What did you need from me?"

"I wanted to let you know that I am asking the judge to be considered as a kinship placement for Amanda and Peter. But I am going to request doing respite first," Charity said excitedly. "Is that okay?"

Barbara looked at Charity and remarked, "Oh, Charity, that would be wonderful. I think the children would do well with you."

"I was thinking that maybe the Monday after Thanksgiving would be a good day to move them so Jeff and Melanie can start their moving," Charity explained, trying to be efficient for the move.

"I think that would be perfect. You are very thoughtful," Barbara uttered, putting her hand on Charity's arm.

Over the intercom, Daniel directed the Ferguson case to proceed to Room Five. They all walked in and took their seats. The room felt as gloomy as the expressions on the faces of the participants. No one dared to utter a word.

The clerk was already seated and after about five minutes, Judge Grimsby shuffled into the room and everyone stood up. They all sat down as the judge sat down. For a brief instant, Charity thought of her last time in court before aging out at eighteen.

Judge Grimsby sat in repose for a moment and voiced, "We are here today before our original date of December 21st because of a change in the transfer of Captain Henderson. It seems the children will need to be moved earlier than originally planned. Does anyone have anything to offer at this time?"

Barbara stood up briskly, "Your honor, we are nearing the end of the TPR appeal phase with just a few days left. Charity Walters has asked for the court's permission to take Amanda and Peter Ferguson for respite. She requested it to begin the Monday after Thanksgiving to allow the children time with the Hendersons before having to leave that home. The DCS is okay with this request if it pleases your honor."

"Thank you, Ms. Frederickson. Miss Walters are you sure you are up for the responsibility for caring of these children?" the judge asked point blank.

Charity rose stiffly, pressing down her jacket and blouse, her body shaking all over, "Yes, your honor. I have given this a great deal of thought. I have the space at my home, the finances to support them and the flexibility to work from home. I have followed their case for almost a year now. I am extremely attached to them. As a former foster youth, myself, I feel it is my job to be a support for children like Amanda and Peter." She lowered herself to the seat, now more firmly in control.

Judge Grimsby was surprised by her powerful words and her evident conviction. Scanning the room across the top of his black rimmed glasses, "Are there any reasons why this request of respite should not be granted to Charity Walters in relation to Amanda and Peter Ferguson?"

All the people in the room with the authority to say so, shook their heads and replied, "No," in euphony.

"Miss Walters, you have been granted respite for these children to begin the Monday after Thanksgiving and go through the first of the year. We will meet again on January 4th at ten o'clock to discuss further permanency options. If there is nothing else, case continued on January 4th." The judge banged his gavel, "Happy Holidays."

Charity and Melanie met in the aisle. They only had a few minutes. Jeff escorted Amanda and Peter to the lobby.

"That went well," Melanie said.

"Yes, I'm glad the judge approved my request. I'm thankful I have the space for them. They can each have their own rooms. I need you to write down their school schedules, doctors, everything I need to know so I am prepared when they come after Thanksgiving. Just text me when you're ready for me to get them," Charity said with some excitement, but also some sadness. She knew what the children were about to go through. Putting all your stuff in boxes or bags and leaving somewhere you feel comfortable. She knew they liked her place, but how soon would the newness wear off?

Barbara Frederickson summoned Charity, "I will see you on the Monday after Thanksgiving to check on the children."

"Okay, that's right. You need to have a visual of their living arrangements," Charity remembered. "See you then. Text me when you know what time you are coming."

"I will. Thanks for being so accommodating," Barbara uttered thankfully.

Normally Charity would engage the children, but today she let them leave without addressing them. They needed this time with Jeff and Melanie. She left the courthouse and headed out for a drive. She needed to do some thinking driving. She wouldn't go far.

She took the long way back to the ranch. As she pulled up in the driveway, Henry called her.

"How did it go?" Henry asked.

"It went well, the judge approved my request for respite. I'll have the children through the first of January. It will be decided then what happens to them next," Charity replied.

"That's wonderful. Good news. I talked to my parents. They have changed their plans for Thanksgiving. Is the invitation to the ranch still available?" Henry wondered.

"Of course. But why do I feel there's more to it than that? What did you do?" Charity asked curiously.

"Nothing, honest," Henry lied.

"See you on Thursday. I will text you the time details. Talk to you later. And thanks," Charity finished.

"You're welcome," Henry replied.

Charity summoned her strength and went inside. She just wanted to put on some music, flop down on the couch, and do nothing. In the last month, she had felt more emotionally drained about everything. She put on her favorite Mozart CD and grabbed her blanket. Funny, that is the quickest way to attract a cat. So, she and Max just relaxed there until Theresa called her for dinner.

****

On Wednesday, Charity helped Theresa clean the house for Thanksgiving. Though Theresa kept an already sparkling clean house, Charity clean bathrooms, swept, dusted bedrooms, and vacuumed the carpeted areas. She had always done these things herself and felt a little weird that Theresa took care of it all. They had only a small list of food items to prep for cooking for tomorrow. Once Theresa gave the all-clear on the meal prep, Charity decided to go on a leaf-looking drive. She didn't know what to do with herself and didn't want Theresa to feel like she had to entertain her all day. She hugged Theresa and advised she would be home in a few hours.

Henry was also driving, but he was going to see his parents today since he told Charity he would spend Thanksgiving with her. She hadn't been fooled when he said the plans had changed. Right now, he really needed to talk to his father. The ride was pleasant. His family lived in Kingsport and the view was always enjoyable. As he drove, he spied leaves falling from the trees. When the sun lit up the treetops, the colors were just breathtaking. Tennessee in the fall is a beautiful place to be. The Northeast, like Boston or places in Connecticut, was also beautiful in the fall, but he loved his Tennessee home.

He pulled into the driveway of the Thompson house and Brian met him at the truck. "Hey, what are you doing here? Thought you couldn't make it for Thanksgiving?" Brian asked puzzled.

"I came to spend today with you and talk to Dad about a few things," Henry explained.

"Sounds serious," Brian said. "Is everything okay?"

"Yep, all's fine. I just need a bit of fatherly advice. To make sure I am seeing the clear picture," Henry countered.

Going inside, Henry wrapped up his mom in a big hug. She stopped her work and returned the hug. "Hey, honey." Deborah uttered, "Thought you weren't able to come home."

"Well, I thought I'd spend today with you. Plus, I need to talk to Dad about something important," Henry explained. "Let me know if you need me to help with anything while I'm here." Scanning the area, Henry pressed, "Where is Dad?"

"You're lucky. He's out back in his man shed. I think he may be hiding Christmas gifts out there, so watch out," Deborah warned.

"I'll be careful not to sneak," Henry said, winking at his mom. "Be back in a little bit."

Henry went out the back door, finding his dad in the shed just as his mom suspected. The shed was an actual shed. It had built-in shelves for holding tools. It also had a mini air conditioner for the summer. And a small heater for the winter. Mike was listening to Christmas music when Henry found him. "Hey, Dad. What are you doing? Are you hiding gifts out here?"

Mike looked up from his cell phone and expressed, "Oh, hey. I was just reviewing my Christmas list for shopping on Friday. I want to get all the Black Friday sales. What are you doing here?" He closed his phone, pointing to an open stool.

"Well, I was hoping to get some advice," Henry began.

"This must be serious, because first you cancel Thanksgiving with us, and now you drive all the way here for advice," Mike said with a smile. "Is it about Charity?"

Henry was caught off guard. Whoa… his dad already knew. "Yes, it's about Charity." Henry confessed as he grabbed a stool, running his hand through his hair. "I've never felt like this about anyone. And, no, it doesn't have anything to do with the fact she has a fortune. I met her before *she* even knew she had a fortune. I enjoy spending time with her. She makes me laugh. She has the most generous nature of anyone I've encountered, even after living her life in foster care and not having a forever family," Henry rambled on like an actor delivering a soliloquy. He missed his dad's expressions.

"You've known her barely a month now," Mike mentioned, clearly seeing how much Charity affected Henry. "Are you sure you aren't rushing things a bit with her?"

"I don't know. Well, how did you know you and Mom were meant to be a couple? How long did it take before you knew?" Henry earnestly wondered.

"Your mother and I knew each other in high school. Her family relocated from a different school district. It wasn't until after we graduated from high school that we tried dating. But once we did, it was obvious we were meant to be together. Well, she knew it first, but it took me a little longer," Mike said reflecting on all the things they had accomplished in their years of marriage. "My advice to you would be if you are convinced that she is the one for you, take baby steps. If what you said is true, she feels things deeply. She may be fearful of taking a chance at love because having a family didn't work out for so long. She's just settling into her new environment at the ranch. Didn't you say she's heavily involved right now with foster children?"

Henry stared blankly at a nut and bolt he'd picked up, screwing, and unscrewing the nut on and off. Never looking up, "Yes, she wants to make sure children in the system know someone is advocating for them. Though it was her choice to age-out of foster care, she still feels let down by the system. She just asked for permission to take the children for respite," Henry said admiringly, glancing into his dad's weepy face.

Mike adjusted his stool toward Henry. "Okay, so let's think about this. Say she gets the children and they do well during respite. What are the chances she will want to keep them permanently? Are you sure you would have adequate time to get to know Charity as a possible mate? Would you be able to share her with these children whose world is falling apart?" Mike intently looked at Henry and then gazed across the yard through the dirty window. "Henry, you know as well as anyone what these children lose when they can't go back home. Are you strong enough to love the children as much as you think you love Charity? You all could be meshing as a family in the end," Mike said wisely.

"That's a lot to consider. But Dad, I would really like to try and do that. I think about her all the time. Her innocence is remarkable for someone who has lived in a crazy world like this one. Thanks for asking the tough questions. All I can do is give it my best shot," Henry said thoughtfully. Henry looked up and glanced from his father to the window as well.

Mike stood erect, stretching, and caught Henry's eyes. "Well, the fact you have asked for advice means you are on the right track. But maybe you should do one last thing before finalizing your decision. Use the Benjamin Franklin method of making decisions. Create a Pros and Cons list. If the Pros outweigh the Cons, then proceed, but slowly," Mike grabbed Henry's shoulder lovingly as Henry stood, tossing the bolt into the bin. "Maybe we should go back inside and see what your mom is doing."

Henry and Mike went back inside and found Deborah and Brian watching a movie.

"Hey, mom," Henry beckoned. "Can you do me a favor?"

Deborah looked surprised but said, "Sure, what do you need?"

"I feel really funny asking, but can you help me figure out a perfume? I can only tell you what it smells like. I don't know the name," Henry started.

"That's not much to go on. Let me see what I can find out," Deborah supposed. "What does it smell like?"

"The best description I can think of is that it smells like Christmas. Almost like gumdrops. It makes me crazy every time I smell it," Henry divulged honestly, though slightly embarrassed he had said that to his mom.

"Well, I'll do what I can. She must mean a great deal to you, honey. I hope she makes you happy," expressed Deborah.

They spent the day watching holiday movies, eating good food, and enjoying each other's company. Henry stayed until dark. It was only about an hour and a half drive back home. He found himself thinking about Charity. Is it too early in their relationship to be giving her a gift? Is it okay to try and kiss her beyond a kiss on the cheek? Henry realized he was just as afraid of admitting how he felt. Maybe even more than Charity. He would follow his dad's advice and take baby steps. The first one being to show up for Thanksgiving.

****

Thanksgiving Day arrived at last. Charity found herself a bundle of nerves. The bed was piled up with outfits not making the right impression. She couldn't decide what to wear. She finally selected a pair of jeans, a red sweater, and her brown knee-high boots. She put her hair up in a red bow that matched her sweater. She put on the only jewelry she ever wore, earrings and a necklace.

Theresa had a light breakfast of bacon and toast ready for Charity. Since they were having the Thanksgiving Dinner at noon, she didn't want folks to eat too much.

"Thank you, Theresa," Charity said as she scraped jelly across her toast. "What do you need me to do?"

"Well, nothing presently. The turkey goes in the oven in about twenty minutes. It will be ready on time. Luckily, we have two ovens. I'm baking two pies, an apple one for you and pecan for everyone else. The stuffing will need to bake quite a while, too. I don't like making stuffing inside the turkey," Theresa offered, frankly.

"I am excited to get the tree up today," Charity said with excitement.

"Real tree or artificial?" Theresa challenged curiously.

"Theresa, with my allergies, I *have* to have an artificial tree. I hate it, but I can't help it. Besides, Max behaves better with a fake tree. It doesn't feel the same when he tries to climb it, so he leaves it alone," Charity expounded.

"Oh, no!" Theresa exclaimed. "We have always used real trees. We don't have one stored anywhere. Did you keep your tree?"

"Actually, no. It fell apart after last Christmas and I threw it away,"

Charity said sadly, looking skyward. "I know. Maybe Henry can help me get a tree before we eat. I'll text him. He has that truck, and it would fit better in there." Before she could grab her phone, she heard it buzzing. Charity glanced at her phone and then Theresa, "Speak of the devil...I mean angel."

"Hey, I'm at the gate. I came early and thought I should check before just coming through to the house," Henry explained.

"Well, you must have sensed a 'tremor in the force', because I need your help. I'll meet you outside. Give me a minute to get my stuff. I will explain in the truck," Charity texted back happily. She turned to Theresa and said, "We will be back in a flash. I'll be sensible, I promise. Thanks, Theresa."

Chuck walked into the kitchen just as Charity dashed away. "What's all that about?" he asked curiously.

"Henry came over early, and Charity is talking him into taking her to get a Christmas tree from the store before we eat," Theresa explained with a grin. "Things are going to be remarkably interesting around here with these two. They are perfect for each other, aren't they?"

Chuck moved to the sink and lathered up with soap. "Yes, I reckon they are perfect for each other," Chuck said shaking his head. "Never a dull moment. Pass me a towel, please."

Charity went outside and climbed into Henry's truck. "I'm so glad you came over early. We need to go get a Christmas tree. I want a big one with colored twinkle lights. So where can we go to get that?" Charity asked excitedly.

"A tree, well, I think I know just the place. It won't take long to get there," Henry said confidently. "A huge tree with colored twinkle lights...here we come."

Fortune was on their side as the very first store they came to was open. They went in. After some time, Henry noticed Charity selected a Christmas tree much like a child in a toy store. Or was it like a buyer at a cattle auction? She had to touch them all, circle it, noting every condition and flaw. Finally, Charity found the one she wanted, "What do you think?" she asked Henry.

"That tree is taller than you! How do you plan to decorate the top?" Henry posed curiously.

"A step ladder of course," she offered soberly, wondering how he couldn't figure that one out. "Or a tall person could decorate the top. Can you handle that job, Mr. Thompson?" Charity joked.

"Oh, now it's on. You just wait," Henry kidded. They giggled the entire way to the cashier. They packed the tree in the truck and returned to the ranch. Charity helped Henry carry the tree into the living room. They stowed it in the corner for later.

Charity and Henry found Theresa and Chuck almost right where they were when Charity left earlier. Theresa had made coffee and they were both drinking a cup. "Oh, that smells good," Henry declared inhaling the aroma.

"Grab a cup and have a seat," Theresa said commandingly. "Did you find the Christmas tree?"

"We picked a great one," Charity boomed excitedly. "It's bigger than me, and it will be awesome once decorated."

Henry was bowled over by her excitement. It was just a tree. It must be the thrill of having people around her this year. Trying to make conversation with Chuck, Henry asked him, "Chuck, what is the hardest thing about working with horses?"

"Well, the thing with horses is that each horse has its own personality. A horse can be trusting or untrusting, just like a human. Take Sinbad, for example. When Frank had gotten him, Sinbad was very standoffish with people. Frank died three weeks after bringing him to the ranch. Sinbad hasn't really been interested in much since then. He appears to have taken up with Charity and seems to find her when she is standing by the pasture fence. It takes lots of patience to get a horse to trust you and work with you. I reckon that is much like dealing with the children you encounter in foster care. Some children buck and fight because they are less trusting and are afraid to let their guard down to like and trust people again," Chuck uttered with the wisdom of a sage.

"I never realized that concept could cross over like that. It's true in both worlds," Henry replied. "Charity, don't you think that corresponds with how children feel in foster care?"

Henry hadn't realized it, but Charity had become melancholy, "Yes, that's exactly how children feel. When they leave their homes under terrible circumstances, they often don't express the fact they may or may not have trusted their parents. Then they get to the foster home and if it is nice there, they feel like they have betrayed their family. If there are adoption attempts that don't work out, they feel like there is something wrong with them and they are unlovable," Charity trailed off.

To lighten the moment, Theresa brought out the plate of sugar cookies she had made while Charity and Henry were shopping. She knew food wasn't the answer to all emotional problems, but she was desperate. "Look what I found! Who wants a cookie?" Theresa asked cheerfully.

"Oh, these look delicious. Sprinkles and everything," Henry responded admiringly. He quickly snatched a big reindeer. It was the best sugar cookie he had ever eaten.

"These are good," Charity replied, holding a decapitated snowman, tooth marks visible. Theresa kept the best selection of cookie cutters. There were cookies shaped like Christmas trees, snowmen, reindeer, angels, bells, and sleighs.

Chuck stepped outside, and Henry found him for just a quick minute. Chuck stood looking out at the pasture. All the horses were out there, and he was conducting a visual count. Henry approached Chuck and started to ask him about Charity, but Chuck started speaking before Henry could say anything.

"I've known you and Charity for just a short time now. I can tell you care deeply for her. She needs someone like you. Just treat her with respect and give her the time, love, and attention she deserves," Chuck said softly. "You both are like two peas in a pod. You have the same passion for helping children…the kind of children like Charity. Give her time and you both can accomplish great things together. A relationship is like that of horses. Give it what it needs, and your partner will give you their heart in return."

"Wow, Chuck. I don't know what to say. I want to build a future with her. Even if she had never inherited the Silver Horseshoe. She is so unlike anyone I've ever met. Her heart is bigger than she is," Henry stood there for a moment as he didn't have a good out for this conversation.

"Go on back inside. Help her have a good day," Chuck suggested.

"We still have about forty-five minutes until we eat. Why don't you go check on the horses, if you want," Theresa suggested to Charity as Henry was just coming back inside.

"Come on, let's go see which horse meets us at the fence," Charity ventured, grabbing Henry by the hand.

Chuck entered the barn and collected some treats. "Horses like it much better when they are greeted with a snack," Chuck explained. All five horses meandered toward the fence. Mr. Whiskers made it first. Then Sinbad, Maverick, Ginger, and Lightning arrived all at once. Sinbad stood in front of Charity and she gave him a treat. Ginger stood in front of Henry. The others found Chuck and he fed them the treats. "I haven't heard you sneeze lately when out here near the horses. How do you explain that?"

"Well, I've been doubling up my allergy medicine and supplementing that with honey," Charity said proudly. "I want to be involved with the horses. Amanda and Peter will want to ride them. I have to be able to help them with that."

"When do they get here?" Chuck asked.

"Probably Monday," Charity said with both excitement and a little sadness. "I'll get their rooms ready this weekend."

Theresa called from the back door, "Dinner's ready." Everyone went inside to wash up.

Since they were in the kitchen, Charity asked, "Before we eat, can I say the blessing?"

"Of course," Chuck said proudly, "that would be wonderful."

Charity grabbed Henry's hand and prayed, "Dear Lord, I want to thank you for the year we've had. It has brought us together. I'm so thankful to have additional family who care about me this year. Let us be helpful to those we may think don't deserve it as You love us when we don't deserve it. Thank you for Theresa who cooked this great meal and takes care of the house. Thank you for Chuck who looks after this ranch. And thank you for Henry. He makes me feel like I'm not alone. Amen."

"Amen," Theresa, Henry, and Chuck all said together. Henry glanced at Charity after hearing her words. And Theresa glanced at Henry.

"The plates are here on the bar to make it easier to get your food. Don't be shy. Get your plate and load up," Theresa said excitedly.

"You don't have to tell me twice," Henry agreed funnily. Truth was, he meant it.

In the dining room, Charity and Henry sat on one side of the table. Chuck and Theresa sat on the other side. They enjoyed delicious food and thoughtful conversations. Theresa staged the pies and coffee pot at the end of the table. Theresa cut a piece of apple pie for Charity. The rest of them ate the pecan pie. It was heavenly.

Everyone pitched in to clean the kitchen. Now, there was a Christmas tree to decorate.

Chuck volunteered to retrieve the boxes of Christmas ornaments from the storage area. Henry and Charity took the tree out of the box and assembled it. Theresa relaxed in a chair marveling at all the excitement. Hard to believe that next week, there would be two additional people in the house. Luckily, there wasn't a lot of expensive or breakable things here. It was a house to be lived in and the things could be picked up and looked at.

The tree was pre-lit, which was a blessing to both Henry and Chuck. They did not have to put on numerous strands of lights. They put the tree in the corner of the living room sending one chair to the office for the next several weeks. Charity fetched the step ladder and Henry laughed that she truly planned to stand on it.

"I can put the decorations on the top," Henry said seriously, trying not to laugh. "Just tell me which ones go where."

"Oh, I need to get my box of decorations. Hang on," Charity stated as she retrieved the box from her closet. She opened the box and started hanging ornaments. Henry and Chuck put the other ornaments on the tree. Theresa snapped a few pictures, chronicling the transformation, then joined in herself. "Wait, what about the tinsel?" Charity exclaimed. "We have to have tinsel!"

"What's so great about tinsel?" Henry asked innocently. "Isn't that dangerous for cats?"

"What's so great about tinsel? It makes the tree sparkly when you look at it with the lights blinking, sitting in the dark. It looks magical," Charity explained. "It can be dangerous for cats. But Max has learned to leave it alone. It just took one time of it getting stuck somewhere awful," Charity revealed with a funny expression.

They realized there was no festive music playing so Theresa queued up several Christmas CDs. When they had finally finished the tree, they all stood back, admiring their handy work. It looked beautiful. Charity's tree had programmable lights. She tested the settings and finally chose a slow-chaser, blinking speed. It had grown dark, so they sat there and just absorbed the Christmas lights. Theresa served hot chocolate. The delicious warm goodness oiled their conversations. They lounged around and listened to the carols. Sometimes they would break into song when they knew the words.

It was late when Henry realized he needed to get home. Henry said good night to Theresa and Chuck. Charity followed him to his truck. "I had a fun time with you today," Charity began. "Thanks for taking me to get the tree."

"I had a good time, too and you're welcome," Henry said taking her hand. "I will always be here for you. I have to go," Henry whispered as he leaned down giving her a gentle kiss on the lips. His heart raced. He gave her a hug and said, "I'll check in with you tomorrow."

"Bye," she whispered as she touched her lips. She waved to him as he climbed in the truck. She watched him drive out of the gate then went back inside. She returned to the comfort of the couch with Chuck and Theresa and the lights of the tree. The sounds of the season drifted in and out of focus as did her thoughts. It had been an exceptionally pleasant Thanksgiving.

CHAPTER 12

The rest of the holiday weekend progressed without incident. On Sunday, Henry came over to assist Charity in preparing the bedrooms for Amanda and Peter. Charity asked Henry to look at the rooms to see which ones he thought would be appropriate for the children. Since there were five bedrooms upstairs, Charity wanted to be sure Amanda and Peter were in the right place. Logically, he chose the two bedrooms closest to the top of the stairs. All she had left to do was hang the pictures she purchased for them and put their new bedding on the beds. Charity's room was downstairs so she had to be sure she could hear them at night.

They were standing in what would become Amanda's room when Charity confessed, "I'm really nervous about this move for them. Do you think they will be okay here?"

Henry sat her down on the corner of the bed and said, "Charity, you are great with the children. They know you and feel safe with you. And they feel comfortable with Theresa and Chuck. Remember how they did with the horses? Just be yourself." He stooped down on the floor, his eyes level with hers, "You have the extraordinary ability to meet children where they feel things because you have lived it. Just use your instincts and everything will be fine."

"Max is easy to care for. These are children who must get to school. They'll have homework, class functions, and doctor's visits. What if I blow it?" Charity uttered fearfully.

"Can you honestly do any worse than their parents? That's not a pleasant thing to think about. The reality is that the parents are not getting the children back. Have you thought about what you want to do after the respite period is over? Do you want to make this their permanent home?"

"I *do* want to give them a home. I'll leave that up to the court. You won't think of me as a failure if they can't stay here, will you?"

"That's a ridiculous question, honestly. Whatever happens, we'll take this one step at a time, I promise," Henry leaned in to convey sincerity.

Charity hugged Henry then decided, "Come on. Let's go get them at least one cool gift." Charity advised Theresa they were going shopping for the children.

"What a wonderful idea," Theresa interrupted, walking by with fresh towels. "Do you have a list of their favorite foods? We will need to make sure we have those tomorrow."

"Great thinking," Charity pointed toward Theresa. "I will consult with Melanie while we're out. Anything you need from the store?"

Shelving the towels, Theresa replied, "I don't need anything. It will be Tuesday before I need to buy any house supplies."

Henry and Charity set out shopping. They had absolutely no idea where to go. They started the trip looking at leaves, then Charity pulled out her phone and texted Melanie. A few seconds later Melanie texted her reply. "Well, that's no help," Charity said with frustration. "They don't need anything right now. Now what do we do?"

"Well, let's take a page out of your playbook. What about having a craft, you know, something they can assemble? Christmas tree picture ornaments? They can take them wherever they end up," Henry proposed triumphantly.

"That's a great idea. We need to go to the craft store. Maybe I should invest in stock in that place," Charity joked. "I know just the kind to get, too. We'll just need a small picture of each of them. We can do that tomorrow evening after dinner."

At the craft store, they found enough picture ornaments for all of them to make an ornament...Chuck, Theresa, Charity, Henry, Amanda, Peter and even one for Max.

On their way to check out, Charity spied an end cap full of puzzles. Charity loved putting puzzles together, especially Christmas ones. She found a beautiful puzzle with three hundred pieces. It was a farmhouse with a frozen pond, a pickup truck, snowman, and trees decorated for Christmas. Picking up the box, she asked Henry, "How do you feel about puzzles?"

If she only knew, Henry thought. "I like to unravel a good puzzle now and then," he winked at her. "Why do you ask?"

"What if we get this puzzle," showing Henry the cover, "and put it together later while we listen to Christmas music? I can't believe I didn't think of doing this before."

"Wow," Henry remarked looking at the puzzle, "except for the pond and snowman, that almost looks like your house."

"I know, crazy, huh?" They checked out with their items and left the store.

Henry and Charity got back to the ranch and placed the crafts in the office. They checked on the coasters Henry had made for his coworkers. They needed to cure just a little longer.

"Oh, no. We forgot to ask about the cereal," lamented Charity. "I better ask Melanie. Hang on." Charity rang Melanie. Melanie explained she was going to bring all their belongings over before they got picked up from school. She would bring the leftover snacks they eat so they would have some consistency. "Whew, she'll bring their stuff over sometime tomorrow. Ready to put the puzzle together? We can sit on the floor in the living room and use the coffee table. That way, we can reach all around the puzzle."

"Sure, let's grab a snack first. Shopping always makes me hungry," Henry declared as they went to the kitchen and looked for a treat.

Once they were set with a snack, Henry helped Charity slide the coffee table out a little bit, giving them both room to sit on the floor. Henry queued up his Christmas classics playlist, and Charity dumped the puzzle pieces on the coffee table.

"Let me tell you how this works," Charity began. "First, we separate all the straight-edged pieces so we can assemble the frame of the puzzle. Then, we assemble it from the inside out."

"I have put puzzles together before, you know. How good are you at putting these together?" Henry jabbed.

"Well, since I usually do them alone, I guess I'm fairly good. Want to make it interesting? The person who puts the last piece in is the winner?" she challenged.

"You're on," Henry said rubbing his hands together in anticipation.

They both set to working on the frame of the puzzle. They sometimes reached for the same piece and quickly pulled back when their hands touched.

Henry was working on the part of the puzzle that was the pond when he asked, "How did you get into doing puzzles like this?"

"Well, for me, when things in my life were a little mixed up or unpredictable, assembling puzzles helped me get all the nervous energy out that builds up when you worry. I focused on the picture and then I felt much better," Charity detailed as she kept finding and putting pieces together, not looking up.

Henry touched her hand and said, "I'm sorry things were so hard for you." He waited for her to look up at him, then smiled. She looked up and returned the smile.

"Well, I'm okay now, and will beat you under the table," Charity started seriously, then turned it into a laugh.

"Oh, you," was all Henry could get out as they got back to the puzzle.

Henry was amazed at how well she really did do puzzles. He sat there for a few minutes, just watching her look at a piece, scan the puzzle, then find its destination and place it in the hole. He saw that she still crinkled her forehead when in deep concentration.

Noticing he wasn't working, Charity nudged, "Hey, what are you doing? We still have loads of pieces here. Are you purposely trying to throw the contest?"

"And let you win? Absolutely not. Let's finish this," Henry winked.

They worked another twenty minutes and had a handful of pieces left. One by one, they filled the gaps until only one piece was left. But where was it?

"Do you have the last piece?" Charity probed. "Are you holding out on purpose?"

"I wouldn't do that! Besides, how do I know you're not holding out on the last piece?" Henry bounced back to her.

"I don't have it. It must have fallen off the table. Let's look around," she suggested as she walked on her knees, looking on her side of the table.

Not able to keep from laughing any longer at her frantic search for the puzzle piece, Henry held up the piece and asked, "Looking for this?"

"You mean you had it all along and had me looking all over?" Charity asked incredulously, her competitive nature really stoked now.

"What are you going to do about it?" Henry taunted wriggling his eyebrows.

Before she could answer, she was tickling Henry. "I'm going to make you laugh so hard you drop the puzzle piece so I can win." As hard as she tried, she could not make Henry laugh.

Henry gently dropped to the floor, pulling her down with him. Though he wiggled at her touch, mainly from the sensation of her fingers on his body, he was not ticklish. "Charity, this isn't working...I'm not ticklish. But I bet you are!" He turned her over, gently tickling her in the ribs. Just as he suspected, she wiggled and writhed to get away from him, laughing hysterically.

"Stop, stop," she said in surrender trying to catch her breath. Her head was spinning from the feel of the warmth of his hands on her side. "I give up. You win."

"What did you say?" he asked just to be sure.

"I said, *you win*," she repeated, trying to regain her composure. She sat up and smoothed her clothes, trying to calm her breathing. "So, what should we do now?"

Needing a moment to compose himself as well, he stood up and said, "I don't know about you, but I need to stretch after all that sitting. Maybe we can go for that horse ride now."

Standing up as well, she agreed, "That would be nice. Let me see if Chuck would mind getting the horses ready. I haven't learned to saddle them myself yet." They wandered around to find Chuck.

"Sure thing, I will get the horses ready," Chuck said accommodatingly. "Give me about ten minutes." In no time at all, Chuck saddled up Sinbad for Charity and Ginger for Henry.

"You should be okay as long as you stay close to the fence, at least until you get familiar with the property," Chuck advised.

"We will," Charity waved settling herself in the saddle. "I don't want to get lost out there."

Henry tipped his pretend hat, "Thanks, Chuck, any other bits of advice?"

"Nope, you are all set. Just keep an eye on how long you ride," Chuck tipped his hat in response.

"Got it. Let's go, Henry," she said as they started off down the fence line, riding side by side.

Charity was surprised how well she remembered her technique for riding a horse. Things like keeping your heels tilted backwards so you can stay centered in the saddle. Moving the reins just a little will make the horse go left or right. Squeezing a horse around the belly caused them to trot and sometimes gallop.

"I can't believe how long it's been since I've been on a horse," Charity expressed to Henry. "I always wanted one growing up. Besides, foster care isn't the normal place to be able to have a horse. Then I found out my allergies were so bad. I can't believe I haven't sneezed yet."

"I guess that would be disappointing. Well, now you have a ranch and several horses. Do you think you will stay at the ranch your entire life?"

"Whoa, I've only been here a few weeks. I haven't given much thought to the rest of my life. I don't even know how to make sure the money I inherited lasts my entire life," Charity bit her lip. "I need to talk with an investor, I guess."

"Hang on, I didn't mean to cause you panic," Henry touched her shoulder gently. "I was just wondering out loud. Besides, I'm sure your Uncle Frank had a plan for that, as well."

"Maybe. He seemed to think of everything else."

They enjoyed the ride until Sinbad got spooked and ran off. Charity tried to rein him in but couldn't. She wasn't strong enough. Before Henry could help her, Sinbad came to an abrupt halt sending Charity over his head into the grass. Henry jumped off Ginger and ran over to her. Luckily, the tall grass had cushioned her fall.

"Are you okay?" Henry asked, scanning her quickly as she lay there stunned. His heart was beating out of his chest in panic.

"I don't know," Charity confessed, still winded from the fall. Henry eased her to a sitting position.

Her hair falling away from her face revealed a mouth wound. "You're bleeding!" Henry exclaimed.

Realizing she tasted blood, Charity touched her mouth then looked at her covered fingers as Henry grabbed his handkerchief and dabbed her lip. When

Henry touched her face, she pulled back slightly.

Henry removed the cloth, lifted her chin, and inspected. "It isn't too bad, just a bloody mess. Mouth wounds usually bleed a lot. Can you stand up?"

Charity lifted herself up but immediately fell back to the grass. She clutched her left ankle, "I can't put any weight on it."

Sindbad had run off, so Ginger would have to carry them both. "Come on, let's get you back to the house." Henry stood behind Charity, gently lifting her to her feet. She still showed pain in that left ankle. He picked her up and walked over to Ginger. Charity grabbed the saddle horn. Placing her right foot in the stirrup she swung her leg over to sit in the saddle. Henry climbed on carefully, sitting behind Charity on Ginger's back. He took the reins and said, "We'll have to trot back. Can you hold on a few minutes?"

"I think so. Sorry I made a mess of everything. This is *not* how I wanted things to go today," Charity expressed in exasperation.

"How did you make a mess of things?" Henry probed. She didn't answer his question, so he didn't press her. Truth be told, his mind was racing and his heart pounding. His mind raced to get Charity to the house and tend to her injuries. His pounding heart, that was another matter. Ever since they met, she captivated him. Each encounter drew him in like a drowning man fighting a riptide current. The memory of her fingers tickling him earlier made his body quiver on the inside. His arms were closed around her, ensuring she wouldn't fall off again. For a moment, he shut his eyes and just breathed in. Her hair was in his face, but he didn't care. He just knew he wanted her with him, always.

Charity felt extremely embarrassed and loathed feeling out of control. Here she was injured and bleeding all over Henry. Her head still ached slightly from the fall she just endured. She was more shaken up than she realized. In addition to the ache in her head, she was conscious of the fact her heart pounded quicker than normal. Was it Henry? Or the fact she was just thrown from a horse? She remembered the tickle fight and how her body reacted to his touch. He was unlike anyone she had encountered before. With Henry, she could let her guard down and not worry about anything. She didn't feel so alone when she was with him. His arms around her gave her comfort.

Fifteen minutes later, they reached their starting point at the pasture gate. Relieved they were back, Chuck dashed to grab Ginger's reins.

"Thank goodness you're okay. Sinbad showed up here about five minutes ago. Charity! You're bleeding."

Charity stated, "I don't know what happened. We were walking along and suddenly, he just bolted. Maybe Ginger was too close to him. He abruptly stopped and I flew off into the grass."

As he eased off and moved to get Charity off Ginger, Henry explained, "It all happened so fast. There was no time to keep Sinbad from running off." He carried Charity into the house, Chuck going ahead to hold the door open. Henry sat her down on a bar stool.

Coming into the kitchen, Theresa exclaimed, "What happened?" Seeing Charity's bleeding mouth, she grabbed a cold rag.

"I was thrown off Sinbad. I've hurt my ankle," Charity explained, taking the rag from Theresa.

After washing his hands, Chuck demanded, "Let me take a look at it." Chuck first felt to see if her ankle was broken. She jumped when he put pressure on the bones. Certain it was okay, he took off her shoe, "It's not broken, but definitely swollen. And it will hurt quite a bit. She needs to start by icing it down."

"Great," Charity moaned. "I don't have time to be hurt right now. I have too much going on."

"Well, sometimes we get slowed down whether we want to or not," Chuck expressed truthfully. "Let's get her to the living room where she can elevate this ankle and get it iced."

Henry gladly scooped Charity up again and carried her to the living room. All she could do was look at him and smile. Charity despised feeling helpless. He placed her on the couch, pulling the coffee table back to the usual position so she could place her leg on there.

Theresa fetched the ice pack and plugged in a heating pad for later. She then stated, "I think we have a pair of crutches around here somewhere. I'll go look for them."

"Thanks, Theresa. You are a marvel," Charity confessed. As Theresa left to find the crutches, Henry took a seat beside Charity.

"I need to keep an eye on the time. Work waits for no man…" announced Henry. Noticing her gloomy countenance, Henry changed the subject and asked "So, aside from the children arriving tomorrow, what's the next thing you have coming up?"

"Well, the Christmas Eve party. I need to connect with Penelope and find out what she needs from me. Plus, we can officially decorate the rest of the ranch. The biggest thing will be creating a routine with the children, making sure they get to school on time, and stuff like that. I can tell a mean bedtime story," Charity said proudly. Then, as if someone flipped a switch, her mood quickly changed again. "How can I welcome Amanda and Peter here tomorrow when I can barely walk?"

Henry shrugged his shoulders, "Maybe the soreness will work itself out quickly. Take some pain reliever, keep it elevated, alternate between heat and ice, and stay off it as much as possible. Your lip will heal soon enough." Trying to lighten her mood further, he asked, "What can I do for you before I leave?"

"Nothing, I guess. I will probably sleep here on the couch since I need to stay put a while. Theresa can help me get my things from my room." Charity took his hand, catching his gaze, and said, "I want to thank you for coming to my rescue in the pasture. I don't know how I would have managed by myself."

"I'm glad to be of assistance," Henry grinned, raising her hand to his lips to kiss it. "You're certainly no damsel in distress and able to take care of yourself. But I confess, I did enjoy being your knight in shining armor." Henry leaned in and kissed Charity on the cheek.

Before he pulled completely back, she closed her eyes and pressed her lips to his, wincing slightly from the pain in her lip. She didn't know why she had done that, but oh, it felt divine. There was a sizzle of electricity between them as she felt his body tense.

Wrapping his arm around her, he drew her closer. He felt like he would never breathe again. She was warm in his arms and sweet on his lips. He tried to be gentle for her injury but found himself devouring her lips with each breath. Needing to clear his spinning head, he pulled back. Eyes still closed, he whispered, "Charity, that was…"

"Yeah," she agreed.

Trying to regain his composure, he said, "I'd better go."

"Thank you, again for all your help with the horses," she stated as he stood up to leave.

"Of course. See you later." Henry walked out the front door.

She leaned back on the couch and exhaled a long breath. She had a major shift happening in her life once again. She had handled all the shifts that were thrown at her for the past four weeks. Wow! Had it been that long already? She had been oblivious to all things related to the Silver Horseshoe Ranch. She was twenty-six, a former foster youth, and now a millionaire. She was blessed with so much and wanted to use it wisely. There were the Aspiration Station grants she wanted to implement. She was providing respite for the Ferguson children. But she felt like she should do one more thing…but what?

Theresa came in with the crutches. "Here they are, Charity. I'll lean them against the end of the couch. What do you need?"

"Well, I will just sleep here. Can you bring my pillow and hand me that blanket over there?" Charity asked, feeling like a mess.

"Of course, I can. Want me to put on *The Polar Express* to keep you entertained?" Theresa posed.

"That would be so nice, thank you. It *is* my comfort movie," Charity uttered as she adjusted herself on the couch.

Theresa brought in her things and set the movie to playing. "Good night, honey. Text me if you need anything during the night."

"Thank you. I think I'll be okay for now. I'm staying put right here. I've used crutches before, so I know what to do," Charity replied. "Good night."

****

On Monday morning, Henry was back at the DCS office after a week and a half vacation. Honestly, he had a hard time concentrating after the kiss they shared last night. He had to put that thought on hold as Erica was the first at his desk.

"Good morning, Henry. It's nice to have you back," Erica said truthfully. "Did you enjoy your time off?"

"It was great. I really appreciate you letting me do that," Henry stated gratefully. "I had some things I needed to work through and found the answers I needed."

Erica clearly wanted more information. She stepped closer. "Charity was absolutely perfect with the Thanksgiving Shindig. So many families have emailed the department and asked us to thank Charity for the gifts. And the table decorations, people were so excited to have them," Erica shared merrily.

"She loves to make people happy. Did you know she's taking the Ferguson children for respite since their foster family is moving sooner than expected?" Henry announced.

Erica nodded in response to his question, "I just hope she doesn't get overwhelmed. She's had many big changes in her life in the last month."

"I know. She's proceeding cautiously. The children arrive at her house today. The foster mom will be dropping their stuff off to her. I promised to stop by tonight and give her emotional support. We're going to make Christmas tree ornaments."

Erica raised an eyebrow. "What a tremendous idea! That would be a good activity foster parents can do with their foster children. The kids can take them back home if they are reunited with their families," Erica affirmed excitedly. She really liked Charity.

"I know. Charity said she likes making them so she can see smiling faces on the Christmas tree. Well, I need to get to work, Erica. I'll talk to you later," Henry moved closer to his desk. He worked on his cases all day. He alternated between checking his watch and phone as he counted down the hours to see if Charity was holding on okay.

****

Charity was waiting on Melanie to come by with the items that belonged to Amanda and Peter. Though her ankle still hurt quite a bit, she was able to bear some weight on it and was slowly walking around the living room. While she was walking around, Buzz texted her.

"Sorry to bother. Got a notice in the ads in the paper you need to see. I sent a copy to your email. Buzz"

What in the world would cause Buzz to text her at home? She limped to the office, pulled out her computer and checked her email. The message read:

Horse equine therapy organization lost their lease due to sale of property by previous owner. The Bit and Bridle provides equine therapy free of charge to children with disabilities. Beth and David Franklin hope to find another location to continue providing services to these families. Many children are current and former foster youth. They have a driving buggy, horse gear, three horses, and a lovable miniature donkey named Albert. Any assistance finding a place to have the sessions and board the horses would be greatly appreciated. Please contact Beth Franklin.

Well, could this be the answer to the 'one more thing' dilemma? She didn't want to overload herself, but if this organization just needs a place to store their gear and board the horses, the Silver Horseshoe could partner with them. First, she would need to check with Chuck and Theresa because it would mean increased traffic at the ranch. She would need to learn whether the ranch would require additional insurance. She would wait until tomorrow before touching this one. Right now, she was waiting for Melanie.

Wincing with every step, Charity made it to the kitchen. She sat down with a soda and a small bag of barbecue kettle chips. Forgetting her lips still hurt, eating chips wasn't a good idea since the salt made her lips burn. Melanie texted she was at the gate. Charity remotely opened the gate for her, and Melanie drove up to the house. Charity met Melanie on the porch as she carried in the first set of items from the car.

"What happened to you?" Melanie queried.

"I was thrown from a horse yesterday. I just have to move very slowly." She walked Melanie to the stairs and said, "Amanda's room is at the top of the stairs on the left. Peter's is on the right. You head on up and I will be right there."

Melanie carried Amanda's belongings to her new room. Melanie took a moment to take in the new décor. Charity had purchased a new bedding set in Amanda's favorite color, lavender. She hung a few unicorn paintings on the wall. Charity finally made it up the stairs, meeting Melanie in Amanda's room.

Melanie handed Charity a folder containing important DCS paperwork, appointment schedules, health insurance information, and school pick-up instructions. "They are expecting you in the carpool line today. The kids get out at two forty-five, so you should be in the line no later than two o'clock." Melanie slowly handed a school parking tag to Charity, "You need to hang this from the rearview mirror."

Charity could see Melanie was struggling to keep control of her emotions. Charity placed the folder on the dresser and sat in the chair to get off her ankle.

"Melanie, would you help me organize Amanda's room? You know how she likes things. I would hate to put them in the wrong place."

Melanie nodded and began to hang up Amanda's clothes in the closet. She had cared for and protected these children for almost a year. She remembered how much Amanda had grown during that time. Coming across Amanda's favorite dress, she took a moment to touch the fabric one last time. She couldn't contain her tears any longer.

Charity stood up and slowly limped over to Melanie, pulling her into a hug as Melanie sobbed. Charity understood in that moment the depth of pain that both biological and foster parents feel each time they experience a loss, no matter the circumstances. Charity had always been the one leaving and never saw, or even considered how her leaving may have affected her former foster parents because of the wall she had built to protect herself.

Charity quietly whispered, "I promise to make sure they remember how much you both love them."

Melanie nodded and said, "Let's get Peter's room done. I'll go get his things from the car." She was gone and back in just a few minutes.

Peter's room was decked out in red bedding with superhero pictures on the walls. Melanie placed his things as closely as possible as they had been at her house. "Now then, Peter will be able to find his things."

Melanie assisted Charity down the stairs then went to retrieve the last items from her car.

"These are the food items that were leftover. This should last you the rest of this week. Amanda can tell you what they normally eat. Peter likes showers, not baths, so just ask him to take a shower. He can run the water by himself. Amanda needs at least one book before she can go to bed. They both wake up easy and are starving when they get home from school. Barbara is extremely easy to work with and is always just a text away," Melanie trailed off. "I need to go," Melanie choked back tears as she gave Charity a quick hug and dashed out the front door. Charity felt like her heart would break in two right along with Melanie's.

Melanie had just barely left the ranch when Charity got a call from Barbara Frederickson. "Hello, Charity. I'm out doing visits and am close to the ranch. Can I come on by?" Barbara inquired.

"Of course, come on over. The gate is open. I was thrown from a horse yesterday, so I'm moving kinda slow," Charity replied. Charity slowly walked to the door and stepped outside as Barbara pulled up.

Barbara got out of her car. "Hello. Thanks for letting me come over right now. I thought it may be best to see you before the children arrived," Barbara explained.

"I understand. Come inside and let me show you around the house,"

Charity gestured. She introduced Barbara to Theresa.

Theresa looked at Charity then butted in, "Barbara, let me show you the children's bedrooms upstairs. Charity, you sit there and rest a few minutes." Theresa escorted Barbara upstairs.

"Oh, wow," Barbara began, "these rooms are great. I see Melanie has already dropped off their belongings."

"Yes, you literally just missed her. She's not taking this very well," Theresa voiced sadly.

"I know. Being a military family and fostering can be an especially difficult challenge. They are remarkable foster parents. And that Zach is adorable," Barbara gleamed.

"We thought so, as well, after seeing them here for the Thanksgiving Shindig," Theresa agreed.

Theresa walked Barbara out the back door and showed her the barn, the pasture, and where the horse equipment was located. Chuck waved to them from the pasture as he was looking for something he dropped earlier. After a few minutes, Theresa had Barbara back in the living room with Charity.

Charity realized it was one forty-five. "Oh, I need to head to the school to pick them up from the carpool line. Anything else I need to do right now?" Charity escorted Barbara to the front door.

"No, we're all set. I'll check in with you in a few weeks. Have a good afternoon. I hope your ankle gets better soon."

Charity waved from the front door as Barbara drove away.

Taking a minute before she left for the school, Charity went up to Theresa and hugged her saying, "I can't thank you enough for putting the finishing touches on the children's rooms. I was planning to do that myself…until I fell off Sinbad."

"You are most welcome. I enjoyed having the chance to be involved in this new adventure we're setting out on," Theresa replied. "It will be uncharted territory…for all of us."

It took her a few minutes, but Charity got in the jeep and headed to the school. Luckily, her driving foot was uninjured, and she was able to drive okay.

The elementary school wasn't as far from the ranch as she thought. There was, in fact, a bus that went past the ranch, which would save a lot of time. Two forty-five came quickly and the teachers began letting the children out, reading the names on the tags hanging from the mirror. She was next in line and she could see Amanda and Peter. She waved excitedly. The teacher opened the door and they climbed in and buckled themselves up. She gently pulled out of the school and they headed home. The children were excited to be back in school after being on Thanksgiving break. Though Peter still didn't say anything, he nodded his head vigorously when Charity asked if he had a good day. In just ten minutes, they were back at the ranch. They exited the jeep and carried their backpacks in the house. Charity walked very slowly, and Amanda stayed back with her.

"What happened to your foot, Charity?" Amanda questioned. "And your lip looks funny."

Charity explained, "Oh, Henry and I were riding horses. Sinbad got spooked and I fell off. I hit my mouth when I fell."

Remembering what Melanie said, Charity took them straight through to the kitchen to get a snack.

Theresa had a few things on the bar for Amanda and Peter to choose from. "Hello, Amanda and Peter, I am so glad you're here. Please ask me for anything you need while you are here," Theresa said softly.

"Thank you, Theresa," Charity gave Theresa a squeeze. "After you finish your snacks, I'll take you upstairs to your rooms and let you get settled in. Do either of you have any homework?"

"None for me," Amanda said happily. Peter shook his head.

"Well, Henry will be coming over to have dinner with us and we'll make a craft for the tree," Charity explained.

They finished their snacks, and moving slowly, Charity took them upstairs. Charity took them to each room. Amanda gasped when she saw the unicorn pictures. Peter quickly found his toys and retrieved his favorite one, a *Captain America* action figure. She showed them where the bathroom was and told them they could spend some time in their rooms. "I'll be downstairs if you need me. Take as long as you need up here. We're having pizza for dinner," Charity said as she eased herself downstairs.

At five o'clock, Charity found Theresa to ask her what she needed to do about the pizzas. Theresa explained they would be delivered notified when they arrived at the gate. Charity's phone buzzed. Henry texted he was on his way and added that if she would pay for the pizzas, he could bring them when he arrived in twenty minutes.

Not wanting to add extra work for Theresa, Charity grabbed the paper plates to reduce clean up tonight. She didn't want Theresa overloaded since two little people would be added to the household for a while. Charity set out the plastic cups for drinks.

Henry texted Charity that he was coming up to the house. Charity opened the front door for him as he stumbled in with the pizzas.

Charity called the children for dinner. Chuck had come inside, washed his hands, and grabbed something to drink.

"Hey, guys," Henry nodded to Amanda and Peter. "Are you hungry for pizza?" Henry pointed them out like a cheesy game show host. Amanda giggled.

"Thank you for picking these up," Charity smiled touching Henry's shoulder. "We're going to have some fun. We do have to keep an eye on the time since there is school tomorrow."

"Amanda, what do you and Peter drink with dinner?" Charity inquired.

"We drink anything, but Peter likes milk most of the time. I'll take milk, too, please," Amanda said politely.

"Here you go," Charity said as she placed their drinks in front of them, sloshing a bit out. She turned to Henry, "Here is your tea." She brushed against him and he suddenly felt warm. Charity grabbed a napkin and cleaned up the milk mess.

Like curious scientists, Theresa and Chuck watched Charity and Henry as they interacted with the children. Except for a few noticeable winces on her face, Charity didn't complain once about her ankle. Both couldn't help but smile affectionately. As everyone finished eating, Charity ambled to the office, retrieving the crafts.

"Okay everyone, now that we've finished eating, I have a craft for all of us to make…Chuck and Theresa, you need to come over here, too," Charity said enthusiastically. Henry was beside Peter. Charity sat beside Amanda. "We're making Christmas tree picture ornaments. Once we get these decorated and dry, we will put pictures of ourselves in them and hang them on the tree in the living room."

It was fun watching everyone decorate their ornaments. Henry had just as much fun as Peter. Charity couldn't tell if Chuck or Theresa was having more fun. They giggled and talked about how long it had been since they did something like this.

At seven-thirty, Charity announced it was time to clean up and take showers for school tomorrow. Peter went up to the shower first. Amanda went over to Charity and said, "Charity, thank you for making this first night here so much fun. I know we won't be here an awfully long time. Well, we thank you for asking us to stay here." Amanda hugged Charity and went upstairs to get ready for her shower.

Charity stood there stunned. Henry noticed her struggling and put his arms tightly around her. She didn't resist. He pressed a kiss in her hair for comfort. Releasing her, he helped her clean up the craft mess and put the ornaments in the office on some newspaper so they could dry. He had to get home.

Charity wobbled back to the kitchen. Chuck and Theresa were sipping coffee. "You did a good job tonight, Charity," Chuck said proudly. "You really connected with those two. I had a good time myself, and I am not easily entertained." He gave her a side hug and went to his part of the house.

Theresa collected the mugs. "Chuck's right, you did a great job. Henry was right there with the children, too. There's something you need to know. Chuck isn't too free with compliments. If he says it, he means it. Take it to the bank."

"Thank you," Charity said humbly. "That means a great deal to me. I just want to make sure everyone stays happy. I know that is an impossible thing, but I know I can do this."

"No doubt. Just keep your eye on the goals you wanted to make for yourself and you will land in the right place. I think you have some tucking into bed to do," Theresa said as she motioned upstairs.

"Right, that means I need to read at least one book," Charity added. "See you later."

Charity went upstairs and started with Peter since he was out of the shower. He jumped in bed and pulled the covers up to his neck. He didn't need any water or a story but did need the bedside lamp left on and the door left open. She kissed him on the forehead and went to check on Amanda.

Charity reached for the light switch in Amanda's room and froze. Amanda had already fallen asleep. Charity pulled the covers up a little higher and kissed her on the forehead. She left the door open and went downstairs.

Charity went to her room and with some effort, put on her pajamas. She decided to sleep with her door open so she could hear the children if they called out in the night. She thought for a moment she might get two monitors so she could hear what was going on upstairs. She set her clock to get them up and ready for school. She turned on the rain app. Max suddenly appeared and was ready for bed. Apparently, it was too noisy for his liking and he hid until it got quieter. "Good night, Max," Charity said.

CHAPTER 13

Over the next week, Charity and the children set a great routine. Her ankle was back to normal and her lip had healed. Charity located the bus that drove past the ranch, so she just stood with them at the road in the mornings. She was so engaged with Amanda and Peter that she had forgotten all about the Bit and Bridle situation. She went back inside where Theresa and Chuck were having coffee.

"I'm glad you're both here. There's something I forgot to ask you about. Last week, Buzz sent me a copy of a notice that was put in the paper about an equine therapy group who lost their lease where they boarded their horses. They provide free sessions for children with disabilities."

"Bit and Bridle?" Chuck interjected, his hand hugging his cup.

Surprised, Charity continued, "Can I reach out to them and offer letting them do that here? The notice said that some of their students were foster youth."

"Well, I see no harm in talking to them and finding out just what they need," Chuck tossing the question with his eyes to Theresa.

"Just be careful that you don't get overloaded. You don't exactly know what you are looking at with Amanda and Peter," Theresa coached gently.

"I won't make any decisions without getting the facts and then checking with you again. I just wanted to know if I could contact the lady," Charity voiced respectfully. Though the ranch was hers, she wanted to include them in all the decisions.

Charity went to the office and closed the door. She found the number for Beth Franklin and called her up. "Hello, is this Beth Franklin?"

"Yes, this is Beth," Ms. Franklin replied.

"My name is Charity Walters, at the Silver Horseshoe Ranch. I wanted to speak to you regarding your needs for your horses."

"Oh, thank you very much for calling. I have three horses and a miniature donkey. We have a driving buggy and lots of saddles and other horse gear. We need a place to board the horses and store the equipment. We do therapy lessons two days a week, but all day each day. We begin in April and finish in October. We fundraise during the winter. All lessons are free to the families we serve, and all our staff are volunteers," Beth recounted.

"Wow! Well, we have five open stalls in our barn. That would be plenty of room for the three horses, the donkey, and the equipment. Since inheriting the ranch, I've been trying to find a way to make a difference. We just may be able to make this work. Why don't you come by the ranch tomorrow and I'll show you around? How about eleven o'clock?" Charity offered.

"That's perfect. Thank you very much for reaching out. I look forward to seeing you tomorrow. I can't tell you what a blessing this would be for us," Beth exhaled a sigh of gratitude.

Charity sensed relief in the pitch of Beth's voice. "Let's see if we can get this done. Good-bye."

"Well, that was interesting," Charity said to Theresa. "Beth Franklin will be by here tomorrow at eleven o'clock to see if the ranch would meet their needs."

"Okay, what else did she say?" Theresa asked curiously.

"They only do lessons two days a week, going from April to October. So, it won't be as intrusive as I figured. I will know more tomorrow," Charity said as she got a drink from the refrigerator. "Now I need to go contact Penelope about the Christmas Eve party. So, besides the dinner, what was given to the families? Toys? Money?" Charity wondered.

"Typically, the families receive a check for $1,000 before the event. That way they can purchase additional presents for their children. The night of the party, it's just a delicious dinner, Santa Claus, and some dancing for the parents," Theresa explained.

"Wow, that sounds like a good time. Is it in a tent again?" Charity wondered.

"This time we decorate the garage. It is large enough and not dirty with oil and grease. We can regulate the temperature and not have to worry about rain or snow," Theresa continued.

"Okay, I'll go check in with Penelope. This sounds fun." Charity called Penelope from the office as she straightened a book on the shelf.

"Penelope, this is Charity Walters. I just wanted to check in with you on the specifics of the Christmas Eve party," Charity started with enthusiasm.

"Hello, Charity, things are proceeding as planned. There are only fifty families attending this year. They are sent a $1,000 check about a week and a half before Christmas. We have the Santa retained, activities to keep the children entertained, the food picked out, the holiday music selected, and the family ornaments made," Penelope checked off the list.

"Family ornaments?" Charity asked curiously.

"Mr. Ledford always gave out a silver horseshoe ornament with the year printed on it in gold. They are incredibly beautiful," Penelope opined.

"So then, I really don't need to do anything this time?" Charity asked incredulously.

"Not a single thing," Penelope explained. "It lasts for about two hours maximum. We start at six o'clock. That way everyone gets to enjoy Christmas Eve after the party. We set up the garage on December 23rd, so there is no intrusion on the daytime activities of Christmas Eve."

"You really have thought of everything. I'll check in with you the week before Christmas, unless you need me before then," Charity complimented.

"I will keep you posted if there are any changes. Have a wonderful afternoon," Penelope said, ending the call. Charity stretched widely, smiling as well.

Charity felt accomplished. The children were building a good routine. She checked off with Penelope and had absolutely nothing to do for the Christmas Eve party. Tomorrow she would meet with Beth Franklin regarding the therapy lessons. She monitored the time, as it was close for the children to get off the bus.

Charity went out to see the horses while she waited. Chuck went into town for supplies. Sinbad was waiting at the fence when Charity arrived. He wanted her to pet him and stared intently, flicking his ears, smelling for treats.

"I don't have anything today, sorry," Charity voiced. "What have you been doing today? What makes you so scared, huh?" Crazy to ask a horse a question. Horses can't talk. She stood there just absentmindedly petting Sinbad. He nudged her to keep loving on him. She checked her phone, as it was time to head around to the front of the house and get the children.

Charity stood attentively when the bus came to a stop and Amanda and Peter bounced off. Amanda shared how she had a good day. Peter held Charity's hand as they walked back to the house. They went inside and Theresa had a selection of snacks on the bar for them to choose from. Like a tour guide, Amanda narrated what she did in the second grade. She liked music and going to the library. Peter was quietly focused on the rest of his apple slices.

After checking for homework, Charity let the children watch a Christmas movie in the front living room. It was a little while until dinner. She peeked in on them and they were having a good time.

Charity set their plates at the bar. Theresa pulled chicken nuggets and French fries from the oven. There were apple and orange slices on a plate shaped like a big orange.

"Time to eat, guys. Go wash up," Charity paused the movie. "You can finish this after dinner."

Charity served Amanda and Peter dinner. She ate with them. They worked together and cleaned up their dishes. Charity allowed them to finish the movie. Then she sent them through the shower.

Diving into bed, Amanda's reddish-brown hair covered her face. She raked it to one side as she wedged her legs between the layers of her quilt and blankets. She wanted to read the unbelievable book, *My Lucky Day*. It was about a piglet who paid a visit to a fox to trick him out of dinner. The piglet almost became dinner himself.

"The piglet grabbed the rest of his cookies and headed home. He looked at the list to see who he would visit tomorrow," Charity read, showing Amanda the picture of the piglet looking up at a bear. "I think I like this story just as much as you do," Charity attested.

"It is funny," Amanda agreed, "I loved the part where the fox is giving the piglet a massage and passes out," Amanda finished giggling as she flopped backwards on the bed, making the blanket rise.

"Good night, Amanda," Charity whispered as she kissed Amanda on the forehead.

"Good night," Amanda replied, pulling her covers up to her chin.

Charity went into Peter's room and asked him, "Doing okay? Need the music on tonight?" Peter liked to have a little bit of music playing while he fell asleep.

Peter nodded his head and climbed under the covers. He popped back up, quickly hugging Charity. It took her by surprise. And then just as quickly, he was secure beneath the covers once again. Luckily, the radio station played Christmas music all the time. She set the timer for thirty minutes. "Good night, Peter. Sleep well," Charity said softly as she kissed him on top of his head.

Charity drifted to the living room and put on *The Polar Express* to relax a little until bedtime. Her phone buzzed.

"Hey, how have things been going? Sorry I haven't seen you much. Work is heavy now. Are the kids adjusting okay?" Henry wondered.

Charity really wanted to hear his voice so she asked, "Can you talk for a few minutes?"

"Sure, I'll call you," Henry replied. An instant later he said, "You okay?"

"Yeah, I'm fine. We've gotten into a good routine. Max tolerates the children pretty well. Sorry work is heavy," Charity responded empathetically.

"Want to meet for lunch tomorrow?" Henry asked hopefully.

"Can't unless we meet around twelve-thirty. I'm meeting the lady from the Bit and Bridle Equine Therapy Group here at the ranch to discuss using our place to continue the lessons. They serve children with special needs and have helped many foster children," Charity added.

"Wow, that sounds tremendous! We can meet at twelve-thirty. Where would you like to go?" asked Henry.

"Not sure. I'll let you know tomorrow," Charity advised Henry.

"Okay. I gotta go. Just wanted to tell you I was thinking about you. Good night."

"Good night, see you tomorrow." Charity and Max watched the movie all the way through, only once, and headed off to bed.

****

Preparing for Beth's visit, Charity decided to head out back to the barn where she found Chuck. "What are you doing out here?" Charity asked Chuck as he moved equipment around to make it look neater.

"I was just trying to make sure we looked organized when Beth Franklin gets here. She will probably want to see where she would keep her equipment. I think we could accommodate what you said she had…the driving buggy and the horse gear. I wonder what Mr. Whiskers would think of a miniature donkey. Wouldn't that be a sight?" Chuck pondered humorously. Charity had never noticed the warmth of his laugh before. It was calming.

"That would be pretty funny. Thank you for even considering letting me do this. I have made a huge intrusion on how things run around here. I certainly don't want to upset the *donkey cart*." Charity mused.

"Oh, you would be surprised at the things your Uncle Frank had going on a time or two. Besides, I like to believe that if you have the means to help people, you should do it without regard for what you get out of it. It may not mean much to you, but it could mean the world to someone else. The money and the ranch are just things. We should be more concerned with people. Things can be replaced, people cannot."

Charity stood there thinking of what Chuck just said. He was so right. Her phone buzzed and it was Beth. Charity remotely opened the gate and Beth drove around to the right side of the house. She went to the driveway and waited.

"Oh, this place is beautiful," Beth said placing a hand over her heart. "It is better than the previous location." Beth was a tall woman about fifty-five. She was slender and well-toned from her work with horses. She had a very slight touch of gray in her light brown hair and wore her sunglasses on her head.

"Thank you very much. It's a beautiful place. I find it very tranquil to do a lot of heavy thinking. Come on, let me show you around," Charity said heading toward the barn.

"Beth Franklin, this is Charles Hobby, but we call him Chuck," Charity introduced Beth to Chuck. "Chuck had been with the Silver Horseshoe all the way back when my Uncle Frank first acquired the property. He takes great care of the ranch and the horses."

"Pleased to meet you, Beth," Chuck nodded, removed his glove, and shook Beth's hand. "What would you like to see first? The barn is this way."

Charity and Beth followed Chuck into the barn where he showed Beth that there was a total of ten stalls, five on each side. The left side was the side that she could use for her horses, donkey, and gear. Chuck led them back outside to the pasture, showing Beth how large the area was and that it could easily handle all the animals. There was an arena where Beth could do the buggy driving.

Beth gasped when she saw the arena. It was the perfect size for the buggy and the obstacle course items she used for lessons. "Oh, Charity, this is more than I imagined."

"Thank you, Chuck, for showing Beth around the ranch. Beth, what other needs do you have besides the physical location to do the therapy sessions?" Charity asked curiously.

"Well, honestly, we have money saved up for things like hay, vet care, and the like. It would be the biggest blessing just to have a location to keep these children attending therapy. We do not charge for one single lesson. We have donors and we are grateful for any financial assistance we receive. There are some children who have overcome physical and emotional obstacles while working with horses. Dave and I, as well as our volunteers, are glad we can get these children to come out of their shells. We provide lessons for children who are nonverbal, children in wheelchairs having serious physical restrictions. There are not many places who have services to help children in this category," Beth said sadly.

Charity looked to Chuck for guidance. He shook his head "yes" to agree to partner with Beth Franklin and the Bit and Bridle Equine Therapy Group. "Beth, I believe we can meet your needs, so you continue to provide these needed services to the children. Make plans to move your animals here at your convenience," Charity reported gladly.

"Thank you very much," Beth said wiping a tear from her eye. "We tend to the horses every morning, or evening, whichever is better for the ranch. Chuck, do you have a preference?"

"No, no preference. You are welcome to be here as often as you need. Just set a schedule or text me when you are heading this way," Chuck suggested.

"We will make a schedule and a plan to get the horses and our equipment here as soon as possible," Beth said gratefully.

"I am so glad we met, Beth. I happen to have a small boy living with me as a respite case who may benefit from some horse therapy. I know your lessons are from April to October, but do you have any advice?" Charity asked earnestly.

"Well, there is a saying that the outside of a horse is good for the inside of a man. Maybe when we bring the horses over, I can spend a few minutes with him," Beth suggested.

"That would be great. I have to tell you, he hasn't spoken in an awfully long time," Charity warned Beth. "But we did get a giggle a little while back, right, Chuck?"

"We sure did. I believe the same thing, Beth, that the outside of a horse *is* good for the inside of a man or child," Chuck said quietly. "It has helped many a man through some deep thinking and tough times."

Beth nodded. "That is a quite common thing with any trauma situation. We just need to get him back on track where he derailed. It may still take a while, but don't give up on him," Beth affirmed earnestly. "I have another appointment I have to get to. Thank you for your generosity. We look forward to partnering with the Silver Horseshoe Ranch."

"Take care and the gate will open when you approach it slowly," Charity said as Beth was leaving. She walked over to Chuck and said, "That went really well. What a wonderful program they have, providing services like that to special needs children."

"Indeed, it is remarkable. I do believe you have satisfied your 'what do I do' dilemmas, don't you?" Chuck asked coyly.

"Yes, I have. Thanks for the push in the right direction," Charity said as she gave him a big squeeze. "Oh, I have lunch with Henry. I have to go."

"Yep, never a dull moment," Chuck grinned.

****

Charity was on her way to meet Henry at the steakhouse. While waiting, Henry ruminated on his father's advice on how to proceed with Charity… Benjamin Franklin's Pros and Cons list. He selected a booth facing the door. He didn't have his notebook, so he used a napkin. He scribbled 'Pros' on the left side and 'Cons' on the right side. He scribbled 'Fun to be with' under the Pros side. Then he added 'Share same interest in mission work…pushes me to be my best…makes me crazy…and has a very generous spirit.' He struggled to find any Cons. Obviously there were some because no one is perfect. But he could not find one that seemed qualified to write down.

"Okay, Mr. Benjamin Franklin, I think you proved my point. She's worth wanting to build a future with. And, thanks to you, too, Dad," Henry said out loud. Henry saw Charity walk in the restaurant and quickly shoved the napkin in his pocket while quickly standing.

Charity seemed incredibly happy. "Hey, thanks for letting me come a little later. The meeting with Beth was a huge success. The Silver Horseshoe Ranch and the Bit and Bridle Equine Therapy Group will be partnering up. Beth and I will have a brainstorming meeting sometime after moving the horses and equipment to the ranch," Charity said excitedly. "She may even be able to help Peter work through his trauma."

"That's wonderful," Henry declared proudly. "I knew you could do it. What are you hungry for?"

"I'm thinking a burger and some fries," Charity said surely. "What are you getting?"

"I'll have the same thing," Henry replied.

Henry and Charity shared a nice lunch and talked excitedly until it was time for Henry to get back to the office. "I have to get back. Thanks for meeting me," Henry verbalized. Henry paused as if to say something. He opted to wait.

"I am glad I got to come," she said in a low voice, leaning toward him.

He slid out of the booth touching her shoulder as he left. She grabbed his hand with hers as he rounded the corner and disappeared.

Charity sat there for a little while longer. She marveled at the tremendous opportunities that had been placed in her path in just a short time. She left the server a little something extra in the tip. She took one last sip of her drink, then left for home. She had become quite good at this new life she was living. The next two weeks went by amazingly fast.

CHAPTER 14

The Monday before Christmas, Beth and David Franklin transferred their horses and equipment to the ranch. Amanda and Peter were captivated by the trailers that held the horses. Chuck was directing David were to park the trailer for the best position to let the ramp down and get the horses out. It was very noisy with the banging and clanging of the gates. Charity tried to keep the children out of the way. They could hear the whinnying of the horses. They wanted to see Albert, the miniature donkey, up close. Charity went out to see if it was okay for them to come out, as long as they didn't get in the way.

"Hello, everyone," Charity began, "I have two peeping Tom's who want to get a closer look at Albert. Can I bring them out?"

"Absolutely, give me a moment to put a harness on Albert," Beth retrieved a harness. "We can move him to the side and not be in the way for Chuck and David."

"Great, they will be thrilled. Back in a flash," Charity declared animatedly. Charity led Amanda and Peter outside calmly so they wouldn't spook any horses. Someone could get really hurt if a horse felt scared, reared back, or ran off. She knew that from experience.

Beth stood away from the trailers with Albert. He was chomping on the mini carrots Beth lured him with so the children could pet him. She had stashed some in her pockets to ensure cooperation from the horses. "Come on over. He is a nice donkey."

"Charity, he looks a lot like Mr. Whiskers, doesn't he?" inquired Amanda.

"He does resemble Mr. Whiskers a little bit," Charity replied. "He feels so soft."

Peter was rubbing Albert on the back. He didn't say anything but sported an enormous grin.

Beth observed him and smiled. She had previous experience with children like Peter. It takes a long time for them to feel safe enough to find their words. Maybe Charity would let Peter do some things with her during the winter. There was always horse work to do. It would be age appropriate, of course. Chuck and David successfully unloaded the horses that were still in the trailer and turned them loose in the pasture. Now they had to unload the buggy and the gear.

"Okay, guys. I have to put Albert in the pasture so I can help Chuck and David get this stuff unloaded," Beth explained. "You will be able to see him more later. Besides, he will be here ALL the time, now."

"Thank you, Beth," Charity grabbed Peter's hand and turned toward the house. "Come on. Let's go see what Theresa is doing in the kitchen."

Charity directed Amanda and Peter back inside. They took off their shoes at the back door to keep from tracking mud in the kitchen. In a moment of irony, *Dominic the Donkey* was playing on the stereo. Theresa covered the counter with the ingredients to make sugar cookies. "Stay here with Theresa and get started on these cookies. I have a couple things to take care of. I won't be long," Charity told Amanda and Peter. She looked at Theresa, "I need to check in with Penelope for Thursday. Then with Henry for just a minute."

Handing out aprons to the kids, Theresa assured, "We'll be fine right here. We will make these the best cookies ever, won't we?"

Charity went into the office and dialed Penelope. "Hello, Penelope? I was just confirming that everything was going smoothly for Thursday. We have decorated the ranch and it looks very Christmassy around here."

"That's terrific. We are all set and will set up on Wednesday, per the usual process. Oh, did I mention the dress code for the event?" Penelope queried.

"No, I don't think we covered that. What is the dress code, black tie?" Charity summoned.

"Oh, no. We don't do a black-tie affair for this event. It is more a business attire dress code. Many of these families don't have the extra income for tuxedos and gowns. We just make them feel as comfortable and dressy as they can within their finances. Your attire will need to be a little dressier, but not a full-blown gown. Does that make sense?" Penelope asked.

"I understand. Theresa can help me choose something that fits the need. And will I need to make a speech on behalf of the ranch?" posed Charity.

"Yes, but just a brief 'Thank you for coming' kind of thing. Don't emphasize *why* they were there. If things are said the wrong way, they could be very hurt instead of having an enjoyable evening," Penelope explained.

"Then how do I know what to say?" Charity fretted.

"You will be fine. Just speak from the heart. If you still feel unsure, write down what you want to say and send it to me to review," Penelope suggested.

"Got it. Thanks. See you on Wednesday," Charity placed the phone on the hook.

She sat there for a moment in immediate panic. What in the world would she wear to this party? She decided to call Henry and see what he was doing. "Hey, what are you doing?" she asked curiously.

"Just trying to finish up paperwork before Christmas. You?" Charity usually just texted. Henry figured her calling must have meant something was wrong.

"I'm freaking out right now. I learned a special dress is required for the Christmas Eve party. Penelope said it needed to be dressier than church, but not a ball gown. I don't have *anything* like that. Can you come over this evening and stay with Amanda and Peter while Theresa and I go shopping? Anyway, you need to get the coasters. They are ready to give your coworkers," Charity reminded him.

"Sure, I can come over. Why don't I take them Christmas-light looking? Have they done that before?" Henry wondered.

"Oh, I have no idea. That would be wonderful. Theresa is making sugar cookies with them right now, so they wouldn't need any sugary treats while riding around. Just plan to eat with us. I owe you, big time."

"I will see you around five-thirty!"

Charity went back into the kitchen where a wonderful pan of decorated sugar cookies was about to go into the oven. "You did these already?" Charity was amazed.

"Theresa said we're naturals at this. It was fun," Amanda beamed with pride in their work. "Can we go watch a Christmas movie?" Peter nodded licking the sprinkles from his fingers.

"Sure, you can. Do you know how to work everything in there?" Charity asked Amanda.

"Are you kidding?" Amanda said half sarcastically. "Kids know everything about how to work a tv." Amanda took Peter in the living room and started *Rudolph*.

Charity looked at Theresa with wide eyes. "I think they're feeling extremely comfortable now. Cheeky, isn't she?" Charity declared laughing.

Theresa looked at Charity and said, "Okay, what is it?"

Charity was always floored at how perceptive Theresa was to her expressions. "How did you-oh, well. I spoke to Penelope. First, I have to say something to the guests at the party. I need to be careful to phrase my words so not to remind them of the 'why' they come here every year. What if I blow it?"

"And two?" Theresa pressed.

"Two, I need an appropriate dress to wear. I don't have a 'dressier than church but not a ball gown' dress," Charity uttered in a panic. "Henry plans to take the children Christmas-light looking tonight. Would you go shopping with me, so I have the right dress?" Charity pleaded with Theresa.

"Oh, honey, I will gladly go shopping with you. I'm honored you would ask me," Theresa exclaimed, giving Charity a hug.

"Henry will be having dinner with us. He needs to take his ornaments home to give to his coworkers. What would you get a man like Henry for Christmas, anyway?" Charity added in the same breath.

"I don't think it would matter what you gave him," Theresa stated matter-of-factly.

"Don't want to do a gift card. I'm at a total loss," Charity bit her lip then grabbed a cookie.

"Don't worry so much. You know he loves just spending time with you. Think about what he likes to do, and then pick something that would go along with those activities."

"Good idea. Maybe I can find something while we're out tonight," Charity said hopefully.

By mid-afternoon, Chuck and the Franklins had all the equipment, horses, and instructions for things wrapped up. Chuck came in and sat down at the bar. Theresa poured him a cold glass of tea as Chuck wiped sweat and dirt from his brow.

"I think the Franklins can help Charity accomplish a lot of the things she feels so strongly about. They are genuinely nice people. Did you know they provide horse lessons for children who have Down's Syndrome, Cerebral Palsy, and other major health issues that many equine therapy places won't assist with? It is a blessing to the families they take care of, that much is certain," Chuck admired.

"Charity has certainly matured in the short time she's been here. Her folks would be so proud of what she's doing with the ranch," Theresa offered, wiping the cabinets down.

"Oh, yeah, they would. I still think we're going to see the Christmas Eve proposal from Henry," Chuck stretched forward in his chair to relieve pressure.

Theresa stopped wiping and spun around, "You just may be right. Henry is watching the kids so Charity and I can go dress shopping for the party. She will look beautiful. Don't you worry about that," Theresa schemed, "Henry won't stand a chance." She tossed the cleaning cloth into the sink.

Chuck sat up and chuckled, "You don't have to tip him over too hard. He's already hooked on her as it is. I'm going to get cleaned up. See you later. All the horses have been tended to for the day. They seem to mesh well together. Even Albert."

Henry arrived at the ranch right on time. He passed through the gate tapping on his steering wheel and humming. When he came in the front door, Amanda yelled, "Henry!" She jumped up and gave him a big hug. Peter wrapped around his leg.

"What's everyone doing?" Henry gasped from the pressure of the hug.

"Theresa and Charity are in the kitchen. It's almost time for dinner. Are we really going Christmas light-looking tonight, Henry?" Amanda asked.

"We sure are. Have you ever done that before?" Henry asked.

Both Amanda and Peter shook their heads no. "We haven't. Zach got carsick a lot. So, we couldn't just take rides unless they were absolutely necessary," Amanda stated sadly.

"Well, we'll have a great time!" Henry exclaimed. "Come on, let's go wash up and get ready to eat." Henry walked the children to the bathroom. They all washed their hands and wandered into the kitchen.

Charity set the plates at the table. Theresa served pork chops, macaroni and cheese, peas, and apple slices. Peas were one of the vegetables Amanda and Peter ate well.

"Okay, let's get seated. Are you hungry?" Charity asked.

Suddenly, Albert starts braying catching Henry off guard. "What is that?"

The kids giggled and Amanda explained, "That's Albert, the miniature donkey. He does that sometimes."

Charity and Theresa left partway through dinner so they could get the shopping done as early as possible. The first store had a good sale on dresses. Charity picked out a few and tried them on. Theresa just didn't think they looked quite right for the occasion. They went to the next store and Theresa found two dresses that looked promising. One was a burgundy dress that stopped just above the knees, and the other was dark blue dress a little past the knees. Charity tried on both dresses, and Theresa had a hard time deciding.

"Well, which one do you like better?" Theresa asked Charity.

"Blue is my favorite color, but I'm leaning toward the burgundy," Charity hesitated.

"I like the burgundy one, too," Theresa agreed. "How will you wear your hair?"

"I don't know. What would you suggest, up or down?"

"Probably up and wear a necklace and dangly earrings."

"Then, I'll do that. Does this store have jewelry? Let's just get everything while we're here," Charity stated, pleased with how the shopping trip turned out.

Charity purchased the dress, the jewelry, and a pair of dress shoes. Charity treated Theresa to a cup of hot chocolate as they drove home. "I wonder how Henry is doing light-looking with Amanda and Peter?" Charity asked curiously.

"I bet they're having a good time. Riding in a truck is always fun for children," Theresa reminisced about her own childhood.

Charity and Theresa arrived home before Henry and the children. They quickly cleaned the kitchen. Chuck joined them as they sat in the living room watching *Elf*. Henry, Amanda, and Peter quietly entered through the door. Peter had fallen asleep, and Henry carried him like a sack of potatoes over his shoulder.

"I'm going to bed, Charity. Henry, thanks for taking us out tonight," Amanda said thankfully.

"Do you need help?" Charity offered.

"No, I can do it," Amanda replied as she gave Charity a hug. "Good night, everybody."

"Good night," Theresa responded.

Charity followed Henry and Peter upstairs. Charity pulled back the covers as Henry put Peter on the bed. She took off Peter's shoes and helped cover him up. She turned on the bedside lamp and pulled the door almost closed. Charity and Henry sat on a step at the top of the stairs.

"Thank you for your help tonight. I don't know what I would've done without you. Did they do okay?" Charity inquired.

"Aw, they were great. They're good kids. Amanda is very polite and Peter...well, Peter loved the big colored lights. Though he didn't say anything, Amanda would tell me when he got excited," Henry explained.

"You *are* coming to the party on Christmas Eve, aren't you? I don't know if I can officially *not* have an escort," fretted Charity.

"Of course! I wouldn't miss a good Christmas Eve party. What time does it start?" queried Henry.

"It starts at six o'clock," Charity informed. "It won't be a late party…so the guests have time to do other Christmas things with their own families."

"I *will* be here," Henry whispered as he squeezed her hand. "I have to get going."

"Oh, what do you want for Christmas?" Charity posed seriously.

"I'll let you know when the time comes." His eyes looked at her lips. He wanted to reclaim them in a kiss as they had done weeks before. Reaching out, he lifted her chin then dropped a light kiss on her lips. Wanting more, he crushed his mouth to hers as she wrapped her arms around his neck. He could lose himself in her embrace. Realizing he needed to stop, he pulled back. "I'd better get going. See you later." He touched the side of her face then stood up to walk downstairs.

Charity walked him to the door and watched him leave.

Theresa and Chuck sat in the living room as the movie finished playing. "Everything okay?" Theresa summoned.

Hoping her face wouldn't betray the emotion from a few minutes before, she replied, "Yeah, Henry helped me put Peter to bed. He said he would be my escort for the party. The children were well behaved."

"They seemed to have a good time with him. He's a natural with children. You both are," Chuck concluded. "Well, this movie has been fun to watch, but I need to go on to bed. Good night, ladies."

"Good night," Charity responded.

"Good night," Theresa replied. "Charity, I need to be getting to bed as well. See you tomorrow."

"Good night, Theresa and thanks for going shopping with me," Charity said gratefully.

"Of course, any time… you will be lovely," Theresa touched Charity's cheek.

My Forever Christmas

CHAPTER 15

December 23rd began with the transformation of the garage into the party room. Penelope and her crew arrived at noon to begin working their Christmas magic. The garage was gigantic, so it easily held the tables needed for the evening. They assembled the wooden pieces, creating a beautiful dance floor covered with Christmas applique embedded beneath the deep lacquer finish. It was bordered with strands of frosted garland with a lit arch way of mistletoe at the center. Green strands of garland sprinkled with silver and gold were draped in breathtaking patterns. There were several tall, slender Christmas trees with white lights decorating the room. The workers connected a covered tent and walkway off the side of the garage for Santa Claus and the children's activities. This would minimize noise, letting the adults enjoy the evening. The tables and chairs had been arranged, each decorated with the silver-gray tablecloths and beautiful centerpieces. There were balls of mistletoe hung strategically throughout the garage. It promised to be a beautiful event. Speakers were wired to play the best Christmas classics.

Charity located Penelope and could only manage, "Oh, wow. This doesn't even look like a garage. You've made it stunning. Does it look this way every year?" Charity queried.

"Thank you. We try and mix it up a little from year to year. Some of the families do attend more than once. Our goal is for everyone to have a magical experience and forget…about things while here. Have you thought about what you want to say to the guests?" Penelope inquired.

"No, every time I think about it, I panic," Charity laughed nervously, following Penelope as she inspected the room.

"You're overthinking this. Just tell them you are glad they have attended the annual Silver Horseshoe Christmas Eve celebration. Tell them to enjoy the evening. Say thank you. That's it," Penelope coached. "Your Uncle Frank wouldn't want you to be worrying so much. He and Marion always let the guests know they mattered and were important." Penelope finished touching up the lopsided bow, "Just do that, and the night will be great."

"You're right. I can do this," Charity assured herself as she fixed a bow, as well.

"I will check in with you when we get here tomorrow around four o'clock. We will be ready to start the festivities by six o'clock," Penelope stated efficiently.

"See you tomorrow," bade Charity as she left Penelope to finish her work.

Charity, Amanda, and Peter skipped out for a bit of last-minute Christmas shopping. The stores were incredibly crowded. Charity held their hands so they wouldn't get separated in the store. They picked out gifts for Theresa and Chuck. They also pleaded to get a present for Henry. She looked for a gift for him as well, but nothing seemed exactly right. Hungry from their shopping, they decided to have a quick bite to eat. They cruised through the drive thru and ate in the jeep listening to Christmas carols. A memory from her first year working at the paper came to her mind. She had just purchased the clunkiest car she had ever seen…but it was hers and it got her to work. She had eaten more meals than she could count sitting in that car. Amanda's need to use the bathroom jolted her back to the present and they drove on home.

Back at the ranch, Charity helped them wrap the presents. There were already a few gifts under the tree with their names on them. When giving gifts to children in foster care, there are two important things to remember, she thought. First, if you have them at Christmastime, be sure you don't put Santa's name on gifts that are extremely expensive like iPads, computers, and other items a child's family would not be able to afford. They would not understand why Santa gave some children and not others expensive gifts. While it did not happen to her, she observed it happening to friends at school she knew were also in foster care. The second thing that is particularly important is to not give children gifts that overshadow what their parents could give them. They feel conflicted if they must worry about having nice things with foster parents and know their parents can't afford them. Charity picked out a few sensible things she knew they would like.

They finished wrapping the presents and arranged them under the tree. The presents overtook the tree, and it wasn't even Christmas morning yet. Some were piled in the corner and others stashed wherever they could find room. The lights reflected off the paper and the ribbon tempted Max. Several times Charity caught Max in a compromising situation with the ribbon in his teeth. Charity let Amanda and Peter watch a Christmas movie while she went to check in with Theresa.

"Hello!" Charity patted Theresa as she snatched a drink from the refrigerator and a sugar cookie from the cookie plate. "Shopping was crazy out there. We just finished wrapping presents."

"I wondered where you all got off to," Theresa grabbed a cookie as well.

"I wanted to get them out of the house and give you and Chuck some quiet time," Charity opened her drink and it let out a loud 'whoosh'.

"Wow, that's a fresh one! Honey, you don't have to worry. They aren't an intrusion. They've found their stride here with us," Theresa reassured. "Are you ready for the party tomorrow night?"

Charity drank deeply. "As ready as I will ever be. Part of me is so scared to upset the guests at the party." Charity reached for another cookie. "What did Uncle Frank say to them when he was the host?"

"Well, he would start by saying, 'Here we are celebrating another Christmas with our friends. The year may have had challenges, but we have worked hard and have the blessing of our families. Have a wonderful evening and Merry Christmas.' Or something to that effect," Theresa remembered grabbing a napkin and clearing her eyes.

"Wow, he spoke eloquent words. He really did care for all people, didn't he?" asked Charity.

"He did." Theresa poured herself a cup of coffee. "They both did." Both stared quietly at their drinks.

Clearing her throat, Charity asked, "So, what normally happens here on Christmas Eve? What should I do with the children until time to get ready for the party?"

"Well, you can't really look at lights in the daytime. Dollywood would be really crowded. Maybe you could take them to the aquarium in Gatlinburg. I would check the hours first, to make sure they were open," Theresa warned.

"That's a great idea. You're the best," Charity said as she hugged Theresa.

Charity went to the office and shut the door. She didn't want to have Amanda and Peter overhear what she was doing in case it fell through. Great, she confirmed the Aquarium would be open. They would need to leave by eight o'clock to get there when they opened.

****

Henry worked himself into a fit trying to select the perfect ring for Charity. Christmas Eve was the night he planned to ask her to marry him. Not wanting to take any chances, he went to Jared's Jewelry store in the Tanger Outlet Mall in Sevierville. He wanted to make sure the diamond was exactly the right size. The sales associate, Mary, patiently pulled out different rings for him to view. Henry's hair had become disheveled from running his hand through it after each rejection. After twenty minutes, Mary finally decided to ask him a few questions.

Mary was a tall, young woman with black hair. She was festively dressed in a Christmas sweater. She could see Henry's frustration. "Sir, I have a couple of questions that may make this a bit easier for you. First, do you want a diamond with a gold band or a silver one?"

"I don't know…I think gold would look better on her skin," Henry stuttered.

"Do you have a picture of her?" Mary inquired and Henry's face immediately registered terror.

"No! I don't have a picture of her. I never thought about a picture," Henry uttered gripping his hair again.

To put Henry at ease, Mary probed, "Okay, tell me about your girl. What is she like? I need character details, not physical ones."

Mission accomplished. Henry's face lit up when he voiced, "Well, she has the most generous nature of anyone I've ever met. She can be fiercely confident one minute and deathly afraid of making the wrong choices the next. Material things don't mean as much to her as personal relationships do."

Mary nodded her head as if she knew exactly what to choose. "How about this one?" Mary pulled out a one carat, heart-shaped diamond. It was classy and unfussy at the same time.

"Wow! That's perfect," Henry said excitedly. "I can't believe you did it!"

"I'm so glad you are pleased. Your girl is one lucky lady," Mary said admiringly. "How do you want this wrapped?"

"Oh, I have no idea. I'm proposing at a party tomorrow night. What do you suggest?" Henry solicited.

Mary smiled, "I know just the thing." She produced a ring box tied with a red ribbon. She placed the ring inside, tied the bow, and put the box in a small bag. Mary cashed Henry out and said, "Merry Christmas."

"Merry Christmas to you!" Henry yelled, as he waved back leaving the jewelry counter.

"Whew. Glad that's over," Henry thought. Tomorrow night seemed an eternity away. His level of anticipation was like that of a child waiting for Christmas morning and all the presents Santa brought. It would be nearly impossible for him to sleep tonight. When he got home, he put on *It's a Wonderful Life* and thought of his future with Charity. He couldn't wait to see what her reaction would be to his proposal. This time, he fell asleep in front of the tv.

****

Christmas Eve morning brought much excitement. The weather was perfect. It offered clear blue skies and a crisp, cold morning, but a warm afternoon. Charity woke up Amanda and Peter. After breakfast, they trekked to the aquarium. Neither Amanda nor Peter had ever been to one, so they had no idea what to expect. They arrived after a thirty-minute drive. They bought the tickets and went inside.

After going through the turnstiles, the first tank they encountered contained piranhas. They all faced the same direction. A monitor continuously played a video of facts relating to piranha fish. The fish appeared to stare at the monitor, having their mouths open like zombie fish. The next series of tanks were interesting, as well. The flat flounders shimmied back and forth burying themselves in the gritty sand. By contrast, the sea worms popped up through holes in the sand. There were sea dragons that looked like they were growing plants off their bodies.

A traveling sidewalk that moved under a large tank with the sharks and other sea life fascinated Peter. They viewed huge turtles, sting rays, and a sunken ship. While all the creatures were interesting, he pointed up to the shark that had the sawblade-like nose. Amanda enjoyed the jellyfish and the coconut crabs.

"What is it with sea creatures and food? Jellyfish aren't made of jelly. And these crabs are not coconuts," Amanda chattered as they walked behind the other viewers.

They ventured into the children's area where Amanda and Peter touched the horseshoe crabs. Charity was shocked they even tried it.

"Charity," Amanda pleaded. "Put your hand in here with us. They feel really weird."

Charity eased up to the pool and stuck her hand in and touched a horseshoe crab as it cruised past. "These do feel weird. Not what you would think they would feel like. Much smoother." Peter had moved to Charity's side and stroked the same crab.

They cleaned their hands and kept going to the refreshment area. This area contained the big window highlighting a diver show in progress. A diver in SCUBA gear was feeding the manta rays and sting rays. As the rays were swimming around from all directions, Peter moved closer to the glass. At first glance, he seemed to be watching the diver feed the rays like dogs begging for treats. Charity stepped in and observed Peter's gaze was fixed past the diver on a large fish tucked in a dug-out chest. She wondered what he thought so interesting about this fish. She put her hand on Peter's shoulder and he just looked up at her smiling. Before going further, they had a snack to hold them over until the party.

They continued further looking at the fish and finally came upon the penguin exhibit. The penguins were amusing to watch. They waddled all over the place but swam fast and straight like torpedoes. After the penguins, they worked their way up to the gift shop. Pachelbel's Cannon played repeatedly on the speakers. It was extremely loud. Charity let them select one souvenir. Amanda chose a sweatshirt. Peter selected a huge shark stuffed animal. They left for home so Charity would be on time to meet Penelope at four o'clock.

When they pulled up to the house, they saw Chuck tending to the horses before the night's activities. They walked around and addressed Chuck. Chuck saw Peter with the huge shark and asked him, "Did you have fun at the aquarium?"

Peter nodded his head lifting his stuffed shark. He eased up and gave Chuck a hug then ran off to the house. "We have to get through to that boy… somehow," Chuck cleared his throat, catching himself. "Amanda, what did you like best about the aquarium?"

"I liked the piranha fish that looked like they were watching tv. They even had their mouths open. It was funny. Charity took pictures," Amanda said with a giggle. "See you later."

"Bye," Chuck said as she dashed away. Charity stood there looking a little anxious. "Did you have a good time?" Chuck fanned his hat.

"Oh," Charity replied, coming back to the moment, "I always love an aquarium. They are better when they have dolphins and seals, though. The kids had a blast."

"Are you ready for tonight? Know what you want to say?" Chuck wondered.

"I think so. Theresa helped me figure that out last night. Good thing we have just a slight chance for snow tonight," Charity declared thankfully.

"What? You mean you don't like having a white Christmas?" Chuck posed in shock.

"No way. I was in New York once over Christmas covering a story. Though snow is pretty, I'm glad we don't get much of it here," Charity said flatly.

"Why on earth not?" Chuck summoned incredulously.

"Well, just because I was born under the water sign, doesn't mean I like water. I hate to get wet. I hate to be cold. But I especially hate to be wet *and* cold," Charity declared.

"Well, I'll be," Chuck was flabbergasted, "I would never have thought that about you."

"I need to check on the kids and explain to them what they need to do tonight. I hope they have a little bit of fun," Charity voiced optimistically. "Penelope will be here shortly."

Charity had the children dressed in their nice outfits for this evening. Luckily, Melanie and Jeff had taken formal pictures back in the summer and had purchased dressy clothes. She sat the children down at the bar with some crayons and coloring books. She needed to check in with Penelope before she dressed for the party.

Charity located Penelope directing the people in charge of serving the guests. Penelope was impeccably dressed in a purple, knee-length dress. She looked very business-like. Her hair was worn up in a loose bun, with thin ribbons of hair covering her ears. She wore flat dress shoes so she could move around quickly.

"This looks amazing! I am excited about tonight. Thank you very much for your hard work and that of your staff," Charity grabbed Penelope's hand.

"We are scheduled to start on time. Be ready to address the guests at five minutes after six. The microphone will be set up for you," Penelope said efficiently. Penelope certainly didn't waste words. Charity could hear people testing the sound system.

"Five after six. Got it," Charity repeated. "See you then."

Charity wandered back to the house. She went into her room and pulled out her dress. The top section of the dress was modest but showed her shoulders. The waist fit closely then flared just a little stopping right above the knees. She put on her earrings and necklace. She curled her hair and pulled it back and secured it with a burgundy clip. She only had on a little lipstick as she didn't wear much makeup. She slipped into her shoes, feeling a bit like Cinderella. Opening her door, she drifted to the kitchen and saw Henry standing there. He was not wearing flannel, but a dark blue suit, white shirt, and a crisp, red tie.

Henry had to keep himself from staring like those zombie fish piranhas. Stumbling for words, he uttered, "You look…beautiful. Ready for the party?" He walked over to her and turned, extending his elbow.

Amanda covered her mouth and let out a giggle thinking about those piranha fish and how Henry resembled one just then.

Henry realized she laughed and asked, "What?"

Charity glanced at Amanda then quickly replied, "It's nothing," as she took his arm. "You look handsome. I've never seen you in anything but flannel."

"Well, there was a dress code for this party, or I would have been in flannel," Henry raised his eyebrows twice. "What do we do now?"

"I think we just head on out to the garage and find a seat. I have to address the guests at five after six," Charity explained.

"Okay, let's head on out. Let's go guys," Henry said to Amanda and Peter.

They walked out together, but Henry walked holding Charity's hand. Theresa and Chuck joined Charity, Henry, and the children. Amanda and Peter had never attended an event like this one. They couldn't wait to see Santa Claus and do the children's activities. Charity had about ten minutes before addressing the guests. The room was filling up with families, some of them long-time friends of the Silver Horseshoe Ranch. The longer she watched them come in, the more nervous she became. The clamor of friendship grew by the moment.

It was obvious to Henry she was anxious. "Hey, you can do this," he soothed as he squeezed her hand. "Just relax…and enjoy the night. It's Christmas Eve. Some people believe it's the most magical night of the year."

"Whew," Charity exhaled fully, "I just need to hold on a few more minutes. Then I won't have to think of anything important the rest of the night," Charity uttered, trying to psych herself up.

Henry realized she didn't want to talk. They sat at the table watching the guests arrive and admiring the festive environment Penelope and her team had created. Henry made a mental note of the hanging mistletoe to use at just the right moment.

Noticing the time, Charity slipped over to the microphone, just a few minutes more. She stepped up to the mic and scanned the room. "Good evening." A hush grew over the crowd. She gained confidence from the warm smiles before her. "We are here to celebrate another Christmas with our friends. Though the year has had many challenges, we have worked hard and have the blessing of our families. Have a wonderful evening and Merry Christmas." The audience clapped as she stepped down and found her place at the table. Chuck and Theresa glowed proudly as she sat back down. Theresa patted Charity on the back.

"Your folks would have been so proud to hear you repeat those words," Chuck offered humbly. Theresa nodded in agreement, reaching for a napkin.

"You sounded great," Amanda praised.

"Yes, you were wonderful," Henry added proudly. Christmas music began playing in the background. "Feel better?"

"You wouldn't believe it. I was shaking in my shoes." Charity changed the subject, "I'm ready for some good food."

The servers were efficient. The meals were served effortlessly to each table. The clamor of joy rose as the guests talked with other families seated around them. Amanda and Peter scarfed their food. They wanted to visit the children's area, explore some activities, and see Santa. Folks made their way to the dance floor to enjoy the holiday music.

"Would you like to dance?" Henry stood extending his hand to Charity.

"You two go ahead. We'll stay and watch for the children," Theresa encouraged.

"Thank you, Theresa." Charity rose and turned toward Henry, her dress fanning out as she took his hand, "Of course, I would like to dance." As they walked to the dance floor, *The Christmas Song* began playing. "This is your favorite song!" Charity remembered.

"It is, and now I like it even more because I am dancing to it with you," Henry said softly, pulling her in close. "Have you ever decided what your favorite song is? *The Train* is not a song…it's a story," he reminded her.

As they moved to the music, Charity thought for a moment then said, "I think *Tennessee Christmas* is my new favorite Christmas song. I finally have a concept of a home and people who care for me. I no longer feel like the woman alone on the train."

Henry planned to wait a little longer in the evening to ask her his question, but *this* particular moment seemed the right time. "You're not alone anymore, Charity." He moved her to the side of the room and continued, "I was going to wait a little later before asking, but will you marry me?" Henry pulled the ring box out of his pocket. "I have loved you since the day I met you. I can't imagine being without you." He opened the box and looked to her eyes for an answer.

Meeting his gaze, Charity exclaimed, "Oh, Henry. It's beautiful." Tears streamed down her face. "Yes…I'll marry you! I love you."

He slipped the ring on her finger. "Why are you crying?"

"You don't understand. For the last eight years, I've been alone. Now, I have my forever Christmas, and I can't believe it," Charity spoke through her tears, turning to locate a napkin. Henry handed her his handkerchief.

"Forever Christmas?" Henry asked trying to understand what she meant.

"You know, when a child gets adopted, it's said they found their forever home. Well, this is my forever Christmas," Charity dabbed her eyes and sniffled quietly. "But what about Amanda and Peter? I can't just abandon them."

"We won't abandon them. Let's petition the court and have them stay with us. We can all be a family." Henry took Charity by the shoulders, pivoting her into a chair and then sat face to face with her, his hands holding hers. "Do you remember one of the questions you asked me at the Anderson's party? You know, the one about what would make me decide to walk away and leave my job? I said that situation hasn't happened yet?"

"Yes, I remember," Charity nodded not following his thought.

"I want to leave my work at DCS and join you in what you're doing here...with the children, Aspiration Station, and the equine therapy. We're a good team. And we can make a difference for these children. Not just Amanda and Peter, but all the children. I love you, every part of you." Touching the side of her face and drawing her to him, Henry kissed Charity with the passion of a thirsty man longing for a drink of water.

Returning his kiss, Charity put her arms around Henry and hugged him tightly. She felt dizzy from the overload of emotion. Henry took Charity outside for a little fresh air. They walked from the garage to the front porch. They climbed the steps and sat in the swing. They sat in silence, just holding hands. Henry noticed Charity shivering and took off his jacket.

"Here, put this on, you're freezing," Henry offered.

Slipping her arms into his jacket, she wrapped herself up to get warm, "Thank you, this is much better." She looked at the ring on her finger and asked, "How long have you been planning this?"

"Oh, I had an inkling the weekend Brian and I came out to help you with Amanda and Peter. But Thanksgiving weekend let me know I couldn't let you get away. These last few weeks have been torture," Henry confessed. "I'm so glad I almost knocked you down in the lobby. It was the best accident to ever happen to me." Henry put his arms around Charity as she leaned against his chest.

"Well, truth be told, I am glad you almost knocked me down, too. I think you shook loose a few bricks in the walls I had up for so long. I can't imagine you not being in my life," Charity expressed, turning to kiss Henry on the lips. He met her kiss, pulling her closer to him. When they parted, they sat there enjoying the creaky swing.

At seven-thirty, or so, the guests started leaving. Chuck and Theresa had taken Amanda and Peter back inside and prepared them for bed. Charity checked in with Penelope one last time. "Thank you for a wonderful evening. I know Uncle Frank would have been happy with the way it progressed."

"Yes, he would. And he would have been proud hearing the words you said this evening. You sounded just like him," Penelope reminisced and paused. "We usually get the garage put back to normal the day after Christmas, which will be on Saturday."

"Thank you very much. Have a good evening and Merry Christmas," Charity squeezed Penelope's shoulders.

"Merry Christmas," Penelope turned away, carrying a trash bag.

The party area was empty and quiet. Except for the audience of disheveled chairs, or the odd piece of paper, no one would know a great party had occurred. Inside, Charity and Henry were tucking Amanda and Peter into bed. Charity was sitting with Amanda when she noticed the engagement ring. "What's this?" Amanda placed her thumb and forefinger around the ring.

"Henry asked me to marry him tonight. I said yes," Charity pulled the covers across Amanda's body.

"Does that mean you don't want us anymore?" Amanda recoiled.

"Why would you even think that?" Charity moved closer to Amanda, her pitch rising.

"I don't know. I guess I'm just afraid of losing the feeling I have now. Like I belong somewhere," Amanda explained, beginning to tear up and glancing away toward the window.

Charity paused and fixed on Amanda's face, waiting for a return gaze. "Tell you what, Henry and I want you and Peter to stay here with us at the ranch. We can all be a family, but we must get the court's permission first. Would you like that?" Charity waited for Amanda's gaze.

Amanda bolted up, covers flying back off and piling up against Charity. "Really, we can stay here with you forever?" Amanda announced loudly, causing Peter to run in with Henry tailing behind. "Peter, did you hear that? They want us to stay here with them forever!"

"Forever?" Peter finally spoke out loud.

"Peter!" Charity exclaimed as she scooped him up and hugged him hard.

Henry gaped in surprise. "Charity is right. We're going to ask the court to let us be your family," Henry hugged Amanda and Peter tightly. "Looks like you two get your forever Christmas, too."

"Thank you! I love you guys," Amanda proclaimed to Charity and Henry.

"Me, too!" echoed Peter.

"We love you, too. Now off to bed or Santa won't be able to leave any presents…if he can find room under the tree," Charity teased them. Henry took Peter back to his room and Charity finished tucking Amanda in bed.

Charity and Henry went downstairs and were met by Theresa and Chuck. They couldn't help but notice the hand holding and the sparkles coming off Charity's hand.

"Yep, he did it alright," Chuck mused with a grin.

"What's he talking about?" Henry asked a little confused.

Theresa had to stifle a giggle herself, "We had a feeling the night would end with a proposal. You two are perfectly made for each other. Just took you a while to see that."

"I gotta go," Henry stated. "I'll be over bright and early to open presents with everyone. Good night."

Charity walked Henry to his truck. Cupping Charity's face in his warm hands, Henry kissed her with a lingering kiss. He knew he'd go crazy if he stayed any longer. She watched him leave. She glanced upward into the starlit, ever expanding sky. Her heart felt as if the joy inside it could fill that chasm. Back inside she placed presents under the tree for Chuck, Theresa, Amanda, Peter, and Henry. She hung up the stockings…even one for Max. Her heart was filled with happiness as she touched all the picture ornaments and saw the smiling faces.

She moved to her bedroom and Max followed her in. She dressed for bed. She tucked herself in listening to her Christmas playlist. As she lay there, she just stared at the ring on her finger. Never in her wildest dreams did she expect to meet someone like Henry or inherit a horse ranch, for that matter. She quietly sang a few of the songs on her list and fell asleep the happiest and most content she had ever been in her life.

****

Christmas morning brought a surprise light dusting of snow. As is typical with children, Amanda and Peter awoke incredibly early on Christmas morning. Charity asked them to wait until at least seven o'clock before getting Chuck and Theresa up. Besides, they had to wait for Henry.

Henry, also a bit childlike, bounced exuberantly and festively through the door at seven o'clock. "Merry Christmas, everybody!"

Breakfast would wait until *after* the presents. Charity had everyone sit around the tree while Amanda handed out the gifts. Each of them had a pile of presents. Charity snapped a few pictures… even Max had a blast photo bombing. They put on the movie *A Christmas Story* and rifled through their gifts.

Henry stole Charity away for a few minutes, taking her to the kitchen. "I've been thinking…what do you say we get married on New Year's Eve? That way, when we go back to court on January 4th, we can show we have a plan to permanently take care of the children."

"How wonderful! We can have the wedding here at the ranch. We can invite your family, the gang from the paper and your DCS coworkers," Charity counted on her fingers. "Oh, that means we have lots to do."

"Yes, we do. But it can wait…until tomorrow. One thing at a time. Let's enjoy Christmas today with Chuck, Theresa and the kids." They walked back into the living room and spent the day enjoying themselves together…as a family.

CHAPTER 16

Christmas Day had been one of the best days Charity ever experienced. Now able to focus on the upcoming event, Charity asked Theresa about having the wedding at the ranch. Theresa teemed with excitement bubbling up all over.

"Oh, Charity, this will be sensational! We should just tell Penelope to leave the garage as it is and use it for the ceremony. I will give her a call before she sends the clean-up team. First, you need to decide who will be your maid or matron of honor. You have a few people you can choose from. You have Julie and Rachel. What were you thinking?" Theresa wondered.

"Julie is on a job that started this morning. It's a hush, hush kind of thing and she won't be able to get free." Charity poured a cup of coffee for Theresa and handed her a gingerbread woman. "Actually, I hoped you would be my maid of honor." Theresa looked up from sipping. "You have become like a mother to me since I arrived here at the ranch. I prefer to have you fill that role…if you want to, that is."

Theresa was left speechless which didn't happen very often. Sitting her cup on the counter, nearly spilling at the edge, she stated, "I would be proud to be your maid of honor. I'm guessing Amanda will be the flower girl and Peter the ring bearer? Are you going to ask Chuck to give you away?"

"You are good…" Charity replied with a grin.

She wandered off to find Chuck. He was out back looking at the horses. It had been a peaceful transition adding Charlie, Bear, Silver, and Albert, from the Bit and Bridle organization. Except for the additional horses to feed, there wasn't much of an intrusion from Beth and David. They came out a few times a week to make sure their horses were okay and clean out the stalls. Chuck saw Charity coming up to him and greeted, "Hello, Charity. Beautiful morning, don't you think?"

"Hello, Chuck. It certainly is. I have something I need to talk with you about. Since I don't have a father to walk me down the aisle, will you please consider standing with me?"

Chuck paused a moment, then spoke, "I think your Uncle Frank would approve. Yes," he turned and faced her, "I would be honored to stand in as your father. I've come to love you as if you were my own daughter. I believe you and Henry will create a great partnership. Now go on, you have things to do for your big day," Chuck encouraged as he gave Charity a side hug, hiding the tear in his eye. "I'll see you later."

Charity knew Henry was having the same talk with his parents from his house. Henry was on speaker with his mom and dad, "Charity and I are getting married on New Year's Eve at the ranch. Can you make it? Dad, will you be my best man?"

"Of course, Henry," Mike said proudly. "Sounds like old Ben Franklin talked you into this after all, huh?"

"You know he didn't have to push me too hard. It will be a small ceremony. Just you, Mom, and Brian. You know Jake and Patricia are doing their yearly mission trip and can't make it. Carla is hip deep at Children's Hospital this time of year. They are regretful they cannot attend. I told them I understood. I certainly didn't know I would be getting married so soon. Charity is also asking the gang at the paper to come and get this, my DCS coworkers," Henry mused fondly.

"Well, I know it will be a beautiful ceremony," expressed Deborah. "Just let us know what time. And oh, Henry, the name of the perfume you were asking about is Love Spell."

"Wow! They sure named that right," Henry mused. "You are just going to love her, Mom."

"I can tell since you seem to hold her in such high regard," Deborah replied.

"Oh, I need to get going. We have some planning to do," Henry said as he ended the call.

****

The next few days were busy getting the wedding details planned. They contacted Penelope and advised she leave the garage intact. She would just need to remove most of the tables and the arch way, and then set up the altar.

Charity's friends at the paper were thrilled to be invited to the wedding and said they would be present on the big day. Buzz promised to give them the biggest write up the county had ever seen.

Likewise, over doughnuts, Henry had a quick meeting informing Erica and the staff that he would be leaving his job at DCS to work with Charity, Chuck, and the Bit and Bridle folks to help children with disabilities through equine therapy. Erica, Alex, and Randi said they were happy to attend the wedding.

"I think that's a great way to amplify your love for the children we care for in foster care," affirmed Erica. "You two will do many good things together." Remembering she had a letter for Henry, Erica said, "This came to the office for Charity. Can you give it to her? It may clear up some of the things she has been carrying around with her all this time."

Henry looked at the envelope and saw Jennifer Ryan's name in the return address. "Yeah, I will be sure to give this to her. Thanks."

Charity, Theresa, and Amanda went shopping for wedding attire. Chuck took Peter with him and shopped, as well. Charity needed a dress and Amanda needed just the right dress to be the flower girl. Theresa knew exactly where to shop. Keeping with Charity's no muss, no fuss personality, Theresa helped her find the perfect one. It was breathtaking. It showed her bare shoulders, tapered slightly at the waist, and went out with a flare to the floor. It was very lac+

y, without sequins. She would be a beautiful bride. Theresa picked out a dress appropriate for the maid of honor. Amanda picked out an adorable dress perfect for being a flower girl. Chuck had Peter fitted for the cutest tuxedo a little boy of five could wear, but Peter insisted on cowboy boots. Chuck already had a tuxedo and didn't need to purchase anything for himself.

My Forever Christmas

****

On December 30th, Charity and Henry had a family dinner with his parents, Brian, Amanda, Peter, Chuck, and Theresa. It was a pleasant afternoon. As they finalized the wedding plans in the formal dining room, Brian, Amanda, and Peter watched a movie.

"We are going to have the ceremony in the garage," Charity began. "It made sense to keep the decorations from the party and just change them a little bit. The ceremony will be at noon. Chuck and Theresa have offered to take care of the children for the weekend. We will be back on Sunday afternoon. We have to get ready for court on Monday."

"This is so exciting," Deborah placed her hand on Henry's. "You will have an instant family. But why don't we stay here and help with the children, too?"

Theresa looked to Chuck, who nodded in agreement, "That is a marvelous idea. We have three extra rooms upstairs and you could stay here after the ceremony."

"Wow, Mom! That would be great. That way you could get to know them better. It's a big change, but Charity and I feel we can make this work for all of us." Henry now reached for Charity's hand.

"I'm so excited that the four of us get to have our forever homes together," Charity spoke, fighting back tears.

Mike and Deborah understood exactly what Charity meant. Brian was incredibly young when they gave him his forever home. "We know you all will be a wonderful family. They seem to be so attached to you already," Mike declared.

"We forgot to tell you, Peter has begun to say some things," Charity boomed with excitement. "He's still shy but doing much better."

Chuck finally spoke up and said, "Henry, I just want you to know that in place of Charity's Uncle Frank, you have my blessing to become a part of this family. Charity is incredibly lucky to have a man like you and I know you both will do many wonderful things together."

"I'm also thrilled about this wedding. You two keep things interesting and worthwhile around here, not that Frank didn't do good things. You're just doing things your own way and that's wonderful," Theresa confessed tearfully.

They sat there together until about eight-thirty. Charity put the children to bed. Henry walked his parents and Brian out to their car. They went back to Henry's house while Henry stayed a little while longer with Charity.

Sitting in the living room on the couch, Henry took Charity's hand, lacing his fingers with hers, "Charity, I'm ready to begin my life with you tomorrow. I know it will be a big change, having a full house all the time. I know we can do this."

Leaning her head on his shoulders, Charity confessed, "I'm not worried…can you believe that? I'm ready to begin my life with you, too. Where are we going after the ceremony?"

"Biltmore…It's a beautiful drive and not too far away. It is a lovely house to tour, especially around the holidays, and there are some other things we can see while over there," Henry said as he lifted Charity's hand and kissed it. "Oh, before I forget again, I have a letter here for you. It came to the DCS office and Erica asked me to be sure you got it."

Taking the letter from Henry, Charity read Jennifer Ryan's name on the envelope. "Huh, this is from my last case worker when I aged-out. Wonder what this is?" Charity opened the letter and read:

Dear Charity,

I caught wind of your incredible story from a news outlet all the way out here in Texas. It is great that you finally have a place to call home. I know that meant a great deal to you. I am so proud of all you have accomplished with your career as a journalist. You did it. What's more, I am thrilled at the opportunities you have before you. I know you will continue to be a tremendous force for good and an advocate for children in care. There is one more thing you need to know…as your worker I was not able to show it, but I loved you as if you were one of my own children. You are one of the bravest people I have ever known.

Sincerely,
Jennifer Ryan

Charity sat there with a lump in her throat and tears in her eyes. All that time she thought no one cared. Realizing she saw things through her built-up walls, she missed the fact that Jennifer did have the same kind of feeling for the children in her care that she had observed with Henry. Finding the courage to speak, she said, "Wow, I had no idea she felt that way. Now I feel terrible for all the pent-up bitter feelings I have had for so long."

Seeing her at this moment, finally realizing people did care for her, Henry hugged her to him and said, "You are an incredible person. You always have been. DCS workers must be incredibly careful in how they show affection to the children they care for. We must look out for their best interests as well as be tough on their parents when necessary. We sometimes must put up walls ourselves so we can be objective. It is quite easy to become too attached to a child and become ineffective. I hope now you have some closure."

"For the first time in eight years, I think I do," Charity expressed peacefully.

Henry kissed her on the forehead and said, "I gotta go. I love you. See you tomorrow."

"I love you, too," Charity replied.

****

Thursday morning dawned a marvelous day. Frost sparkled like fields of diamonds across the pasture. The weather was a little cooler than expected, so it was a good thing the wedding was indoors. Everyone lounged around until about ten o'clock. Theresa made a light breakfast, and everyone pitched in to get the kitchen cleaned up. Theresa made several plates of finger foods to have after the ceremony and the fridge was stocked with drinks of all kinds. The rooms upstairs were ready for the Thompson's stay over the weekend.

The guests began arriving around eleven-thirty. Theresa found Charity trying to get Peter dressed and offered, "Here, honey, let me take care of Peter. You take Amanda with you."

"Thank you, I'm finding myself all thumbs today. I'm more nervous than I realized," Charity confessed. This was yet another major change in her life in a short time. "I'll get Amanda. You'll have to tell me when to come out."

"I've got you covered," Theresa reassured Charity.

"Amanda, it's time to get your dress on. Grab it from your closet and come to my bedroom," Charity directed Amanda.

"Okay, be right down," Amanda responded from another room.

In her room, Charity pulled her dress out of the closet. She stood there and just looked at it. Today, she would start another new chapter in her life as Mrs. Henry Thompson. She and Henry would become one. All decisions they made would be done together. They were joining two lives and families and would hopefully soon be adding Amanda and Peter.

Amanda knocked on the door and entered to change into her dress. Standing behind her looking into the mirror, Charity helped Amanda put a hairband of flowers on her head. They stood there smiling together as they decided Amanda looked great. Charity then went into her bathroom and put on her dress. Amanda had to help zip up the back.

"Oh, Charity, you look so beautiful," Amanda expressed lovingly.

"Thank you. I'm so nervous," Charity replied. "How should I wear my hair? Up or down?"

"Definitely up," Amanda said excitedly. "Men like it up."

"Where did you learn that?" Charity asked in astonishment.

"Television. It's my life," Amanda declared.

"Really? Can you see the guests outside yet?" Charity changed the subject.

"Oh, yeah. I can see Henry and his family. I think Henry's DCS friends are here, too," Amanda reported. "They're going to the garage."

"Please go out and see if Theresa can come here for just a minute," asked Charity.

"Sure thing. Be right back," Amanda spun to the door, making her dress fan out.

Theresa came back a few minutes later and knocked on the door, "Charity, are you okay?" Theresa opened the door and entered the room.

"Yes, I'm fine. I just need a second set of eyes to make sure I look okay with the dress and hair and all," Charity explained.

"Oh, Charity, you look beautiful. I think all the guests have arrived now. The violinist is here to play the music. Minister Randolph is standing with Henry. Did you write your own vows?" wondered Theresa.

"We did. I hope it will be a good fit for us," Charity explained.

"Let me go see when Chuck will come to get you and walk down the aisle," Theresa said as she dashed out of the room.

Charity sat there for a few minutes lost in thought. She was disappointed Julie couldn't make it to the ceremony. She was glad that Rachel could be there. Her mind went to her uncle and aunt as she looked at their pictures on the bed side tables. She wished she could have known them while they were living. Would they be proud of her? A knock at the door jarred Charity back to the moment.

"Charity, it's time for the ceremony to begin. Are you ready?" Chuck asked through the door.

Charity opened the door and smiled at Chuck. "I'm ready."

"You are breathtaking," Chuck said as he kissed Charity on the forehead. He offered her his arm, "Let's not keep Henry waiting."

Minister Randolph had Henry take his place with him at the altar. Mike stood beside his son, swelling up with pride. Henry felt a surge of adrenaline.

Amanda and Peter were positioned a few steps back from the starting point of the aisle. The word was given, and the music began. Amanda started down the aisle, dropping flower petals from a basket. Once she was halfway down the aisle, Peter began his way down. Amanda stood on one side of the altar and Peter moved to stand beside Henry. Next, Theresa walked slowly down the aisle and stood beside Amanda.

The violinist began playing the bridal march. Everyone stood and turned to watch as Chuck slowly escorted Charity to her place at the altar with Henry. They made it to the end of the aisle and the music stopped. Minister Randolph began to speak.

"Dearly beloved. We are gathered here today to join this man and this woman in marriage. Who gives this woman to be married?" Minister Randolph posed.

"On behalf of her uncle and aunt, we do," Chuck replied emotionally. Chuck kissed Charity on the cheek and moved her to stand beside Henry. Amanda, Peter, Theresa, Chuck, and Mike all took their seats.

"It is always a blessing when two people are joined in marriage having the same purpose in life. It is just this way with Henry and Charity. Are you ready to recite your vows?" Minister Randolph prompted.

"We are," Charity and Henry replied in unison. Both turned toward each other, smiled, and joined hands.

Henry began first, "Charity Walters, I have loved you since the day I met you. I promise to love you with an unfailing love. Whether we have good times or hard times, I promise to work things through with you and not give up or quit. You help me be a better person and I will strive to be the husband you need and deserve all the days of my life," Henry squeezed Charity's hand.

Breathing in, Charity began, "Henry Thompson, it took me a little while to realize I was someone you wanted to love. I had been alone without family for so long that it was difficult for me to see. But now I do. And here we are," she paused to catch her breath. "I promise to love you with an unfailing love, through the good times and hard times. I promise to work things through with you and not give up or quit. I will strive to be the wife you need and deserve all the days of my life," Charity exhaled into a broad smile.

"Do you have the rings?" asked Minister Randolph. Henry handed him their rings.

The minister offered the ring for Charity to Henry first and said, "With this ring, I thee wed."

"With this ring, I thee wed," Henry repeated as he slipped the ring on Charity's finger. Then she took the ring from the minister and said…

"With this ring, I thee wed."

"Is there anyone here who believes this man and woman should not be joined in marriage?" The minister scanned the crowd smiling. "Speak now or forever hold your peace."

Albert started braying. The minister quickly added, "Not sure if that is an affirmation or something else." After some giggling and a brief pause, the minister said, "By the power invested in me by our Lord and the state of Tennessee, I now pronounce you husband and wife. You may kiss the bride."

Henry gave Charity a lingering kiss as the minister said, "I present to you, Mr. and Mrs. Henry Thompson."

Henry and Charity walked back up the aisle as the violinist began to play again. A photographer was there to take a few pictures of the bride and groom. Then pictures of the families. The guests headed to the house to enjoy the finger foods and company.

Henry, Charity, Amanda, and Peter changed out of their wedding clothes and joined the guests. Charity was met by her friends from the paper.

"That was a beautiful ceremony, kid," Rachel hugged her hard.

"You were a beautiful bride," declared Buzz as he kissed Charity on the cheek.

"Thank you so much for being here today. I wouldn't dream of not sharing this with you. You have been my family for the last several years,"

Charity began tearfully. She gave each of them a hug...Rachel, Marcus, and Mr. Cooper.

"Henry," Marcus extended his hand to Henry, "take good care of this girl."

"Don't worry, I plan to," Henry shook Marcus' hand.

Henry and Charity made their way to see Henry's family. Mike shook Henry's hand and gave him a hug. He also hugged Charity and gave her a kiss on the cheek.

"You looked absolutely beautiful out there, daughter," Mike complimented.

"Thank you," blushed Charity.

"Welcome to the family," Deborah exclaimed, hugging Charity tightly. "Henry, we are so proud of you."

"Thanks, Mom. We are excited to take on the world," Henry beamed. "Please don't forget to get some food. We need to check on the children."

They walked around until they found Amanda and Peter. They were in the living room with Brian playing a card game. Brian stood up and gave Charity a hug and then gave one to Henry.

"Congratulations, guys. I know you'll be happy. You both think about the same stuff all the time," Brian complimented awkwardly.

"Thanks, Brian, I think," Henry replied.

Charity stooped down to talk to Amanda and Peter. "You guys did a great job in the wedding. I'm so proud of you," she said earnestly as she hugged them both.

"It was cool," Amanda replied with a big smile. "Throwing flowers around is fun, but messy."

Peter hugged Charity and then Henry.

"We'll let you get back to your card game. See you later," Charity remarked.

Splitting up, Charity and Henry circulated among the guests. The team from DCS waved at Henry.

"Thanks so much for coming today. It really meant a lot to me," Henry voiced sincerely.

Erica was the first to speak, "I know we'll miss you at the office, but you have an even bigger mission here with Charity. I can't believe all the things she has going on right now."

"Yeah," Alex interrupted, "just knowing that there could be vehicles for aging out youth is tremendous."

"And don't forget the equine therapy," Randi reminded, sipping a drink.

"Nevertheless, you both will be incredibly busy doing wonderful work for children," Erica concluded. "Where is Charity? We want to say something to her."

Scanning the area, Henry quickly said, "Um, I'm not sure where she went. Hang on a minute."

After looking all over, Henry found Charity sitting on the bed in her room. "Here you are. What are you doing in here?" Henry sat beside her.

"Oh, I just needed a minute to compose myself. This has been quite a day, Mr. Thompson," Charity expressed, leaning her head on Henry's shoulder.

"Indeed, it has, Mrs. Thompson. And it's not over yet," Henry replied pulling her across his lap. He held her tenderly saying, "Erica and the gang want to speak to you before they leave. Come out for a minute?"

"Of course," Charity said as they wandered out to engage Erica, Alex, and Randi.

Charity greeted Erica, "Thank you very much for sharing this day with us. And thank you for passing on the letter from Jennifer Ryan. It gave me a sense of closure."

Erica grabbed Charity's hand, "We're delighted you included us. Not only today, but in all the things you have done for children in care. I'm thrilled you were able to find healing from that time in your life. You have so much to be proud of."

Alex chimed in, addressing both Henry and Charity, "Now, don't be strangers at the office. We expect regular updates. It is remarkable, Charity, you have such a big heart."

"Take care of this girl, Henry," Alex charged. "She's one of a kind."

"Don't worry, I will. You guys take care and thanks for everything," Henry replied.

After the last guest retreated, Charity found Chuck and Theresa. "I just wanted to thank you both for making this a truly unforgettable day for me," Charity stifled tears. "I'm so thankful you stepped in for me and I didn't have to do this alone."

"We're so grateful to have shared this day with you," Chuck declared. "We know your folks would be so happy. Oh, forgot to tell you. Henry's debit card to the ranch estate should be here when you get back. He's one of us now."

Meanwhile, Henry walked in the kitchen followed by his parents.

"Don't you two need to be heading off to Biltmore? The children will be fine. We don't want to hear a peep from you until you get back home on Sunday," Deborah dictated.

"Are you sure you don't want any help cleaning up?" Charity asked, not wanting to leave things a mess.

"Heaven's no. Penelope will have this stuff picked up the day after tomorrow. Besides, Mike and Deborah are here to help. You two take off," Theresa ordered.

"Thank you very much," Henry said as he hugged Theresa. He turned to face his mom and dad. "Thank you so much for stepping in and helping with the children. Just ask Amanda any questions about their routine."

Mike stepped in and prodded, "Will you go on? We know a bit about tending to children. Besides, Chuck and Theresa can bail us out of any trouble we get into."

Deborah gave both Henry and Charity a tight squeeze. "Don't worry about a thing."

Henry and Charity said good-bye to the kids. They explained that Chuck, Theresa, and Henry's parents would take care of them for the weekend.

It was two-thirty when they left for Biltmore Estate. "I can't believe we're getting away alone," Charity spoke excitedly sporting her sunglasses. "Have you been to this place before?"

"No, but I hear it's a very romantic place to visit and beautiful this time of year," Henry replied honestly. He queued up some driving music and they were at Biltmore ninety minutes later.

They checked into the hotel and Henry posed, "Want to get something to eat? It'll be dark soon so the gardens will have to wait. Our guided tour of the house starts at seven o'clock."

"I hardly ate anything earlier due to nerves. Now I feel like I could eat a horse," Charity could hear her stomach gurgle.

Not having to rush, they ate a nice dinner in one of the onsite restaurants.

The lighting was dimmed, and a quartet played instrumental Christmas carols. Having about an hour before the tour started, they checked out a few shops while making their way to the front door. They found little souvenirs for everyone. Luckily, Charity was carrying her larger handbag.

It took three hours to walk through the first two floors. The tour was wall-to-wall people and moved very slowly. They would finish the rest of the house tomorrow. Needing some fresh air, they walked around until ten-thirty, looking in the closed shop windows and at the holiday decorations.

When they returned to their room, Charity pulled all the bags from her purse and set them on the table near the window. Henry beckoned Charity to sit down with him for a few minutes. As she moved to sit beside him, he pulled her gently into his lap, putting his arms around her. She relaxed and leaned back against him, his arms still around her.

"What did you think of the estate?" Henry wondered.

Charity didn't know where to begin, "There were many fascinating aspects of a house that large. I think I liked the bowling alley in the basement. Imagine having that game in your house to play anytime you wanted to."

"That was amazing. I thought the deliberate decorations in the rooms were remarkable. The individual wall papers, carpets, and drapes made the rooms inviting."

"Can you imagine getting lost in a house that big? Or having to clean it?" Charity queried.

"Sit here for a few minutes, I have a surprise for you." Henry knew Charity loved to take bubble baths, so he ran a tub full of bubbles and lit some candles. Not ready to give up Christmas, he queued up instrumental carols for her while she soaked in the tub. Thanks to his mother's detective work, he left a set of Love Spell lotion and perfume for her in the bathroom.

Henry had Charity stand up, covered her eyes, and led her to the bathroom. He removed his hands from her eyes, and she exclaimed, "Oh, Henry! This is wonderful. I won't be long. And I just might have a surprise for you, too."

Henry sat on the couch and checked his phone for any messages about the children. Naturally, there weren't any. His parents, Chuck, and Theresa would never bother them even if a problem arose. He changed into his pajamas-a sleeveless top and bottoms and was again seated on the couch when Charity came out of the bathroom. That wonderful, familiar aroma filled his senses. Just when he felt he had his thoughts under control, that she couldn't seem any more beautiful, he was yet again surprised. To keep her hair from getting wet, she put it up in the messy bun and she was wearing an emerald-green, mid-thigh length gown with a robe that had slipped a little off her shoulder. She had the lotion in her hand and a puzzled look on her face.

"I didn't pack mine so how did this get here?" Charity queried. "I didn't know if you had any fragrance allergies, so I brought my unscented lotion."

"Well, that's a story...all the time we have spent together, that scent has become seared into my being. When I smell it, all I can think about is you. When my mom told me that it was called Love Spell, I knew I never had a chance," Henry confessed walking over to her, wrapping his arms around her lifting her up and spinning her around. She almost dropped the lotion.

Charity didn't realize it affected him so. "I'm so sorry if I caused you any discomfort," she smirked as he put her down. She walked to the chest, putting the lotion down, "It's one of the only things I can wear that doesn't affect my allergies. Which I don't understand since it's made from peach and cherry blossoms."

The lights were off except for a strategically placed candle illuminating the room. The 'Do Not Disturb' sign was on their door. Since it was New Year's Eve, the hotel was alight with excitement. Henry and Charity weren't drinkers, but the hotel left them a small bottle of champagne for the holiday. Henry poured them both a glass and they sat on the couch waiting for midnight. Charity leaned against Henry and he had his arm around her, playing with the back of her neck. They flipped through the channels and found the rest of a Christmas movie and watched it as they counted down to the new year.

When the movie ended a few minutes before midnight, Charity got up to peek through the curtains to view the lights below. They left the tv on one of the channels that showed the ball drop from New York City. Though Dick Clark didn't do the specials anymore, they were waiting to see the change to the new year.

"Did you ever watch the Dick Clark specials growing up?" Henry asked Charity as he sipped from the glass, watching her from across the room.

"No, I don't think I even know who you're talking about," Charity said honestly. Turning toward him, she asked, "Wait...was he the American

Bandstand guy?"

"That's him, alright. Come closer," Henry beckoned with his finger. "It's almost midnight. I need a girl to kiss when the clock strikes twelve," Henry joked.

Charity sat her drink down then eased herself onto Henry's lap like a child telling Santa what she wanted for Christmas. Knowing where this could lead, she casually asked, "So, you want to kiss just any girl for New Year's?"

"No, not any girl…just Mrs. Thompson," Henry replied kissing her on the nose. Seeing the ball about to drop on the tv, he counted down the last ten seconds to the new year. "Ten, nine, eight, seven, six, five, four, three, two, one!" He turned toward her, taking her face in his hands and gently pressed his lips to hers. She wrapped her arms around his neck and returned the kiss, fully giving in to their passion. When their lips parted, catching his breath he said, "Happy New Year, Charity."

"Happy New Year, Henry," she whispered. Henry scooped her up and carried her to bed.

Henry was the first to wake up. Still asleep, Charity was curled up against his body. Not wanting to move, he stayed there enjoying the feeling of her next to him. She looked so peaceful as she slept. His heart had never been as full of love and happiness as it was at that moment. Getting up to plan the rest of their day, he let her sleep a while longer. They still had lots of Biltmore to see as well as planning for court on Monday.

****

Monday morning arrived and Henry, Charity, Amanda, and Peter were sitting in Room Three. Barbara Frederickson met them and asked how things were progressing. Charity explained that she and Henry had gotten married and planned to petition the court to adopt Amanda and Peter.

"That is a marvelous plan. I will present this to the judge momentarily. Just remember, they must be with you the full six months, first," Barbara said emphatically.

"All rise for the judge," the clerk announced.

Everyone stood up as Judge Grimsby made his way slowly to his seat. "Be seated," he said flatly. "Good morning, everyone. We are here to discuss the permanency options for Amanda and Peter Ferguson. Is there any news to report at this time?"

"Yes, your honor. Charity and Henry Thompson would like to petition the court to be an adoptive placement for the children, after the end of the usual six-month placement period. They were married last week and have an appropriate home with affection and financial security for the children," Barbara Frederickson proudly presented.

"Henry Thompson…the DCS worker Henry Thompson?" the judge questioned.

"Yes, your honor," Barbara said happily.

"Well, that is quite a change in situation from just a month ago. Mr. Thompson, I am familiar with your work for the department. You have a big heart for these children whom you represent."

Henry respectfully replied, "Thank you, your honor."

Continuing, "So… Mr. and Mrs. Thompson, are you prepared to love and care for these children as long as you live? Once they are given to you, you will be responsible for them their entire lives until they reach adulthood," the judge reminded seriously.

"Judge, we *are* prepared to care for them until they reach adulthood. We have given this a great deal of thought," Charity replied honestly. "I can't imagine the children going anywhere else."

"Children, how do you feel about becoming a family with Mr. and Mrs. Thompson?" asked the judge.

"We love it there with them. Peter and I feel like we belong with them. We want to stay there…if we can," Amanda reported truthfully.

"Do you feel that way, too, young man?" Judge Grimsby asked Peter, not sure what to expect.

Peter managed a very faint, "Yes."

Judge Grimsby was in total shock as he heard Peter's response. "Well, if there is no more discussion on the matter, and DCS is in line with this proposal, then I will grant permission to proceed with adoption between the Thompsons and Amanda and Peter Ferguson, following the end of the six-month placement period. Case continued, pending a date for adoption," said the judge as he banged the gavel.

Everyone stood up as the judge left the room. Barbara went over and congratulated Henry, Charity, and the children.

They all talked excitedly as they drove home. They met Theresa and Chuck in the kitchen and told them the judge would be setting the adoption date.

Over the next couple years, Aspiration Station helped almost 1000 aged-out youth in Tennessee get a vehicle. Charity, Henry, Beth, and David worked hard to keep equine therapy available to children with special needs for many years to come. Chuck and Theresa provided love, support, and guidance for as long as they lived at the Silver Horseshoe Ranch. And Charity did get her book published.

And they lived happily ever after…The End.

My Forever Christmas

ABOUT THE AUTHOR

Marion Rhines lives in Knoxville, TN, with her husband and five children. Working with children for over thirty years in various capacities has provided her with experience from which to draw meaningful stories. She has been a private childcare provider, preschool teacher, a special education resource teacher, substitute teacher, and a foster and adoptive parent. She has previously published two children's books, *Two Ways Home: A Foster Care Journey* and *When Feelings Get Too Big*. She also released *The Amazing Abigail Morgan*.

Made in the USA
Columbia, SC
11 July 2021